1800 Seconds

By Ian Horne

PROLOGUE

20,000 years ago, the land did not carry the name it would be given in 1846. It is said that chief trader John Bell of the Hudson Bay Company canoed down the Porcupine River to where it was introduced to the river the natives called "Yu-kun-ah," meaning great river."

The village was alive with purpose. The precious gift of daylight was fleeting. After so many seasons, and so many hunts, the bones of the hunters were more accurate than the village medicine woman when it came to foretelling the approaching winter.

The fur of the giant beaver would shield them from the cold nights. The elk provided everything else needed to survive the journey to the hunting grounds. Leather bladders for fresh water, meat for energy, antlers, and bones would be forged to take life in order to sustain life.

The hunters left in the light of the full moon and would arrive when the moon was full again. Leaving the shelter of the bluefish caves for the unforgiving icy glaciers that swallowed the land was as dangerous as the hunt itself. The weather and the land were more unpredictable than the mammoth. More a necessity than a risk; the risk would be not going before winter made the trip impossible.

Returning with packs of meat was not a guarantee; returning at all wasn't either. There were no tears, no clingy goodbyes; everyone understood their part. The women assumed the added responsibility of protecting the village as the men were turned into featureless silhouettes and eventually erased from the memory of the tundra by an early snow squall.

The weather had been kind to the hunters, who arrived on the second full moon and set up a more permanent hunting camp than the overnight stops on their journey. For the younger men in the group, this was their first journey to the glaciers, to the hunting grounds.

Their eyes were as wide as some of the fissures in the ice. The men, their senior, were not going to be their protectors.
Being safe and staying safe was an individual responsibility while juggling the focus of bringing down the giant animal that would help see the village to the thaw of spring. If you were on this hunt, you earned the right to be there and earned the trust of the others.

Three cycles of the sun and moon provided nothing more than a steady depletion of supplies. There was no danger of running out yet, but the hunters were in need of a sign that the mammoths had not moved on.

On the fourth day, the sun had firmly settled in the sky, and the hunters were almost half a day's journey from camp. This time, they sought the mammoth in the opposite direction of their empty hunts from the days before. The sky was as blue as the ice, which had softened slightly under the sun's ineffective and indirect light.

Nothing! Just the land and the sound of their own feet crunching through the icy surface. The day was fading, and the walk back would be dangerous in the dark. The camp was still too far away to be seen when a couple of men sounded off and pointed into the snow. There, dissecting the footprints of man, were tracks that dwarfed their human counterparts. The mammoth had been patient after catching the scent of man. They simply waited for them to pass and then continued on their own trajectory.

The hunters knew the risk; if they followed the tracks, the hunt would likely be a battle between man and mammoth and man and the night sky. At least they could subdue the mammoth, the same could not be said of the darkness that would come regardless, relenting, reclaiming the land from the light.

It was decided that the risk was worth taking, so they followed the tracks. Their pace was driven by their hope, and their steps were quickened by the determination not to return to the village with empty packs.

In no time, they found the herd. In the fading light the group of men singled out 'the one' and surrounded the bull that had seen two migratory seasons. He had lost his juvenile size and was now worthy of the name mammoth. The fire of their torches combined with the yelling that fought to be heard in the falling snow, the mammoth's only hope was to drag this out long enough for the dark to provide a possible advantage to escape.

It was not the dark that provided the escape, but a thunderous clap being spat out from a place in the sky beyond the clouds and snow. The hunters and the mammoth, startled by the noise, fixed upward on a glow that was increasing in size, still under the veil of a blend of dark and clouds. Suddenly, a fireball erupted from the clouds that cloaked its approach.

Unsure what they were looking at, the hunters froze and locked on the streaking fire that split open the sky. The mammoth, much more focused on its own survival, used the distraction to its advantage and fled the area that surely would have been the location of a last breath followed by a bloody butchering.

The streaking object, burning with a blinding brightness, rocketed across the sky and slammed into what had been an impenetrable wall of ice on the side of a receding glacier until that moment. Fear of the unknown and the realization that their prey was getting away, the hunters ran from the small crater that steamed and hissed like an angry snake. The hissing stopped, the steam dissipated, and just like everything else, the harsh reality of winter claimed the thing that fell from the sky.

PART 1: ICE

CHAPTER 1
MOM

Be a spark! Javon's mom said that a lot when he was growing up. Javon never really got it. His mom's wisdom never really landed. He just thought it was some rote advice 'old people' dished out. "Be a spark," his mom said, "as that light, that spark relinquished its hold to the darkness as it overtook the last remaining evidence of who she used to be, who she was.

Javon couldn't sleep, not because of the nakedness, not because of what had been shared only a few hours ago. No, he couldn't sleep because it was quiet. The A/C wasn't running. As soon as he noticed that, he also saw the temperature in the room. It was warm. He pulled back the curtain. Bedlam greeted him. It was still early morning; the sun wouldn't be up for a couple more hours, but that didn't matter. Looking toward the Athens city center, smoke was rising from several burning fires, the foreboding clouds highlighted in the forefront of the hellish, orange glow of the fires. That glow penetrated the room, the light dancing in Candace's eyes, who was waking up.

As much as she wanted to beckon him back to bed, she read the room; the look on Javon's face said it all.

"I think panic has officially set in," Javon said in a very matter-of-fact tone. "Power is out, stuff is on fire, I've heard a few gunshots. You know, that conversation about things devolving into darkness, yeah, I think that's happening."

He then yelled, "THAT'S IT!!"

"That's it like – this is the end we're giving up?" she asked.

"No! THAT'S IT!! I get it now; it finally makes sense, the last thing my mom said.

Javon's excitement grew.

"Be a spark", he said.

"What?" Candace found the words very random.

"It's something my mother always used to say. 'Be a spark'. It reminded me that when things seemed their darkest, all it took was one tiny spark to chase away the darkness.

"Be A Spark! Her message was hope. As long as there is a spark of light, there is hope. That idea you had, that's the spark.

We are not done. We are not falling to our knees. Whatever this "GLU" is, wherever it came from, there has to be an answer, a solution, a cure. As impossible and unavailing as that answer seems, you and I will find it."

CHAPTER 2
ICE ICE BABY

Josephine preferred Joey. She only answered to Josephine officially or if she was in trouble with Sam. Neither of those applied as she and her boyfriend of more than three years trekked across the Kaskawulsh Glacier. They had been planning this trip for over a year.
This was an adventure that was more than the hiking, kayaking, and camping that was familiar to them. This was uncomfortable, challenging, and a first.

Still, they had enough respect for the dangers involved that this trip wasn't hastily thrown together. They researched and spoke to others who had explored this unforgiving part of the planet. Despite the risks and the stories that ended with them saying, "Well, that's not going to be us," – Joey and Sam knew they wanted to do this. They both shared that thing. A vibration in their soul that yearned to ripple outwardly in places many wouldn't dare go. The Kaskawulsh Glacier was one of those places.

The Kaskawulsh Glacier is two converging outlet glaciers that, at its widest, span a daunting three to four miles at the widest point. At an elevation between 6,000 and 9,000 feet, it covers more than 15,000 square miles of Yukon landscape, finally meeting its demise at the head of the Slims and the Kaskawulsh rivers, which feed into the Yukon and Alsek River systems respectively.

Sam and Joey talked a lot about this trip. They knew they wanted to be in this part of North America, but it took them a while to land on the Yukon. Alaska was to the west. As big as it is, you can't see it all in one trip, but they had been a couple of times, so that was out. British Columbia to the south would have been for a visit to Vancouver, but Joey wasn't feeling that city vibe. She wanted something a bit more remote like Alaska, but NOT Alaska. So, the Yukon it was.

"Selfie time"! Sam shouted with excitement.

"Just another half mile, then we can stop," protested Joey. "I want to cover as much distance as possible before dark."

"Yeah, but look how perfect this spot is. The sun, the shadows, the amazing blue sky, the spark…." Sam stopped, distracted by a shiny object. Not in the metaphorical sense, like when someone has "shiny object syndrome" and gets easily distracted. In the literal sense. Sam focused on a slight rise a few hundred yards away. So focused, Joey had ceased to exist until she grabbed him by his arm, spun him around, and looked at him with an amalgamation of annoyed, curious concern.

"Earth to Sam, do you read"? Joey playfully asked, trying to keep the mood light.

"Yeah…but …c'mon….there is something in the ice over there. It could be buried treasure. Sam said, starting to slip into a lousy pirate impersonation somewhere between Captain Jack Sparrow and Mr. Smee.

"Avast ye scurvy swab!" he yelled as he ran to where the mysterious object sparkled.

"Who are you calling a scurvy swab? Keep it up, and I'll make you…uh…ye walk the plank". Joey started to play along, now fully caught up in the excitement of this unexpected mystery.

The closer they got, the more their excitement transitioned to uneasiness. That feeling in the pit of your stomach where all the red flags blow in the wind of your hesitation. Just feet from the mound of ice, they stopped. Sam and Joey looked at each other, then the object, then back at the object with a look that matched those little kids in the Life cereal commercial. Sam, in his best "Mikey" impersonation, was quick to announce, "I'm not going to touch it; you touch it."

Joey looked like she was about to burst.

"Well, Sam! Curious is the mind that is not – that's what I always say". With that, Joey put her pack down and started digging for her small ice pick. She began chiseling away at the ice with such care you would think she were this middle-of-nowhere modern-day Michelangelo carving a replica of David for an ice carving competition.

Carefully so as not to damage it, Joey went from chipping and chiseling to scraping. Sam was no longer sitting on the sidelines; he eagerly joined in. Not wasting time searching for the tools in his pack, he removed his gloves and used the warmth of his hand to melt the ice away in the corners to loosen the object from its frozen sarcophagus.

You know those little kegs you would pick up for college parties? The one that said, I want to party, but I don't want things to get out of hand. That's about the dimensions of this, whatever this was. It was smooth, sleek, and unlike the shine it gave off from across the ice when Sam and Joey first saw it, up close, it was something more.

For its size, the 'pony keg' was remarkably light, and the surface, whatever it was made of, allowed the light to dart as if it was being seen through a jeweler's loop. It was almost as if the light vibrated on the surface as it moved and refracted and reflected in every direction. Joey was mesmerized by it in the same way a school of fish darted from one peripheral to another – catching the sunlight from the surface – when she and Sam were on one of their snorkeling adventures.

"We are DEFINITELY getting that selfie now," Sam shouted excitedly. If someone could "fanboy" over what appeared to be an inanimate object, Sam was doing it.

He held it up about chest level, with one hand underneath as if he were delivering a deep-dish pizza to a table at Giordano's in Chicago. Joey stood close to Sam, one arm around him, the other holding the selfie stick with her finger on the trigger.

They smiled. No, they grinned from ear to ear, snapping some pics. Joey grabbed her phone and couldn't get to the camera roll quickly enough. Despite this moment that felt important, Sam knew the rule. It was the same rule that had been in place since they first started dating. NO PICTURE GETS POSTED WITHOUT JOEY'S APPROVAL. At times, on some vacations, this required multiple shots of the same pose to get it right for her standards. If the hair, the smile, the eyes, something in the background, or the lighting wasn't just so, she'd say, "Nope, again."

Finally, a shot that passed the test.

Ten years ago, out in the middle of nowhere, people would have had to wait until they got back to civilization, Wi-Fi, and the internet to post anything. All that changed when Kadima launched its Constellation satellite network to provide internet access to remote parts of the world—internet for everybody was the idea. In this case, the internet was for the adventurer who could now take the world along and instantly share their journey.

Of the two of them, Joey was, without a doubt, the more curious of the two. As a kid, she had to turn over every rock just to see what was under it. One day, clearly by being in the right place at the right time, she accidentally discovered the Juro Spider had made it to North Carolina, where she lived. If not for the spider floating (some say flying) on the breeze and landing in her hair, she may have missed it. But, since it's the size of a softball, Joey's 13-year-old self came unglued and ran around screaming.

Of course, that drew a lot of attention, and days later, the spider was on the Facebook page of the local news station. Turns out, this big, harmless spider made its way from the Asian-Pacific region to the states on container ships. Everyone learned that the web can be a real engineering masterpiece and be several meters wide. The big question everyone's mind was whether they were harmful to humans. The Facebook story said the venom caused a slight rash and minor pain, but humans had nothing to worry about.

Once she had calmed down, she became fascinated with the spider. She got brave and got close to it, half expecting it to launch from the ground and attach itself to her face like in the "Alien" movies. When that didn't happen, she picked it up. At first, it was a hard pass from her Mom when Joey wanted to keep the spider in a small aquarium as a pet, but then she gave in to the parental urge to foster her daughter's curiosity.

Joey launched her social media, started typing, and then stopped. She felt, deep down in her wandering spirit, that this was an important discovery. Something that could change their lives, no, change the world. She felt burdened with the weight of saying something profound. Something like, "That's one small step for man" profound. Joey being Joey, she went with humor instead.

"Even aliens forget the 'Carry In-Carry out' rule when on vacation in the great outdoors."

And she hit post – with no idea that she had just inadvertently killed almost 100 million people on the planet.

CHAPTER 3
MAINE

Travis Grendall was a lobsterman from Kittery, Maine – a small town on the southern tip of the state on the New Hampshire border. The Portsmouth Naval Shipyard, tourism, and the fishing industry drove the economy.

Travis worked from the first glimmer of light to wake up the Atlantic Ocean to the last fading light that put the ocean to bed. Working on the water was all he knew, all he wanted to know. His father had done it; his grandfather, Travis, being a lobsterman, was the answer to the question that didn't need to be answered,

Still, he did it well, committing himself to a livelihood that had provided a comfortable way of life for him, his wife, and their only son, Spencer. Shortly after Spencer was born, it seemed the world had it in for Travis at every turn. If it wasn't unusually strong Nor'easters in the fall, it was category two hurricanes in the late summer. Fuel costs continued to rise, gear wasn't getting any cheaper, and the Maine Department of Marine resources seemed to be squeezing the industry from every corner with this new regulation and that new regulation.

Vents on the traps needed to be bigger; gauge sizes were increasing, and where you could push a trap off the rail seemed to be constantly changing due to boating lanes or the lanes of migrating species.

Travis understood the need to preserve the industry that had been so good to his family, but it was too much, too soon. That money, at the end of the month, that cushion that was dwindling along with the savings.

The only thing that seemed to be In abundance was worry and stress, which took a toll on Travis and his marriage to his wife, Kim.

The headaches weren't bad at first. Kim would take a couple of ibuprofen and go on about her day. She cared for Spencer, kept the home, ran errands, and juggled the finances. Travis had enough to worry about and focus on; this was her job, and she prided herself on doing it well.

The headaches gradually got worse, bad enough that Kim's vision blurred; there was light sensitivity, dizziness, fatigue, vomiting, and then the slurring of Spencer's name.

Spencer, a word, as any hard-working stay-at-home mom will understand, she says a hundred times a day. She was saying it differently the last few days. The "s" sound for the letter "c" was now a "z". This would have been perfectly acceptable if you had lived in Quincy, Massachusetts. The z sound for the c instantly indicated that you weren't a transplant, a tourist, or someone who would receive a very polite "You ain't from around here, are you"? In a New England accent as thick as seafood 'chowdah.'

Glioblastoma. It was the grenade that went off in Travis' world. A fast-growing and aggressive brain tumor that had unapologetically taken up residence in the temporal lobe of Kim's brain. Diagnosis on a Tuesday, surgery scheduled two days later. The plan was surgery to remove as much of the tumor as they could, with the understanding that with this kind of tumor and its location, you never really get all of it. Surgery would be followed by chemo and radiation to shrink what was left of the cancer to relieve some of the intracranial pressure.

There was also the pressure of the medical bills that relentlessly piled up. Sure, Travis had insurance, but the plan he could afford was one he purchased, and he had never dreamed of this scenario. Kittery was a small enough town where the locals all knew one another, so when news of Kim's diagnosis spread, it wasn't long before the fundraisers started. From church suppers and bake sales to the GoFundMe page. Families chipped in with meals and daycare for little Spencer since Travis was splitting time between the ocean and the hospital. Sleep became a rare commodity.

Six months later, Kim was gone. His high school sweetheart, whose hand he held in the halls of Traip Academy, was gone. The loss was crushing, suffocating, extinguishing. Many who knew the family expected Travis to die of a broken heart or broken heart syndrome. Takotsubo cardiomyopathy is rare, but it happens.

The conclusion was Broken Heart Syndrome Is thought to be caused by a surge of adrenaline in the heart after extreme physical or emotional stress. This causes a chamber of the heart, usually the left ventricle to weaken and expand, making it hard for the heart to do its job and pump blood. This can lead to shock, low blood pressure, heart failure, and sometimes death.

It was not Broken Heart Syndrome that took Travis away and left Spencer without both his parents. Travis, for all he was, for all he had done for his family, his final act was selfish. One of Kim's friends found Travis in his bed, the whiskey and pills displayed on a stage that was more tragic than anything the best playwrights could breathe life into.

If anything was forgiving about the monster that had devoured a once proud family and snuffed out any hope of there being another Maine lobsterman in the family, it was that Spencer was still too young to make any sense of this. Just shy of the age of two, Spencer's innocence shielded him from the horror that he would revisit at a time when he was older when he could process it all.

CHAPTER 4
DRIVEN

Travis and Kim both lost their parents when they were in their late teens and as only children with no real immediate family in a position to help, Spencer was absorbed into the foster care system. The first couple of stops didn't work out; only when he found his way into Mary's home did life seem to favor him.

Mary, a widowed woman from Wisconsin who had moved to South Berwick, Maine, thirty years ago, still had so much to give of herself at the age of 58. She loved being a foster mom and had been for 12 years, specializing in young babies and toddlers. When Spencer came along, something shifted in her. Rather than simply providing respite for a short time, Spencer was different. Rather than shuffle him off for placement in a family that wanted to skip the late nights, the potty training, the 'terrible two's' – Mary grew fond of Spencer. There was something about him, something she couldn't quite put her finger on.
Call it God placing something on her heart or just something she was missing that Spencer provided; she dedicated her life to Spencer.

Spencer thrived. No, he excelled. By 6th grade, Spencer was not only taking high school curriculum classes; he was dominating them, especially the sciences. Chemistry, biology, botany, anatomy...all of it. He was a sponge. By the time he should have been a high school freshman, Spencer was applying for and receiving acceptance letters from a list of colleges and universities as long as a drugstore receipt.

After the first year and many late-night conversations with Mary, Spencer was offered a full-ride scholarship to Stanford. The kid was a prodigy. After graduating from Stanford in three years with a Bachelor in Biomedical Engineering, he was then off to John Hopkins University – focusing on microbiology and clinical virology. Ever since Mary told Spencer about his Mom and Dad, the cancer, and the depression, he was determined to understand the brain, the body, and what made it tick. Was his mission to cure cancer? Maybe. But his laser focus was on learning as much as he could as fast as he could and being the best while doing it.

Knowledge is power. With that power comes recognition; in Spencer's case, it was more fame. Naturally, with that sort of genius-level IQ fame came money. Companies were throwing themselves at his feet to woo him to their team, to their vision for the world.

Spencer knew he wouldn't be happy working for someone, under someone. Just the thought of it seemed to make his skin itch, like he was allergic to the restrictions and limitations not being his own boss would bring. No, Spencer knew that to thrive, grow, innovate, and lead, he would have to start something of his own. With that, Kadima was born.

He had liked the word Kadima since he had heard it used in an episode of an old superhero TV show about "The Flash." The Hebrew word that translated to "Forward" – to Spencer, it was a simple, compelling expression of his determination to conquer everything that stood in his way. It didn't take long for his first success to put him on the map, and while he wasn't the lobsterman from Maine who existed in another life-another timeline in the universe, the connection was still there.

That connection eventually led him to a groundbreaking new drug that offered cutting-edge hope for treating cancer. It didn't happen overnight because Spencer needed to ensure the research and science were sound, and then he needed financial backing. He couldn't get the financial backing without testing, something to show tangible proof that he was on to something. The answer to his financial shortcomings was the biotech venture capital firms. After a few failed pitches, the firms started to buy into Spencer's miracle drug that he was developing. That turned out to be beneficial for all involved.

The new drug Spencer had created didn't cure cancer, but in every trial, in every form of cancer, it not only slowed the advancement of the mutating cells—it effectively stopped them from growing. This was a game changer, saving more lives than ever.
While not every cancer was treatable, it gave decades, where there may have only been months or a couple of years. So, Kadima's first pharmaceutical success, Mikurin, was born.

And it was all thanks to Mitsukurinidae – The Goblin Shark.

As old as the dinosaurs and as ugly as sin, this rare shark has been found in the Atlantic, Pacific, and Indian Oceans. With an average size of 10 to 13 feet, they have been known to grow as big as 20 feet. They can be found in the upper continental slopes, submarine canyons, and seamounts throughout the world's oceans at depths greater than 330ft. Some researchers have found them as far down as almost 4300 feet.

So, how did this swimming dinosaur go from the ocean to being the foundation of one of the most significant scientific advancements of the 21st century? Spencer would tell you some dumb luck, with most of the credit going to King Julien, the animated Lemur in the Madagascar movies.

Growing up, King Julien and the other Madagascar characters were a great comfort to Spencer. As an adult, shortly after he made his first million, Spencer decided he wanted to visit the island nation off the coast of Africa.

While there, he, of course, encountered plenty of lemurs. He also went on what he liked to call "photo safaris" with his camera, spent a hot minute on the beach, and went deep-sea fishing. He booked a charter on "Nosy Be Paradise Tours," which, in hindsight, was an ironic coincidence considering the Goblin Shark's large nose.

An overnight fishing trip on the Mozambique Channel side of Madagascar took Spencer and his party from the tiny island of Nosy Be to a few fishing holes around Isla Faly and then into Ambaro Bay. On this trip, Spencer was lucky enough to land a Goblin Shark. With a face only a mother Goblin Shark could love and an insatiable curiosity, Spencer arranged to have it put on ice and shipped back to his labs at Kadima. It was almost a year and a half and thousands of tests later, Mitsuchimera was born.

It turns out that what this shark lacked in looks, it overcompensated for in a particular enzyme found in its liver. The best part: no sharks had to be killed.
The sharks could be tranquilized, the enzyme harvested, and with careful post-harvest care, the animal was returned to the ocean, no worse for wear, ready to swim, eat, and live its best Goblin Shark life.

Mitsuchimera was the catalyst for Kadima's exponential growth. The government usually funds research, development, and the occasional top-secret project. From 3D-printing organs that changed the organ donation landscape to branching out into bioengineered foods and animals for an overtaxed global agriculture that was running out of answers to the question, "Will humans be able to sustain our growth on this planet, or will we eventually strip it bear like a plague of locust?"

At 44, Spencer had more money than he could spend. Private planes, homes in all his favorite places, and security details were comprised of ex-military and private chefs. His list of accomplishments and accolades bordered on the ridiculous. Sure, he dated but found no time to dedicate to family. Maybe in the back of his mind, knowing the troubles that came with family, he chose not to go down that path. His strong upbringing, provided by his foster mom, Mary, kept his nose clean and out of trouble. No matter how hard the news and social media tried to tear him down, he provided them no satisfaction. Outside of his scientific achievements, his world was beige, as if he were staging it to sell it. It was a life well lived where he wanted for nothing.

That's how it seemed, but the truth was he wanted more. More knowledge, more creation, more advancement, more than anything to build his legacy on how he would change the world and humanity. For thousands of years, that change had lay dormant in a shiny little keg in a glacier, unleashed by a couple of adventure seekers just taking a selfie with a piece of space junk.

CHAPTER 5
JAVON

Some days, Javon seemed a world away from his childhood home in Charleston, South Carolina. It had been forever since he had visited. 6 foot, fit, a handsome dark complexion that sadly took a back seat to the conversation piece on the side of his neck. Javon had a noticeable scar, about 6 inches long, on the side of his neck, just above where his collar would rest. It healed fine; it just couldn't have been in a more prominent place. In every social interaction, the scar was his plus one. He could never introduce himself without "oh, that" being placed in a sentence that began an explanation and a story he was tired of telling.

When he was young, he and his sister were messing around, and he fell headfirst into the glass table in the living room. The glass made easy work of his flesh, and the blood loss was substantial. Anything made of absorbent material was the vampire that drank in Javon's blood with an insatiable thirst. Shy of being exsanguinated right there in his living room, he spent a few days in the hospital and learned a precious lesson – Mom was right when she said don't play ball in the house.

Growing up, he was pretty self-conscious about the scar. Of course, kids can be brutal, and he had his share of teasing that went along with it. Scarface, Frankenstein, freak…yeah, he had heard it all. It only strengthened his character while at the same time teaching him patience and how to control his temper when what he really wanted to do was lash out. Thankfully, his mom taught him better than that. However, every once in a while, Javon would get pushed just a little too far.

In sophomore year, Javon was walking home, and Steve Pruitt and a few of his lackeys trailed a few yards behind him. Everything was going as it usually did. Javon ignored his tormentors while they hurled a salvo of insults his way. This day was different, though, because Steve took things too far and threw something at Javon. During lunch earlier that day, Steve had gathered up a brown bag full of food scraps from the school cafeteria. Javon was just 100 yards from home. He almost made it before that bag exploded on the back of his head and shoulders, sending half-eaten lunchroom scraps in his hair and his clothes.

Something inside Javon snapped, and Javon turned, dropped his bag, and went into a blind rage. When he was done, Steve Pruitt's face was bloodied and swollen. Steve's friends ran, and Javon continued home. It wasn't until later that night, when Steve's mom called Javon's mom, that Javon suffered the consequences of his actions. Grounded for a month and very few privileges.

Sadly, the damage was done. Javon kept his walls pretty high, never really making room in his high school life for friends or dating. It certainly wasn't due to a lack of interest. There were several girls who did everything they could think of to get his attention. Unfortunately for them, Javon's lack of self-confidence got in the way.

With decent grades and being the star running back in high school, the scar was suddenly not that noticeable to anyone. His achievements and his character were what people saw. While many expected him to head off to college and maybe get a full ride for playing ball, Javon had always known he wanted to be a Marine. It was a move his mom completely supported. She thought the discipline and structure would do him good.

Fueled by stories about his Granddaddy that his mother would tell him, one could almost blame his mom for watering that seed. Javon's

Granddaddy was a Marine and fought in Iraq after the attacks on 9/11. While his Daddy didn't serve, the fire in his belly stayed lit.

After ten years in the Marines as a member of the Military Police Force, he found transitioning back to civilian life had its challenges. Being a Marine came with a certain edge that life after service wasn't providing. One day, he got a call from a Marine buddy with a lead on being the head of a private security detail for one of the wealthiest people on the planet, Spencer Grendall of Kadima Biotech.

Javon interviewed for and got the job and felt 'normal' again. His life had the structure, discipline, and routine he needed. He became married to his job, an empty chair at family events back in Charleston, but he was good at it. He was damn good at it and paid well for it.

Most of the time, he was a bodyguard for all of Spencer's public appearances and social engagements. Occasionally, an over-zealous eco-warrior with an ambitious and misguided manifesto would get a little too close, and Javon would politely and effectively remove them. As long as they saw the error of their ways, the brief interaction between the Marine-trained Javon and the protester benefited both parties. Javon didn't risk getting his suit dirty, and the protester avoided any uncomfortable or unexpected pain. It was those moments where Javon loved to exist. The excitement, the tension, the adrenaline. Some days, he almost tried to make something remotely dangerous happen.

The phone rang, singing, "Be careful what you wish for."

CHAPTER 6
CANDACE

Khal sat still only when he was in the kayak with Candace. Yes, Candace had a two-person kayak so she and Khal could spend time on the water together. They had since she rescued him from the shelter when he was a pup.
The then little blue pit, just a few months old, was now 40 pounds of loyalty mixed with the energy of the Tasmanian devil, but in the kayak, it was like he was a different dog.

Candace was a different person when on the water, too. When not on the water, she was one of the country's leading blood experts—more specifically, a hematological oncologist. What Candace knew about blood was its origins, how it behaves under certain situations, the life it can give, and the life it can take. So much of her time and life's work had been dedicated to hematological oncology, from her residency at Johns Hopkins to joining the Cancer Center of Kansas team.

There was very little doubt that Candace would end up in the medical field. One Christmas, when she was 8, Santa put the game "Operation" under the tree. That red nose lit up more than Rudolph on a foggy Christmas Eve, and that buzzer filled the house night and day until it didn't. Not because Candace had grown tired of the game. It was the exact opposite. She played it so much that she got very good at removing funny bones and butterflies without touching the sides.

While Candace was more than qualified to work at any of the biggest hospitals in the country, she liked the Midwest because things seemed more honest and predictable. Plus, Midwesterners can make a mean casserole.
She wasn't confident she would have made it living in the city while trying to save every single patient she came in contact with.

That didn't stop her from trying. Candace celebrated with some families and cried with others. Each patient was much more than a chart, numbers, and results. The patients were family, and she paddled when she couldn't save one. Something about the way the paddle knifed through the water, combined with the Kansas breeze, made the grass restless. The sound and the rhythm of it all were disorienting in the best way possible. What was waiting for her off the water seemed a million miles away. Her spirit was still.

Still, a connection to the outside world lay beyond the veil of escapism. Like a string with a can on the other end and the neighborhood kid yelling at her through the other end, her cell phone rang.

"Hi, Mom," Candace answered, although she considered letting it go to voicemail. However, with so much sickness and death in her line of work, she answered more often than not, never taking for granted that her Mom was still able to call.

"Candace, I know it's only August, but as busy as you are, I wanted to see if you'll be home for Thanksgiving this year," her mom asked with a level of hope in her voice that could not be ignored.

"Actually," Candace started.

"Oh, you're not coming; I understand," her mom interrupted

With much more emphasis on the word, Candace started over, "ACTUALLY, I meant to call you last week. I am planning on coming home for Turkey Day. I was going to let it be a surprise, but I know how you hate surprises."

"Jason—she's coming for Thanksgiving," Candace could hear her Mom yell on the other end of the phone; the joy in her voice made Candace smile.

"Will there be a plus one?". And there it was; the sweet and tender moment was ruined. Sure, Candace dated, but there was nothing serious; there couldn't be anything serious. Who had time for love when all you wanted to do was save every patient who walked through the doors? She knew her mom only asked because her grandmotherly biological clock was ticking loudly. It was loud, like one of those old mantle clocks people who ran bed and breakfasts put in your bedroom, thinking it added character when all it did was keep you up at night with every deliberate Big Ben tick.

"No, Mom, no plus one. Besides, it's been a few years since we've been together for Thanksgiving, and I don't want there to be any distractions."

There was a pause on the other end before her mom spoke. A pause just long enough to make the disappointment manifest in a palpable form that could be rolled around in one's hand like clay.

"I understand, Candace, but seriously, I wish you would prioritize yourself and look for someone with whom you can share your heart." With teasing sarcasm, Candace said, "I do have someone. I have Kahl, plus he's a good judge of character, and he hasn't approved of the last several guys I met for coffee."

Knowing she was wasting her breath, Mom said, "Have you ever considered leaving Kahl at home when going on these coffee dates?"

"What? He'd never forgive me if I didn't bring him along for a pup cup."

"A what?" Mom asked. "Oh, never mind".

And with a dose of misdirection and change of topic, the uncomfortable subject of "When are you going to make me a grandmother?" was dropped, at least until the next phone call. Candace said goodbye and smiled. She loved those phone calls.

CHAPTER 7
LIKE AND FOLLOW

The phone rang, and Javon answered; it delivered a voice on the other end that was a mix of excitement and bluntness. It was Spencer

"Javon, pack your things. A ticket is waiting for you at the airport; your flight leaves in 3 hours. Oh, and pack warm; you're headed to the Yukon."

"Sir" is all Javon could muster as he refueled his alertness, which was still lost between REM sleep and the half-awareness of needing to go to the bathroom.

"No time to explain everything; all I can say is I came across this viral video of this young couple up in the Yukon that found something."

"Something"? Javon asked, fully expecting a mountain-sized dose of misdirection and evasiveness.

Like a kid with too much candy on Halloween, Spencer kept going and would not slow down to allow Javon to catch up.

"I just sent you the link to the social media page. Look at the pictures; that is what you will retrieve."

In no time, his Marine training had his mental agility running stride for stride with Spencer, and he could respond with more than one word at a time.

"This couple, you've spoken to them?" he asked before he could stop himself. He knew Spencer was a man of means, meaning if he saw something he wanted, he meant to have it. "Have they agreed to meet somewhere to handle the exchange?"

"Yes, I was able to track them down, and let's just say I have funded many of their future adventures, plus donated generously to the charity of their choosing in exchange for the object." He said with the satisfaction of a person used to getting their way.

"They will meet you at a little place called the Burnt Toast Café. It's close to the river on the corner of Steele Street and 2nd. I've forwarded you their names, contact info, and everything. You can get up to speed on the rest of the details, including the plan, after you have the object in your possession on the flight there."

Javon knew to ask only a few questions. He was paid well to provide security and obedience. Javon had grown to trust Spencer because he had never been put in a position to do something illegal or immoral. At least, not that he knew of. Everything he did for Spencer felt above board. While sometimes borderline eccentric, Javon shrugs his shoulders and mutters, "Crazy rich people."

What else was there to say? Like many who came in contact with Spencer, he soon realized that he was accustomed to getting what he wanted, regardless of the cost.

A few years ago, a curator named David Aaron, who specialized in ancient antiquities, was auctioning off the essentially complete skeleton of a juvenile T-rex discovered in Montana. The body was 55 percent intact, the skull over 90 percent complete, and in great shape for somewhere between 68 and 66 million years old. That T-Rex, the Spencer has since named "Chompy," welcomes visitors as they walk through the center foyer doors at Kadima. It's so in your face on display one would expect Spencer to come walking out with a white suit, hat, and cane and say, "Welcome to Jurassic Park."

"Awwweee Crap!"

"Something wrong?" a woman in the seat next to Javon in business class asked him.

"I'm sorry?" Javon asked because he could barely hear her over the movie in his earbuds. He paused "Avatar," a perfect long movie for a long flight, removed his earbuds, and turned to the woman. In her late 70s or early 80s, she could have been Betty White's twin sister.

"You seem a little frustrated," she said as she tried to give a nosy side-eye to his computer to see what was on the screen.

"Love those screen protectors that don't allow snooping," Javon thought.

"Oh, nothing so dramatic. I left in such a hurry today at my boss's request that I forgot to cancel my date and my reservations at Halls Chophouse."

"I'm sure your wife will understand."

"My future wife or future ex-wife," he said, smiling. The woman looked confused.

"It was a first date," Javon explained. "No telling how it was going to work out."

"We hit it off over Facetime, so I was hopeful."

The woman looked at him. Her eyes dwelled, full of core memories. Her face reflects years of love's greatest moments and life's most challenging trials. Smiling, she patted him on the knee and said if it was meant to be, nothing in the universe could stop it.

"Sir, please put your laptop away and your tray upright; we're on final approach," a 40-something, a little extra weight, the effeminate male flight attendant asked.

Javon was so wrapped up in his conversation with his neighbor that he lost track of time. The Airbus A320 was 10 minutes out from his layover at Chicago O'Hare. He had about an hour for a quick beer, to get to his gate clear on the other side of the airport, and to stop for a cheese/caramel mix of Garrett popcorn.

Never getting her name, he watched the sweet old woman disappear into the masses on Concourse G, and he continued; he couldn't help but sing,

"Thank you for being a friend."

CHAPTER 8
MIDDLE OF NOWHERE

Javon spent another 90 minutes in the air while reviewing the material Spencer had forwarded him in an encrypted file. That alone seemed odd to him. Why all the secrecy? After all, to the best of his knowledge, he was meeting up with a couple of travel bloggers and influencers to retrieve an artifact that Spencer would just add to his collection of weird stuff.

Whatever happened to collecting comic books? Javon wandered through his collection as a child and sold it to pay off a couple of bills. He never did get his hands on Incredible Hulk #181, the first full Wolverine story. These days, it lacks the retirement value of Action Comics #1.

In the right condition, it would go for anywhere between $6,000 and $10,000. It was more sentimental since the Hulk and Wolverine were two of his favorite characters.

Scrolling through the documents, images, and maps seemed pretty pedestrian. The way someone would mindlessly browse a copy of "Highlights" in the dentist's office. Then, before the next page finished scrolling into sight, the words at the top of the page caused Javon to look around to make sure no one else was trying to read over his shoulder.

"What the Fuck?"

There, in bold letters at the top of a document that had been redacted, were the words "Extra-Terrestrial."

There was a dryness sweeping over the inside of his mouth, like a sandstorm burying and hope of words forming for him to speak out loud.

"Excuse me, could I get a bottled water?"

The flight attendant was back in no time; he drank the whole thing like a frat boy "shotgunning" a beer.

He read on.

From what he could gather, this thing these kids found was not just some artifact—not a piece of primitive metal smithing in the ice from a long-forgotten Indigenous people.

The following pages were from the Canadian and U.S. governments confirming a UAP.

UFOs are so 2020. Around 2023, when former military members who wore a display case worth of medals on their chest testified before Congress about the existence of UFOs and little green men, they decided it would be a good time to change the acronym to UAP—Unidentified Aerial Phenomena.

At a time when the world was focusing on or fighting against inclusion, acceptance, and being woke, this term appeared to open the door to a whole litany of mysterious things in the sky.

Back in the early 1900s, the two governments, despite dozens of military and civilian eyewitness accounts, had no other alternative than to agree that something fell from space. A joint task force of scientists and military types was formed, but no matter how hard they looked, burdened by the lack of the technology that exists today, they couldn't find a trace of it.

A century, a couple of decades, and several dreadful, extra-snowy Canadian winters later, it was slowly forgotten about. Other than the documentation Javon was examining now, it was like it never happened.

That's not what his computer screen was telling him. It very much happened, and now, Todd and Margo, the adventure enthusiasts, may have just confirmed it.

"What is this shiny thing in the ice Todd? I DON'T KNOW MARGO"

Javon chuckled.

"Man, great movie," he mused.

The plane landed at Erik Nielson Whitehorse International Airport. Javon made his way to the rental car counter with just a carry-on and a duffle.

Spencer Grendall had thought of everything for his trusted head of security so far. In no time, he had the keys to a sizeable four-wheel-drive SUV. Checking his phone, his bank account had been advanced plenty of money to ensure no surprises couldn't be matched with the right amount of financial leverage.

He threw his gear in the back and put the coordinates for the Burnt Toast Café in it. The meeting was scheduled for 5 p.m. he looked at his phone. It was 4:36. There was no time to head to the hotel, and the café was 10 minutes away, so business first, hot shower at the hotel later.

Josephine and Sam, otherwise known to Javon as Margo and Todd, were at a corner table when he walked in.

The couple, whose faces in that selfie were so full of wonder and adventure, now displayed something more akin to a mixture of profound curiosity with a touch of fear of the unknown.

CHAPTER 9
UP THE CREEK

Candace stopped paddling. To decompress from the chat with her mom, she just floated on her back on her kayak. The call wasn't bad; every time she called home, it came weighed down with a certain level of anxiety with a dash of "I must be such a disappointment to them because I didn't settle down, instead focusing on my work."

She put her earbuds in, shuffled her playlist labeled "Chill," and breathed.

Suddenly, Ed Sheeran competed in her ears with a muffled sound. It sounded familiar, but not.

"Mmmfs Stnnntn". Mmmfs Stanton"

Was someone calling her name? She opened her eyes only to have the sun blocked out by the silhouette of a man, possibly wearing a military uniform. As her eyes came into focus, Kahl, an outstanding judge of character, let out a low, rumbling growl – the shadow spoke.

Mrs. Stanton?

"Ms." Candace quickly corrected him.

"Sorry, Ms. Stanton. Dr. Candace Stanton?"

"Yes, that's…." She froze. The soldier came into focus, but now he wasn't the only thing blocking the sun. A Blackhawk helicopter, she was guessing from the Kansas Air National Guard base in Wichita, had found a place to land about a half mile from her earlier position, and now it dominated the landscape.

"You guys run out of gas and need me to paddle back to civilization to get help?" she said with a wry, sarcastic smile lost on "G.I. Don't Have A Sense Of Humor."

"No, Ma'am." I'm Colonel Eugene Brighton."

"As in beach," she interrupted.

"Ma'am?"

Candace had forgotten that the sense of humor gene was non-existent with this one.

"New York City? Nothin'?"

"I'm a West Coast native, ma'am."

Then, with more rigidity and seriousness Candace didn't expect, Colonel Brighton got down to business.

"Dr. Stanton, I need you to come with us. We will explain everything along the way."

"I'm not going anywhere," she protested as she pulled her boat and her very protective "pitty" onto the river bank.

"I have my orders, and I'm afraid this is not up for discussion."

"But my dog, my kayak, MY JOB!! I'm supposed to be back to work tomorrow."

"My team has already made arrangements with your job, and two of my men will stay behind to ensure your things and your dog are safely transported back home to friends and family."

Colonel Brighton continued.

"Dr. Stanton, you are not in trouble; the United States Government needs your expertise on a sensitive matter."

"Like, national security kind of stuff?" Candace asked in a way that revealed she streamed way too many spy movies.

"Nothing like that, Dr. Stanton, at least not yet. It all depends on what insight you can provide," the Colonel explained.

"Again, I can fill you in along the way, but we need to leave now," the Colonel demanded as his water broke and the contractions were four minutes apart.

"Okay….here",

Candace dug into her backpack and pulled out a Kong and dog treats.

"You'll need these to win the big guy over."

The Colonel handed them over to a couple of team members and ushered Candace into the helicopter.

As he was helping her strap in, put on a helmet, and set up a headphone/mic so the conversation could be heard over the powerful helicopter, Candace asked, "So, where are we going?"

"Juneau, Alaska, doctor."

CHAPTER 10
POSSESSION IS NINE-TENTHS OF THE LAW

Javon spent the last 90 minutes listening to Josephine and Sam rehash their adventures on the Kaskawulsh Glacier.

Sadly, they did not just get to the point. There was the night Sam swore he could start the fire, the Aurora Borealis, and the argument about polar bears and penguins only being seen together at zoos because they live at different poles.

Once that was settled, they shared everything with Javon. Everything they could, after all, they knew as much, actually less than the man sitting across the table from them. That didn't matter; this was a delicate situation, and he needed to make them feel like their time was worth something and what they were doing by surrendering the object was worth something. It would have seemed rude and suspicious if he had given off an "eat and run" vibe.

The three wrapped up their visit as the late spring sun was fading. Josephine and Sam still had a few more days in Whitehorse before returning to the States. Javon put the object in a hard case lined with a memory foam-type material, another Kadima prototype.

Western Gold Rush Inn. Nothing fancy like what Spencer was accustomed to, but certainly perfect for the "I don't want to draw any attention to myself because I have an alien object in my possession" situation that Javon found himself in.

After a hot shower at the end of an incredibly long day, Javon's stomach took over all thought and reason and prioritized a trip downstairs to the Gold Pan Saloon. Decorated as one might imagine an establishment with that name might be, he found a small table under a deer antler chandelier and took a deep breath.

Man, it felt good to get off his feet.

"What'll it be, ay?"

Javon looked up to see a 30-something waitress with freckles and a friendly smile ready to take his order.

"Dealer's choice," he said.

"You're new in town?"

"I'm new to Canada," he admitted with a bit of shame. He had always talked about making time to travel, but it seemed he was married to his work and, in some cases, Spencer.

"Well," the waitress practically squealed excitedly, "You HAVE to try a Canadian delicacy. It's practically the official foodstuff of our great land."

"Deep-fried moose," he said with a playful smirk.

"We only serve that on Taco Tuesday," she smirked back as he looked at the name tag on her shirt.

"You have to try our poutine; it's the best for hundreds of miles around," Jill replied. "Could have something to do with the fact there aren't many other places for hundreds of miles

"Pou – what?" Javon asked with a healthy level of skepticism.

"Poutine, everything a growing boy like you needs. Potatoes, brown gravy, and squeaky cheese curds."

Javon laughed. Squeaky cheese curds sounded like a name given to someone at a holiday party from a naughty elf name-generating game.

"I'm sorry, squeaky what??"

"Cheese curds, ay!" Jill said with an implied "duh."
"If your cheese curds don't squeak, you got bad cheese curds."

"I see," Javon played along. How could cheese, brown gravy, and deep-fried potatoes be bad? Okay, Poutine and a bud light, please."

"Oh muh gawd!!" Javon said with a mouth full of the most incredible thing he had ever had. He was making audible noises that would have caused frowns on the faces of parents sitting within earshot as they covered their child's ears. Lucky for him, the Gold Pan was mostly empty, shy of what Javon could assume were a couple of regulars.

As he went in for another bite, his pants vibrated.

"Hello!"

"Do you have it?"

"Shit," Javon blurted out. He had forgotten to call Spencer as soon as he had the artifact. Damn, stomach betrayed him again.

"I do. Just grabbing a …"

Spencer cut him off. "Get out of there, now, LIKE NOW!"

The urgency in his voice told Javon not to ask questions. He didn't need to because his boss continued.

"The Canadian government saw the same social media post from Josephine and Sam, and they are heading your way. I called in a couple of favors, and they aren't just coming to take pictures. They know something we don't,' and they are bringing some military units to work closely with local and state authorities."

"Why all the fuss?"

"I don't know, but they aren't doing it for crowd control to keep people out as word spreads; they are keeping the word and the people of Whitewater in."

"WHAT?!" Javon started to get a terrible feeling.

"They intend to cordon off the entire town. At least a 10-mile perimeter in every direction, and they don't plan to make it optional. However, they won't act on it until they arrive, so you still have time. Get to the airport; tickets are waiting for you at the counter for a flight to Juneau."

"How do I get that thing through security?" This was a fair question, considering it was allegedly from outer space.

"Some documents will be with your tickets. Like I said, I called in a favor; now go."

Javon looked around for Jill and didn't see her, so he figured $50 would cover the great food, tip, and friendly chatter. After a quick turn and burn at the hotel, he sped off toward the airport, but not too fast to draw attention to himself; he dropped the vehicle off at the rental counter and accelerated to the ticket counter. Everything was there: tickets, gate assignment, mysterious "this is not the contraband you're looking for" Jedi documentation that was his free pass through security.

Twenty minutes passed until boarding, and he looked at the ticket and his watch. Javon had always wanted to do that O.J. Simpson run through the airport, like in those old commercials. Now was his chance. Fortunately, Erik Nielson International Airport was not Chicago O'Hare, and he was at his gate just as they called Veterans, active-duty personnel, and people who needed special assistance to board.

The following 10 minutes seemed like an eternity as they loitered in the space between, "There has to be a better way to board an airplane that doesn't require people fighting for overhead bin space" and "I'm in first class, and I need my drink before you do help any of the other 180 passengers on board."

Finally, push back from the gate and taxiing along the runway. Javon looked at how blissfully unaware the rest of the plane's human cargo was about the things in motion.
Why would Canada go through the effort to cut off a whole town of over 30,000 people on little or no notice?

The plane made the final turn, lined up, and accelerated. The plane was shaking, his weight was sinking slightly back into his seat, and the flashing lights were not of the beacons on the wings but of the flashing lights from emergency vehicles pulling into the airport. The last thing Javon could make out as the ground pulled away from him was the planes that didn't take off returning to the gate, barricades going up, and a faint perimeter of flashing lights creating an ominous circle around Whitehorse.

The direct flight wasn't recalled. Javon could only assume that the chaos on the ground demanded the full attention of the military and mounted police, and they just had to control what they could at that point.

They were on the ground four hours and forty minutes later, and Javon was grateful. Usually, he didn't mind flying, but that storm they landed in was no joke. Catching his breath, he could tell the plane was within cell phone service. That was obvious from the orchestra of pings, chimes, or other personalized noise people had set on their devices. Javon looked at his phone; there was a message from Spencer.

It read:

"I called in another favor; get off the plane and look for the guy holding the sign with your name in the gate area."

This gave him pause. In the post-9/11 era, this was not a thing. Family, friends, and rides from the airport all had to wait on the other side of the gates and security near baggage claim. He kept reading.

"You will be taken a ride waiting for you on the tarmac that will get you off airport property before they shut it down. MOVE, NOW!"

"What the hell was in the case he pulled out of the overhead bin? This was supposed to be a simple, "My rich boss wants it, and he'll make it worth your while to give it to him and not ask a lot of questions.""

BING!

Another text from Spencer

"One last thing, never do you or anyone else open the package. Protect it at all costs and assure the security of the artifact.

The man at the gate, the side door, and the tarmac were all very "Ethan Hunt" and seamless. It was all frigid, wet, and stormy, too. The weather the plane had been lucky enough to survive landing in had "turned up to 11" like it was pissed at Alaska for being an odd-numbered state when it could have just waited and let Hawaii go first. Not only did the wind and rain intensify, but the temperature was dropping. Right before his eyes, the big fat raindrops were mixing with an amalgamation of snow, sleet, ice, and everything else that would make a fast getaway a bit more of a "white knuckle pucker."

Around the hangers and out a side gate that was as secure as using the word "password" for a password, just like Whitehorse, as soon as the gate closed, the main entrance to the Juneau International Airport was swarming with civilian, military, and government personnel.

Unlike Whitehorse, getting away was going to prove more challenging.

"Sir, seatbelt, head own, hold your questions until we are clear."

"Got it, uh," Javon realized he was trusting everything to a man whose name he did not know.

"What do I call you?"

"If all goes well, you won't need to. Like I said, later."

Later arrived in 10-minutes. On the Glacier Highway, just about to cross the Mendenhall River, the escape was over. With the effectiveness of a Navy Seal terrorist strike force, Javon and the driver were soon forced to the side of the road and out of their vehicle.

"Javon Oliver, I'm special agent Walter Gordon. I shouldn't have to explain how the next few minutes will go, but if it's been too long since your days as an MP in The Corps, let me refresh your memory."

This guy knew more about Javon than what can be found on Google.

"I know you possess a certain artifact. One you know very little about. Not even enough to be dangerous. Therefore, you will hand me that case, tell your boss money couldn't buy it this time, and sit back down at the kid's table while the adults talk."

"I'm sorry, sir. I have my instructions, which were pretty clear about how much effort I needed to put into maintaining possession of this case."

Under the storm, a cacophony of metallic clicks created by safeties being moved to the off-and-ready position could be heard. The four tough-as-nails military types were losing their patience and sense of humor at a rate equivalent to the speed of the worsening weather.

"And I don't think you are clear on the amount of effort it is taking my men to not just put you down with rounds to the head and simply just take the case from you," explained Special Agent Gordon.

"Leave the case, leave the state, forget any of this was even a thing. Can you do that?"

From his sports and military days, Javon was well-versed in compartmentalizing. He knew what was a nuisance and could wait, what was stressing him out, and what needed immediate attention before things got worse.

The latter was Javon's situation, devolving by the second.

"If I hand you this case, what kind of assurances can you give me that you won't get curious and look inside?"

"We have some idea as to what is inside the case." SA Gordon said with a certain amount of smugness.

"Not that!" A frustrated Javon continued. "I need to know that when I hand you this case, you won't open it."

A few glances and moments later, both sides had what they wanted. Javon had a beating heart and life-giving air vibrating through his body as he watched the government Humvee leave like it was late for dinner.

As the tail lights faded out of sight, Javon's last thought was, "They better slow down."

CHAPTER 11
SPEED KILLS

Special Agent Gordon of Homeland Security and his Fab Four detail never returned to the airport. At the intersection of Mendenhall Loop Rd. and Route 7, a panicked driver may have just killed 80 percent of the people on the planet.

The airport was falling under a Marshall Law-type scenario. Frank Trimble, salesman of the year for his local radio station in Juneau, was arriving back from a trip to D.C. and the annual meeting of the National Association of Broadcasters
More 'drink working' than networking, it was a trip Frank took every year. When he got off the plane and was greeted by the chaos, his first thought was "another tax dollar-funded training exercise."

The gunfire cleared up that confusion, and men in uniform explained in a booming voice no one would be allowed to leave. Anyone caught trying to go will be detained. Anyone wishing to try their luck using force to force the issue would be shot.

Frank didn't need to hear anymore. Before being seen, Frank disappeared behind the counter of a Starbucks and into the kitchen. A couple of service hallways later, he was breathing the chilly Juneau air, not jet fuel fumes. Racing to his truck, he gunned it. He wasn't sure what was going on, but he would be damned if he would not see his wife and kids again.

Like Javon, Frank could sneak out of the airport but didn't see the traffic lights. The wind was so strong that it was swinging the traffic lights horizontally, not the optimal position when it came to wanting to obey the rules of the road. However, the rules of the road were only sometimes a top priority for Frank.

The panic bone is connected to the gas pedal bone, which is a bad combination. Fear fueled Frank's gas foot and on a slippery road that proved detrimental to Frank's getting home. A slick spot, loss of traction, and that sickening feeling of the only wheel making contact is the one Frank has a death grip on.

"Fuck, fuck, fuck" was all the English his brain could provide because it was kind of busy trying to remember, is it turn into the direction of the spin or turn in the opposite direction of the spin? The oncoming headlights shielded the answer, but then there was nothing.

Inside the Humvee, a "firearm safety 101" failure was about to unfold. One of Agent Gordon's "fab four," a kid who looked barely old enough to play "Call of Duty," let alone be on this detail, forgot one of the biggest rules of all – safety.

The impact between the heavily armored military vehicle and Frank's half-ton pick-up was one-sided and over in seconds. Physics states that for every action, there is an equal and opposite reaction, which sucks at this very moment if you're Frank. The nearly 3-ton Humvee hit Frank's sideways truck at 45 mph.

In a tornadic explosion of metal, airbags, and shattered glass, it was over in 20 seconds. All that violent noise is a memory now drowning in the storm's wind. Frank died on impact, as his buckling side door was ripped and fabricated into a nightmarish pitchfork whose three tines found their home in his left ear, left lung, and finally, his left kidney.

Everyone inside the Humvee was shaken but unharmed—everyone, but not everything. The impact was still jarring. Enough force was displaced from its original home only to find a foster home in the SIG P320 semi-automatic pistol carelessly held in the hand of "Call of Duty" rather than in his holster. One of the noises in the crash was a distinct gunshot. The bullet was the unintended consequence that, looking back, could have prevented so many lost lives if only the safety were on.

The case holding the artifact at the center of this kerfuffle was nestled between Call of Duty and another member of the Fab 4, who, like Yoko Ono, is about to break this party up and doesn't even know it. Leaping from the barrel of the gun as if to say, "Holy Shit, this crash sucks, and I want no part of it," the bullet pierced the case and the unknown outer shell of the artifact. The faint, green mist – a color reminiscent of Nickelodeon slime – was hard to see in the flash of dark, headlights, and streetlights.

If they could have seen it, they would have noticed that despite all the movement inside that vehicle, the mist seemed to have a mind of its own. While it did not, it was unfortunate for Yoko Ono that she was close and in the path of whatever that mist was. It was a fundamental truth in the universe of unintended consequences that if it could go wrong, it would.

Also, the shortest distance between point A and point B is a straight line. That straight line ended with point B being the open mouth of an unsuspecting soldier. The mist found its new home, settled into her mucus membrane and lungs, and began to come alive.

CHAPTER 12
TSUNAMI

It has been about an hour since the accident. Call of Duty, Special Agent Gordon, and the other two members of the team were all off to the side of the road, clearing up the final details for the report the local police officer was going to have to file. Labeled a terrible accident, it was just a matter of clearing up what was left of Frank's truck and Frank.

The coroner van took care of that while the fire department went back to the station. The wrecker's flashing lights turned what was mostly snow into a disco ball, and one ambulance remained. The back of the ambulance was open, and sitting up on a gurney undergoing a battery of tests was Yoko Ono.

Having discharged a weapon in such close proximity, the paramedics were checking for everything from powder burns to wounds caused by ricochet. Also, Yoko, real name Makayla Reed, had been complaining of feeling tired, dizzy, and short of breath. Suspecting concussion, it was decided that Makayla would be taken to Bartlett Regional Hospital.

Five minutes into the 10-minute ambulance ride, Makayla's health seemed to be deteriorating. All she wanted to do was sleep, and when she wasn't complaining about the headache, she and her very warm and flushed complexation had an impossible time answering questions and staying on topic.

On the radio, one of the paramedics was in constant communication with the trauma center, clearly fearing some severe concussion, brain swelling, brain bleed, or anything along those lines, and told the medical team waiting at the sliding doors of the trauma center, which was presently keeping the nasty storm outside, to be ready.

The ambulance backed up, the doors opened, and the paramedics lowered Makayla out of the ambulance, and that's when the nose bleeds started. Not a nosebleed that was a result of the crisp, dry Alaskan air. Those typically stop after a few minutes with your head tilted back. This was something else. Slow, steady, persistent and after 15 minutes, it still wasn't stopping.

Met at the door to the trauma center the paramedic gave the doctors and nurses a rundown of the basics. "28-year-old African-American female, victim of a motor vehicle crash, complaining of severe headache and presenting with dizziness, flush and warm to the touch, mild confusion is present. BP is 148 over 90 and climbing. Pulse ox is 88 percent and dropping; nose bleed presented just now."

The paramedic continued, "Breathing has become somewhat labored, pupil function normal, no known allergies according to the patient in early Q&A before answers to our questions become challenging."

Makayla had made it to Trauma Bay One and was being slid from the gurney to the table.

"Doctor," one of the nurses called out

"Nose bleed still presenting with no signs of slowing down and now gums are bleeding."

"Maybe she hit her teeth in the impact of the crash"

"No signs of trauma to the jaw to indicate that doctor and I'm no dentist, but her gums seem healthy." The nurse continued, "I'll keep an eye on it; if it gets worse, we'll have to use suction to prevent choking.

The nurse was concerned. This wasn't just a case of too many sweets or Makayla not being diligent about brushing and flossing. Blood was pouring from her gums, something akin to a cut.

The doctor looked over, "Start normal saline drip for now, but be ready for changes in I.V. protocols; I need a full panel of bloodwork. Type her, and call the blood bank. So far, the bleeding appears manageable, but if it gets worse, we'll need several units of AB+ on standby. I want to be notified the moment her condition changes".

The nurse made a visible facial expression as if to say, "No Shit!" She hoped Doctor Assai hadn't seen it.

Stabilizing her the best they could, Makayla was whisked off to imaging for x-rays of her skull and to get some more detailed pictures of the brain. The task was made even more difficult because, as one x-ray tech put it, "Why won't the bleeding stop?"

While more like a trickle than a steady stream, that was the million-dollar question. Blood seemed to be trying to leave the body using any path of least resistance. As the blood continued to slowly stain the sheet and gauze, at first look, Makayla was starting to look like a burn victim and not someone who came into the ER for what appeared to be a mild concussion.

Like a scene out of a horror movie, blood was escaping from everywhere. The ears, corners of her eyes, mouth, vagina, anus, and even the pores of her skin were dotted red with Makayla's blood. The mechanism in the human body, designed to keep the blood on the inside, was clearly failing.

Imaging was done, and just as the front wheels of Makayla's bed hit the threshold of the trauma bay, things went sideways.

The trauma team had been working together in Juneau for a long time and had seen some things. Bear attacks, car wrecks, bodies burned more than 80 percent, falls from high places onto rocky low places – but nothing like this. Everyone took a moment to get the "what the fuck" out of their system, then used every tool in their skill set to save this girl.

There are about 1 and a half gallons of blood in the human body (give or take), that give or take was all over Makayla's sheets and her clothing. While accurately measuring the rate at which the blood was leaving her body was difficult, the trauma team didn't need a machine to see the rate was increasing. The ER was not prepared. Woefully understocked in gauze, bandages, sponges, and even paper towels, the blood was winning. Makayla was losing.

The nurse paged the doctor; the phone rang.

"We need you back here," the nurse said. "It's not slowing down".

"Then just keep her stable," the doctor replied.

"No, sorry, I wasn't clear. She's getting worse. We can't stop the bleeding." The doctor could hear a hint of desperation in her voice.

"Ok, I want the room sealed off and everyone in full PPE, like back in the days of Covid. Seal yourselves up tight and someone notify the CDC in Atlanta."

Not one person was dumb enough to question those orders. Makayla was on the verge of hemorrhaging in a way reminiscent of Ebola, and it was scary.

"One more thing," the doctor said, "you are all quarantined, and anyone you came in contact with within the last two hours needs to be found.

CHAPTER 13
PATIENT ZERO

Answers were at a deficit, blood was at a loss, and time had run out. 6 hours from when the paramedics first arrived to when Doctor Assai ordered Makayla to be put in a medically induced coma. Whatever was killing Makayla, it was nothing they were prepared for.

The exhausted doctors and nurses slumped against walls on the only few clean spots of the floor that were left. Red and white gauze littered the floor like a New Year's Eve confetti and they all knew what just happened wasn't normal. It was miles away from normal, and so …much…blood.

So much blood, more than there should be. Makayla had been moved to the ICU, and the fastidious cleaning of trauma bay one was underway.

"So much blood," the doctor said, standing out of the way of the cleaning, sanitizing, and sealing of the room.

That's all she could think of because her basic med school teachings told his rational mind that it was much more than the gallon and a half that should have been in Makayla. Where did it all come from?

Due to the urgency the last 6 hours had presented, Doctor Assai was pressuring the lab to put a rush on the blood work. She would be the one tasked with talking to Mom and Dad Reed when they arrived. The question is, does she make up some bullshit or simply admit they don't know what they are dealing with. In her career, honesty, and transparency had always served situations like this best

Special Agent Gordon had just arrived at the emergency room desk, which was on the other side of a few walls and hallways.

"I'm here to check on a …" he paused. Co-worker, team member, and soldier all seemed very uncaring in a situation like this.

"I'm here to check on a friend, Makayla Reed."

"The doctors and nurses are working on her now, sir. If you could have a seat in the waiting area around the corner, we'll call you when we know more."

"Working on her? Don't you mean treating, it was just a mild concussion from what the paramedics were saying at the scene."

The nurse repeated, "We will call you when we know more. Someone will be with you as soon as they can."

The last time Walter saw Makayla was in the back of the ambulance. She was sitting up, awake, and cracking a couple of jokes. It turned out that was going to be the last time he saw her.

"Agent Gordon?" Dr. Minnis Assai asked. An easy guess since he was the only one in the waiting room.

"Yes, Makayla, how is she?"

"Was anyone else in this waiting room with you in the last couple of hours?

"No, but ….

Doctor Assai cut him off, "I will explain everything in just a second, but I need you to come with me. I know you have a lot of questions, but getting you quarantined is my top priority right now."

"Hold on", Agent Gordon protested

With a firmness in her voice that she knew a government official like Walter would understand, she insisted. "Agent, I am going to guess someone in your position understands the need for the time of truth, embellishment, and shut up and listen because we are up against it. This, Makayla, all of this is the latter. So, please follow me, and when we are secure, I will tell you what I know."

In the hour it took for Doctor Assai to recap the events of Trauma Bay 1, the six members of her trauma team that worked on Makayla were in an isolated wing of the ICU. All with the same symptoms that Makayla Reed first presented with. The headaches, dizziness, confusion, all of it.

Under close observation by a fresh team of nurses and doctors who were called in under the quarantine protocols that the hospital had in place – Doctor Assai, who hadn't slept much, was reviewing the labs and the imaging.

"What am I looking at? Are you sure?" she asked the radiologist.

"I wish I weren't, but yes, I've never seen anything like this. Not this fast." Doctor Assai read on. The liver, the spleen even the kidneys were enlarged in a way that made no sense. There were several clots in her lungs, and as shocking as all those things were, it made what was next seem downright normal.

With all the blood that ended up on the outside of Makayla, she had a full complement of it inside her, as if she had never lost any at all.

The coroner saw the confusion on her face and decided to interject.

"Dr. Assai, the blood, it was …..", trying to find the right word, "thick." I've seen only a few cases of polycythemia vera, which resembles this in a way.

It's a condition where the blood thickens. It can be treated with certain medications, chemotherapy, or phlebotomy, where blood is basically siphoned off to relieve the pressure."

"Could this be…" she was interrupted

"If the patient had been diagnosed months even years ago. This is way too fast for that and Polycythemia Vera doesn't present with this level of hemorrhaging. The only way I can describe what is causing the blood to evacuate the body from any hole possible is that it is being pushed out."

"Excuse me?" Doctor Assai was all for experiencing firsts, but not like this.

"The only way I can explain it is, well, remember the old play dough fun factory when we were kids or something more grown up, the sausage-making attachment for a stand mixer. The pressure behind pushes the content out of the only available exit.

In this case, the pressure of the thickening blood that was still continuing to replace what was being lost at an alarming rate forced the thinner blood out of the body to allow for the density and volume of this new blood that was now residing in every part of her. The veins, arteries, capillaries. Everything that relies on blood had this thick, glue-like blood forced in.

Seeing Doctor Assai struggling to process all this, the coroner continued.
"Did you try Apixaban or warfarin?" Dr. Assai asked, running down in her head the checklist of things that normally would help.

"No effect." The radiologist confirmed.

"Plavix?" thought Dr. Assai. "Maybe if we can slow down or prevent the production of platelets, it would help the patient turn the corner."

"Sorry." Was all the radiologist could say.

"Normal blood has a viscosity of somewhere between 3.5 and 5.5 cP. Your patient's blood viscosity had a value of 2500 cP, greater than Elmer's glue. Not the original Elmer's glue we all played with as kids, poured all over our hands and let it dry so we could peel it off like fake skin. No, the industrial strength Elmer's glue. The stuff that bonds wood and other household materials. So yeah, Makayla's blood turned to glue."

Stunned, Dr. Assai sat in the coroner's office, trying to make sense of what she had just been told. She looked at the time—3 a.m. The last 8 hours had been unlike any she had ever experienced. All she really knew was it was something highly infectious.

"Lord, help us if this thing gets out," she thought.

CHAPTER 14
SHUT EM ALL DOWN

It only took till sunrise to give Dr. Assai the answer she was dreading.

By morning, the ER had half a dozen new patients. At this rate, it would only be a couple of days before the waiting rooms, trauma bays, hallways, and even conference rooms were made into make-shift spaces for beds. Dr. Assai mind revisited the days of Covid. The New York City hospitals were parking refrigeration trucks outside and using them as makeshift morgues because the bodies were piling up, and there was nowhere to put them.

When the ambulance crew did all they could for Makalya before dropping her off at the hospital, little did they know it was already too late for them. If they had, they may not have stopped at the bar on the way home for a couple of drinks or hit the convenience store for a pack of smokes and a lottery ticket. Powerball was $800 million dollars. That kind of money is life-changing.

Their lives would change after that night, but no amount of money would save them, the people they came in contact with, and those caught in the ripple of death slowly making its way through Juneau.

There was a wailing in the halls of Barrett Regional Hospital, reminiscent of the gale winds of last night's storm. This was a human-generated noise. An eerie blend of sorrow, fear, and physical pain all wrapped up into a singular, ominous, dire note.

Candace Stanton had landed in Juneau about 45 minutes ago, about 13 hours since Makayla first showed symptoms, and it was that death nell that greeted her when she finally arrived at the hospital an hour later. At that time, she was left speechless and filled with more questions than answers.

Before leaving the plane, her military 'escorts' instructed her to put on a hazmat suit. This big yellow thing, not very form-fitting, offered her a brief escape from reality as she yelled, "23-19, we have a 23-19" in her head.

Walking through the terminal that had been transformed into what can only be described as a hybrid medical facility and detainment center, Candace was surrounded by the angry voices of civilians with lots of questions, no answers, and even angrier military and government personnel who had been ordered to make sure no one leaves, period. That building stays locked up tight at all costs and by any means necessary.

At the hospital, there was a different vibe. A very busy ER greeted her, the awful sound of suffering humanity filling the halls. She was also met with officials from the CDC, FEMA, state and local authorities, and even NASA had joined the party. As quickly as the military got Candace to Juneau, it appeared other government agencies were quick to drop everything. Their advantage was they didn't have to go find a doctor kayaking in Kansas with her dog and strongly persuade her to get in the helicopter.

"Why is NASA here?" she thought. "Why am I here?"

She was ushered into a large conference room filled with TV screens, computers, whiteboards, reports and files, and what appeared to be a collection of the smartest people in the room. Whatever this was, it was much more than e. coli or listeria from not washing vegetables you got at the local grocery store. This was bigger, much bigger.

At about the same time, Candace was getting introduced to a room of her new best friends; Javon was getting out of the shower. The ship known as the "M/V Called in Another Favor" had sailed. Not even Spencer Grendhall could manifest influence over what was happening in Alaska. Which meant Javon was on his own.

His phone rang.

"What went wrong? I thought you had it in your possession"

"I did, but then the government, "governmented" and well, here we are." Javon stopped briefly to mentally pat himself on the back for turning the government into a verb.

"We were just a couple miles away from the airport when they surrounded the vehicle. Your escape plan from the airport wasn't flawed; we just needed more time. They had Juneau zipped up tight." Javon explained

"How did they get the airport shut down that quickly?" A curious Spencer asked.

"Not the airport, sir, Juneau. All of Juneau. Perimeters, a Marshall Law kind of presence, and all the dick-swinging and posturing that goes along with it. Remember that scene in Star Wars? Luke, Leia, C-3PO, and Chewy are in the trash compactor?"

"I was more of a Star Trek guy"

"When things calm down you and I need to have a talk. Anyway, the walls were closing, and R2D2 was trying to guess the right combination to stop the walls from closing in and squashing his friends. Luke yells, 'SHUT EM DOWN, SHUT EM ALL DOWN R2'. That is what someone did here; everything from the nursing homes to the gas stations has been absorbed into this mayhem."

Not giving Spence a chance to interrupt, Javon continued. "I'm not able to confirm, but if I were a betting man, I'd guess by now, there has been an order issued for people to shelter in place and not come out of their homes unless ordered to. I'm not sure what's going on yet, but military, state, and local officials ain't playin'".

"Where are you now, Javon?"

"A place called the Silver Bow Inn and Suites in downtown Juneau. It's about 10 minutes east of the hospital and 20 minutes from the airport. I wanted to put a little anonymous distance between me and the shit show north and west of here."

Spencer thought for a moment. "Okay, there is not going to be a lot you personally can do today at either the airport or the hospital. At this point, you need to go into survival mode. Acquire firearms, ammo, survival gear, transportation, food…."

"Sir," Javon cut him off. "10 years in the Marines and a lot of time working for you, I'm already a few steps ahead of you."

"I suppose that's true," Spencer admitted, slightly embarrassed. For all his money and power, Spencer still retained a certain amount of humility. Losing a parent at a young age will probably do that to a person unless it goes in the other direction of anger and hate and wanting to take it out on the world.

"Firearms and ammo were my first priority because as soon as the unsuspecting people of this town figure out what has really rolled up on them, real panic will set in, and it's going to be every salmon fisherman for themselves. I, personally, want to be as far away from here when that happens."

"Good idea!" Spencer said with a shared enthusiasm. "I will put more money in your account. Enough to make up for the fact that there's not much else I can do for now. Take about twenty percent of it out in cash and guard it with your life. We don't know how bad this will get. Worst case, I think power grids could be compromised, looting, gas shortages, short tempers – you'll need all the bargaining power you can get."

His boss continued to robotically list things: "First aid supplies, antibiotics, penicillin, things to sterilize with. If you have a paper cut that gets infected and you don't have basic supplies to clean it, you could get a bad infection or worse.

Ewan Trenholm, Noa Tupoa, and Casey Ledger (a.k.a. Call of Duty") were all waiting at Juneau International Airport for their ride. They had been dismissed shortly after the ambulance carrying Makayla had driven away from the scene.

Their orders were to take a government-provided 2-hour flight north to Eielson AFB in Fairbanks. From there, they would board a flight back to northern Virginia. Four hours post-accident, thanks to rare government efficiency, the three soldiers were on a KC-46A tanker bound for Joint Base Andrews just outside D.C.

That plane would never make it. In close quarters and recycled air, as soon as Noa Tupoa started to show symptoms and was contagious, this extraterrestrial organism had little trouble finding purchase in the immune system of all on board.

The pilot, while still lucid enough to perform the emergency landing, had diverted to Seattle while on a flight path that would have taken the plane over Calgary. Still, less than 5 hours from Makayla presenting symptoms, news had not traveled that fast. Sure, there were the internet and cell phones, but thanks to a healthy skepticism fueled by the misinformation provided by most vexed political landscapes this day, many people did their due diligence to discover what was really true or not. Add that to the fact that local, state, and government military and science types still didn't have their heads completely wrapped around all of this; it made it still quite easy for the spread to continue.

Emergency medical teams on the tarmac in Seattle just thought this was another medical call. Unruly passenger, a bad allergic reaction, maybe a heart attack, but nothing more exciting than that.
When they walked up the stairs and entered the plane that had been parked away from the terminal, it was too late.

So much blood.

CHAPTER 15
JUNEAU FALLS

The briefing in the conference room at Bartlett Regional Hospital wasn't so brief. 4 hours later, Candance had a lot of questions. Where did it come from? How are people getting it? Is it airborne, passed by saliva or other bodily fluids, or both? The biggest question of them all is how it can be stopped.

"Okay, but why am I here?" Candace politely demanded.

"You have all the leading experts in infectious disease, little green men from outer space, military strategists, psychologists, DOD, CDC, FEMA, NSA, CIA, FBI…..only thing missing is KFC."

Candace knew she should have read the room. There were situations that called for a little levity, but this was not one of them.

"Miss Stanton, you are the smartest person in the room when it comes to blood – you've seen the pictures," Special Agent Gordon said.

"So much blood," she mumbled in her brain. "Human blood, I know human blood, not stuff from outer space."

"From what we can tell, doctor, even after the blood has been infected, it still resembles human blood; it just behaves differently. Here is what we know. Symptoms present around 30 minutes after infection. That was about the time it took to get the patient to the hospital from the crash scene. Headaches, mild disorientation, fatigue, slight fever, and a persistent nosebleed are all first to show. About an hour later, the patient started complaining of pain, not in one spot but everywhere. The pain was mild at first, but as it increased, so did the pain meds."

SA Gordon continued. "Also, at this point, the nosebleed hadn't stopped; in fact, it had gotten worse. The patient was now also bleeding from her gums, ears, and the corner of her eyes." He paused for what Candace could only imagine was for dramatic effect or so that she could process all of this.

"Labs were drawn, and this is where it gets weird." Agent Gordon announced. "The blood we drew from the patient was not like the blood that was now drenching her gown and sheets and being discarded on the ER floor in 4x4 squares of gauze."

"I'm not sure I understand." Candace declared feeling safe that she would not be judged.

"Don't get me wrong, Dr. Staunton," Agent Gordon responded. "The blood was the same color; it was just thicker. After further examination under a microscope, there are things in the patient's blood we can't identify. All we know is it didn't flow like blood. It was more like glue."

"GLU," Candace cut Agent Gordon off

"Yes, GLU, the consistency of the blood," Agent Gordon said with an implied "This was covered in the briefing."

"Right!" Candace replied with some confidence she hoped would hide her embarrassment.

"Whatever this "glue" is, it affects several systems all related to blood production and health. The endocrine glands, bone marrow, and stem cells all undergo some sort of change that thickens the blood. Initially, the symptoms of the person infected mirror those of a person inflicted with Polycythemia Vera. Honestly, we thought that was it, but it was just so fast. That also didn't explain the final symptoms right before death. The blood is forced from the body by any means necessary."

"You said that in the meeting, and I was confused. Don't you mean 'draining' or 'leaving'? Forced seems like it was an evacuation, it seems almost to have thought, purpose, intelligence," Candace quizzically stated.

"No," Agent Gordon said as if he wished that were the case. "It's being forced out, replaced. Not reduced, mind you. In fact, just the opposite. Which seems counterintuitive. It's as if the patients have hemorrhagic symptoms similar to Ebola, but unlike Ebola, the body is actually keeping up with replacing the blood lost with new blood. It's fascinating and alarming all at the same time.

In order to keep up with this and give the infected extra time, I am hearing early reports from the medical team on the front line of this thing in the ER that performing a Phlebotomy helps stabilize the patient a little longer. Sadly, it doesn't stop the blood from turning to GLU."

"What's the blood supply like in this hospital?" Candace asked because a light bulb had just gone on.

"I'm not sure; the lead doctor, Doctor Assai, hasn't briefed me on that. Why?"

"Phlebotomy was a good thought and a good first step. Gotta Start somewhere, right? Would I be correct in assuming no one has tried a transfusion at the same time?"

"You'd have to ask Dr. Assai," the slightly confused Agent Gordon said.

"I'm going to guess no," Candace speculated. "Here is what I'm thinking…."

Agent Gordon and Candace governed their speed to a fast walk, kind of like the silly ones in the Olympic sport of speed walking. Running through the halls of a hospital in complete disarray was not advised.

"WHERE IS DOCTOR ASSAI?" Candace demanded.

The startled nurse caught her breath and balanced. "She's in the trauma unit. She's doing her best to keep everyone focused, and that's just the people who normally work here."

"What do you mean?" Agent Gordon asked.

"We are calling in EVERYONE!! EMTs, Paramedics, retired military doctors, law enforcement, and firefighters—not just from Juneau but all over Alaska. From Nome to Ketchikan, if there is anyone with medical experience, chances are they are on a seaplane and on their way here if they haven't already landed.

"You'll have to excuse me; I have to make more rooms in this hospital," the nurse explained.

Candace and Agent Gordon arrived at the trauma unit to a scene of organized chaos. While nothing could have prepared the trauma unit doctors and nurses for an outbreak like this, it's not like they were rookies at this.

Back in 2016, an Alaska Air passenger jet carrying 167 souls on board inexplicably lost power over Glacier Bay National Park while heading for Vancouver. It almost made the runway; another 150 yards was the difference between wheels down and a very bumpy landing. 95 of the 167 were injured, 23 critically.

So, no, not their first time at the rodeo, just the first time at THIS rodeo. The basics were still the same, with a few added steps like isolation, PPE, etc.

In less that 6 hours, the town of Juneau, Alaska, was bowing under the weight of being the epicenter of a story that was slowly starting to creep out from the dark recesses of the internet. News media, Reddit, TikTok, it was everywhere. #PrayForJuneau was trending everywhere along with #UFO #Aliens #GovernmentCoverup #Consiparacy.

All means of shiny paper hat-wearing influence was attempting to bend the free will of the average Joe and manipulate them into their individual 'Cult of Personality'. Anyone at Bartlett Regional Medical Center didn't care about any of that. Their world did not exist outside that campus, and it couldn't.

Bartlett Regional was licensed for 57 inpatient beds, 16 residential substance-abuse treatment facility beds in the Rainforest Recovery Center, and 61 residential beds in Wildflower Court. It was designed to serve the 15,000-square-mile region in the northern part of southeast Alaska, where 55,000 residents resided, many of them in areas inaccessible by road. If you were trying to get in or out of Juneau, it wasn't accessible by roads. You got here by water or air.

That sort of isolation did have an upside. It meant the people living there were already pretty self-sufficient and probably had all they needed for the cold and flu season and the occasional errant swing of the ax. Someone in that part of Alaska had to be in tough shape to need Bartlett. The increasing number of infected filling the over-taxed hospital, were coming from Juneau proper.

Twin Lakes campground, the Office Max by the airport, Hostel Juneau International, and even Deckhand Dave's Fish Tacos. You don't realize how everyone knows everyone until they are all at the hospital waiting to get treated for the same thing. This wasn't the '6 degrees of Kevin Bacon'; this was "How's your mom, tell her hi for me" next-door neighbor, church congregation kind of familiar. Now they all had one thing in common, the question, "Am I going to die?

For many, the answer would be yes.

"YOU CAN'T BE IN HERE" Dr. Assai yelled over the bedlam that was the trauma unit and emergency room of the hospital.

"We need just 5 minutes", Candace begged

Looking at Agent Gordon, like the HOA Karen, who is convinced you don't live in the neighborhood, "I'm sorry. And who is this?"

Candace didn't need anyone to speak for her; the credentials she had earned over decades of dedicating her life to her science did the talking. "I'm Dr. Candace Stanton, lead hematological oncologist at the Kansas Cancer Center in Wichita, Kansas."

"Well, Dorothy, you're……"

"With all due respect Dr. Assai, cut this territorial; I'm in charge bullshit. Cause from where I'm standing, you're in charge of two things, 'Jack' and 'shit'."

Candace continued to exert herself into the hierarchy.

"I have spent years understanding and studying blood and I'm not about to stand here and wait for you to determine if I'm qualified to join your club or not."

Candace didn't wait for the shocked look on Dr. Assai's face to fade.

"I'm here to help, and I believe I have a suggestion that might buy the patients and you some time and slow this runaway train down just a little so that we might get a little closer to understanding what we are truly up against here."

"Give me 2 minutes to clean up, and I'll meet you in the conference room"

A few minutes later, Gordon, Assai, and Stanton were able to hear themselves think, and Candace wasted no time.

"Dr. Assai, the basic pathology of this is old blood gets forced out, blood volume doesn't change, and blood that stays in the body turns to GLU. Is that about right?"

"Yes, simply put, that's the entry-level version"

"I want to try something," Candace insisted. "There is some risk involved because nothing like this has been tried. Nothing like this has needed to be tried. I think we can all agree, these last couple of day, there have been a lot of firsts."

Candace continued, "As a person's blood is being forced out and the 'new' blood is being turned into GLU, in theory, couldn't we, through transfusion, push new blood in? This would keep a constant flow of healthy blood through the body and maybe slow the progression of the changeover to GLU?"

Agent Gordon, who had enough medical qualifications to put a band-aid on, jumped in, "At this point, it's like chicken soup."

Both doctors looked at Andrew like he had lost his mind

"Chicken soup…when you have a cold, everyone says chicken soup. Do you know why? Because it may not help, but it couldn't hurt. Basically, ladies, what have we got to lose?"

They agreed, and a room was soon prepped for the first real experiment to find a weapon against GLU.

CHAPTER 16

TRIAL AND ERROR

The first attempt at simultaneous phlebotomy–transfusion was underway. The patient, a healthy male in his mid-40s, like all the others, started with symptoms about 30 minutes in.

Unlike some who started the bleeding phase about 4-8 hours in, depending on their family history and genetic makeup, Trevor (a restaurant manager here in town) had not yet. He was in great shape. From what they could tell, he was physically active; his records (since Bartlett was the only game in town) showed no history of heart issues, cancer, etc. Never smoked and occasionally drank.

There was no doubt he had it, but the goal was to stay ahead of it before the blood started leaving the body. While in the confused headache stage of the progression, it was determined that sedation was the best course of action. Anything they could do to give him a fighting chance.

A web of tubes, wires, and cords surrounded Trevor, and every sound of beeping and buzzing filled his acoustical airspace. None of that mattered. Anyone with a medical interest in this experiment was gathered around his room.

In a casino, you would have thought there was a craps table in the center of this mob of medical humanity. No craps table, and the odds would have been better if there were.

7 hours since the first symptoms and Trevor's blood was where it belonged. All indications were that the blood that was coming and going was stabilizing his vitals. In the room, a resuscitation of hope that this could actually be working.

9 hours. Trevor was at a threshold of possibly living longer than anyone who was in that 80 percent mortality rate. The collective breath everyone had been holding was easing. Allowing other thoughts to creep in. Thoughts like, when did I sleep last, or eat last, or "God, I didn't realize the coffee we served in this hospital was so bad," Dr. Assai cracked a smile as her train of thought continued.

"If this experiment doesn't work, maybe we can pump the patients full of this stuff; that's bound to work." A few people in the room nervously chuckled, wondering if it was appropriate to laugh or not.

Across the room, Candace, who hadn't slept for about 48 hours was drifting in and out. Even in her dreams, she was kayaking with Khal. The rhythmic paddling, slicing into the water, the warmth of the light of the sun.

That was odd. The paddle was beeping. With each stroke and knifing of the blade into the water, "BEEP" sounded strange. Stroke. Beep. "Looking back to the front of the kayak, where Khal should have been, he wasn't.

"Khal – BEEP -Khal – BEEP!" Her shouting was more distressed and louder. The beeping was louder. Also growing louder, muffled at first, "Dr. Stanton….Dr. Stanton…..Candace"

"I'm awake," she said as if she had fallen asleep during a movie with her person who was getting very frustrated and ready to turn the tv off. In this case, the person was Agent Gordon, shaking her shoulders. Not Dr. Assai, who was tending to Trevor on the table.

So Much Blood!

10 hours and 38 minutes. From headache to heart failure. More than double the time than any other infected person. Losing Trevor was hard, not just because of all who knew him and how personal the medical team took it when they lost someone; death would always be hard. However, there was hope in this death. A day after, Makayla was reduced to a machine keeping her alive until someone made the hard choice to turn it off, and after dozens of less fortunate people who died quickly before help could be rendered, this death brought with it a spark.

"Clean this room and prep it for the next patient," Dr. Assai said very clinically. Clearly, she was compartmentalizing her emotions and was, had been for some time now, focused on saving as many people as possible.

The next patient, Judy, a 64-year-old school teacher, was looking forward to retiring in a year after teaching history at the same middle school in town for 35 years. It was a retirement she would more than likely not live to see. Some of her students would not live to see.

Dr. Assai hand-picked Judy for a couple of reasons. Judy was of a higher age demographic, and the bleeding had just started to present. Dr. Assai wanted to see if they could 'turn the tide' of GLU's progression. Would someone in the upper age bracket, in average health, tolerate the procedure?

Judy provided the answer, one final lesson, 9 hours and 21 minutes from the first symptoms. Again, it sucked, and again about twice the longevity. Six more patients, six more similar outcomes. Male, female, age range 19 to 86. The average time of death from first symptoms is 8 hours 56 minutes.

"What about radiotherapy?" Candace asked.

"What about it," Assai asked with a mild indifference

"In some cases, like patients with Sickle Cell, Radiation Therapy or diagnostic radiation has shown benefits in disorders of the blood. While I've never used it on patients with PV, it makes sense that it might work. Radiotherapy can sometimes slow down the cells in the bone marrow that make the blood cells. The larger the area of the body being treated, the better the results. My theory is, if we can slow the hyperproduction of blood, will it slow the advancement of GLU if it doesn't have the fuel source of red blood cells being produced?"

Not even arguing, "What have we got to lose?" Dr. Assai consented.

12 more patients, wide ranges of age, family health backgrounds, socioeconomic and environmental factors, and activity levels. All were treated with the trio of phlebotomy, transfusion, and radiotherapy. It was a brutal assault on the body, a body that was already on the GLU struggle bus.

With the odds stacked against them, they all died. That's the bad news. The good news, if you can consider it good news, is that the average time of death from the first symptom was 16 hours 54 minutes. The longest holdout, a 37-year-old halibut charter boat captain, just over 18 hours.

The numbers didn't represent hope or comfort, but they did represent progress and knowledge, and knowledge is power.

1,700 miles away in Seattle, Washington, the team of first responders on the KC-46 from Alaska was trying to make sense of what they were looking at.
No signs of a fight or trouble, mechanical failure or attack, but the bodies and the blood. Was it bacterial, was it viral, was it contagious?

The answer to that question would be answered by one of the first on the scene. Bruce Targoli, in his 15 years of law enforcement had never witnessed something like this. No crime scene could have prepared him or his early breakfast for what he saw. He walked from one end of the plane to the other, trying his best not to contaminate the evidence.

Needing fresh air, he ran out and down the ramp. Disoriented by the horror of what he saw, he was not paying attention; a baggage tram hit the brakes hard to avoid hitting Detective Targoli. Trying to catch his balance, he fell head-first into a stack of suitcases, knocking them from the tram that was bound for baggage claim.

"Watch where you're going", the driver yelled
"Sorry, I didn't....see ..."

"Clearly. Seriously, if you're gonna flash your badge to be out here, keep your head on a swivel."

"Got it," Bruce said apologetically. "Here, let me help." An everyday gesture that was the right thing to do unless you consider all the bags Bruce's sweaty hands were touching. All the bags, some that had reached their final destination, others that were connecting to points like Hawaii and beyond into the western Pacific.
Other bags were heading east to Chicago, south to Denver, and Dallas and Atlanta. Soon, all the major hubs would have bags from Seattle transporting personal belongings on the inside and extraterrestrial death on the outside.

PART II: EARTH

CHAPTER 17
LANDSLIDE

Nick Badwey had been called to the office of his station manager at "Today's Country" TAKU 105. Knocking on the door frame, he continued in.

"You wanted to see me?"

Kim Jones had earned every bit of intimidation she portrayed in her 35-year radio career. She had fought and clawed for every ounce of respect she earned, and she wasn't going to apologize for the ways and means by which she got her hands on it. She was fair and kind, just didn't suffer any bullshit. A straight shooter, if there ever was one. That is the woman who Nick expected on the other side of the desk when he walked in; that was not the woman who was waiting for him.

"Was she scared?" he thought. If he didn't know any better, she was.

"Shut the door and sit down, please, Nick." If you can imagine what Jack Nicholson would sound like as a woman, that was Kim Jones.

"What I'm about to share with you can't leave this room, Nick. First, read this." Kim handed him a very official-looking one-page document with the FEMA and Department of Homeland Security logos at the top.

As Nick read, the color drained from his face. He couldn't believe what he was looking at. When Covid hit the U.S. in 2020, and the world seemed to stop, he had been handed one of these letters. It labeled him and other media as an essential part of emergency management, and the letter authorized his travel beyond any blockades or barriers that may be in place, with the right precautions, of course. PPE, gloves, hand sanitizer, etc. After Covid started to subside, he framed that letter as a reminder. Now, he had a second one.

"Does this have something to do with what's going on down at Bartlett Regional Hospital?"

"It has everything to do with that but not just that. This is something else, something worse. I had a visit earlier today from the black SUVs with the tinted windows that all the conspiracy theorists living in the woods talk about on their ham radios.
What is going on at Bartlett makes COVID-19 look like hay fever. Its mortality rate is very high, and it doesn't care if you have a weakened immune system or not."

Nick just sat, quiet, stunned

"Nick, it's fast…like really fast. 30 minutes or so for the first symptoms to show, and the longest they have been able to keep anyone alive has been a little over 18 hours"

"How is it spread, are there things we can do like handwashing and masks and social distancing?" Nick asked, referencing the shallow knowledge pool he had waded into when Covid hit.

"Airborne, bodily fluids, surface contact, from what the suits and the doctors are saying, this nasty little organism has found a way to ensure it will find a way."

"Nature …uh…finds a way", Nick said, delivering the Jurassic Park line in his best Jeff Goldblum. When Nick was scared or nervous, he would fall back on being funny or trying to be. Kim wasn't laughing; she wasn't even smiling.

"I would almost agree with you if this was something natural," Kim stated.

"Okay, now you're freaking me out…what do you mean 'not natural'. This isn't paranormal, is it? Demonic, end of days bullshit? Do I need to find some Jesus in my life in the next 24 hours?"

"The Jesus thing couldn't hurt. Seriously, pray, Nick." Kim said flatly. "If you've never believed in God, pray to whatever part of the universe you think might hear you because that part of the universe may know what this is."

Kim had lost Nick at this point, for just a moment. Nick was a smart dude, and just like that, the confusion was gone.

"You can't be serious, Kim!"

Looking Nick dead in the eye

"They told me this organism that is trying to wipe Juneau off the planet is something extraterrestrial." She reached into her bottom desk drawer and pulled out two glasses and a bottle of Whistle Pig. She didn't even ask; She didn't have to. The look on Nick's face said, "Pour and don't stop".

The key card beeped, and Candace was over anything beeping. The door to her room at the Silver Bow Inn clicked and unlocked, and she dragged herself and her carry-on into the room.

Agent Gordon drove back to the hospital after dropping her off at the hotel, the room arranged and paid for by the same U.S. government that, for lack of a better description, kidnapped her.

Her eyes were as heavy as the odor that clung to every inch of her. She took a quick shower, slipped on some sweats and a Wichita State Shockers hoodie, and did something that resembled crawling into bed. It was more like surrendering to gravity, but she landed on the mattress and not the floor, and Candace considered that a small victory.

In the 45 seconds it took for her to lose consciousness, the last thought that drifted through her mind was Thanksgiving. The one year she told her mom she would be able to make it, and Candace wasn't sure if anyone would have Thanksgiving again.

The next morning, Candace was startled awake by gunshots outside the hotel. She peeked out the curtain, and the scene played out: society breaking down right in front of her eyes. She slipped on her running shoes, grabbed money, cards, and mace from her purse, and put them in her sling bag along with her phone; she paused with her hand on the doorknob.

"Girl, what exactly do you think is going to happen when you open that door?" she asked herself. Her inside voice had a point. She had walked out of 'Avengers: Infinity War' inspired by the strong female leads, feeling invincible just like the next nerd, but she was not Black Widow or Agent Carter. She was Doctor Candace, whose best superpowers were her medical knowledge and fiery wit—not really the best ammo in a gunfight.

Candace grabbed the remote and turned the TV on. The narrative, the spin, and the control that the medical staff and government had tried to keep close to the vest had gotten away from them. Every news channel, local and national, had opened the floodgates to any influencer and budding social media star on the internet.

The days of network news, news with an agenda, verified news—all of that is gone. Welcome to real-time news being filmed, uploaded, and live-streamed for millions to see and digest with nothing more than the disclaimer that "what you're about to see could be upsetting to some viewers."

The first thing that was upsetting Candace was the terrible camera work. Shaking, out of focus, subject not framed right. "Jesus, I've seen better bigfoot footage than this crap," she mused out loud.

To make matters worse, so much worse, the footage wasn't just from Juneau. It was a story about an Air Force K-46 that made an emergency landing, leading to Seattle-Tacoma International Airport being hermetically sealed from the outside world. No more planes came or went, no one left the airport, and no one was told why.

A sinking feeling swept over Candace. She knew the main ingredient for "Dumpster Fire and Dumplings" is to keep people in the dark.

She grabbed her phone and dialed

3 rings, 4, rings, "c'mon Mom…answer….please answer….pick up the da…"

"Candace! What a surp……"

"Mom…listen"

"You've changed your mind, and there will be a plus one for…"

Interrupting again, but this time with an urgency that bordered on rude.

"Mom, Mom, Mom…please, get Dad, put me on speaker; I need you both to listen very carefully to what I'm about to tell you."

"Candace, you're scaring us"

"That's the point. I need you and Dad to pack practical, comfortable, easy-to-wear clothing. Cash, if you have it, would be best, as would first aid supplies, N95 masks, and gloves. If you have that pistol in the nightstand, Dad, grab it."

"How did you know about that?" He said with some surprise.

"Not time for that right now; secure it, get as much ammo as you can, and pack smart."

"Candace, what is this all about?" her dad jumped back in.

For the next 30 minutes, as society devolved outside the hotel, Candace told them everything. The virus, the blood, the spread, Juneau teetering on civil unrest, everything. Her parents were stunned, in shock, non-believing.

"Candace, are you sure you're not blowing this out of proportion?" Mom hoped

"You haven't turned the TV or radio on yet, have you?"

"Well, no," her mom said.

Over the speaker, Candace heard the voices of her parents in the background arguing about the location of the TV remote. She knew when they found it because the only indication that the line was still open was the faint cellular hum.

"Honey, tell me you're okay" her dad pleaded

"I am, but I don't have much time. I need to get out of Juneau while I still can."

"Where will you go?"

"I'm not sure, but as long as cell service holds, I'll call every few hours. If we lose touch, we meet at the cottage at the Homestead on Goose Lake.

Goose Lake is a small 29-acre lake in the middle of Indiana farm country in Warsaw, Indiana. Small-town life is enough for now that her parents should be able to avoid contact with most people.

"We haven't been up there in years, I'm not even sure what kind of conditions it's it," Mom protested.

"Make it work. It's remote, and I have a feeling remote is going to equal safe. The last place you want to be is around other people who could be sick or, even worse, scared. Scared people make bad choices, selfish choices, dangerous choices." Candace continued with her suggestions that felt more like instructions or orders. "When you get to town, stock up on as many essentials as you can. Gas for the generator in the barn, dry goods, non-perishables, over the counter medicines, first aid, water, batteries….

"Slow down, slow down, I can only write so fast," her mom protested.

"Mom, you and dad are smart. We survived many a winter storm without power up there for a week or two. Just multiply all those precautions so that you can last a minimum of at least 6 months. If anyone asks why you're stocking up, make something up. Just don't tell them about GLU. The key is to avoid spreading panic."

Candace finished the call by saying, "I love you. I'll see you soon, I promise," and then she hung up.

Candace had heard her share of gunshots from living in Wichita, so it wasn't so much she was panicked as it was; she knew she needed to get into self-preservation mode and "GTFO".

Back to the door, with essentials packed and in hand, she paused just long enough to picture in her mind's eye what kind of bullshit she was getting ready to step into. It was like having the TV on and turned all the way up on an episode of NCIS. Tires squealing, gunshots, screams, sirens, you name it.

In her head, "One, Two,

"Wait" she said out loud as if there were other people in the room.

"Is it one, two, three GO! OR is it one, two go"?

Maybe it was the adrenaline, the stress, the fear. Maybe she was stalling for time, hoping the insanity outside would simply just get the command to "Move along; this is not the end of the world you're looking for." Maybe she was just stalling for courage.

Or maybe the scientist in her was taking that exact, inopportune moment to ponder the percentages and statistics swirling around the age-old question. If it's "one, two, three, and then GO," everyone in the room better know this.

If one person thinks it's "one, two, GO!" the element of surprise, the cohesiveness of form and function the entire moment was built around, falls apart in that one miscued second. EVERYONE has to be on the same page of chaos breaks out.

Clearly, the people in Juneau, Alaska – and it sounded like the entire population was outside her door – were not on the same page, and the "everyone remains calm" ship had sailed and struck an iceberg when it took a left out of the parking lot.

"Stop stalling, woman – It's 'Bad Bitch O'Clock', so let go!"

Candace swung open the door and inserted herself into the maelstrom.

CHAPTER 18
DERECHO

When Candace told her family and friends she was going to move to Wichita, Kansas, the first question was inevitably, "They have tornadoes there, don't they?" Well, yes, but there is so much more to the beautiful Midwest than this poltergeist of a weather phenomenon that can wipe entire towns off the map in less than 30 minutes.

In fact, the part of the country she lived in was the center of what is known as "Tornado Alley". Over the last few decades, there has been some speculation as to whether that weather corridor has shifted to the east a few hundred miles. More and more damaging storms and tornadoes are landing in places like Nashville, Ohio, and Indiana, and scientists are wondering why. Candace told herself she would make it her mission to dispel everyone's misconceptions about tornadoes and also make an effort to get them to stop saying, "There's no place like home."

She would often counter the "Isn't that tornado country" question with "Derecho is the new tornado."

Once the look of complete bewilderment left the faces of those around her, she would go on to explain, providing examples and historical examples along the way.

A relatively new weather event, only by name and reporting, a derecho is a continuous downwelling of high winds associated with a nearby jet stream and the expansion of dense rain-cooled air in the wake of strong thunderstorms. In August 2020, an exceptionally strong derecho subjected some areas of Iowa to sustained winds equal to that of an EF-0 and EF-1 tornado for over an hour.

Typically, this weather event lasts 20-30 minutes. Before it was over, some wind gusts reached 140 mph. Add torrential rains and large hail to a derecho and when it was gone, millions of people were affected. The Cedar Rapids area was in a blackout for almost a week and damage was estimated at over $11 billion.

Derecho was the first thing that came to mind when Candace opened that door. It's like she had not just stepped through a door but had been transported to an alternative universe, one that couldn't have been more polar opposite of the kayak, the river, and Khal. She missed that goofy dog of hers.

CHAPTER 19
RUN

Candace was having a hard time making sense of what she was seeing. This sort of thing doesn't happen in the United States. The closest version of this was 20 years ago, when Black Friday sales caused injuries from stampeding shoppers and the occasional fight that would break out over the last $10 kitchen counter appliance.

People were violent. It was well beyond pushing and shoving. These people lacked patience, tolerance, and empathy. They were scared and in survival mode. Anything and everything was a weapon. Those who were carrying were at the top of the food chain, but they were few in number. As they soon discovered, they couldn't stop everyone. Crowbars, car jacks, 2x4s, the kids 'sporting equipment they hadn't taken out of the trunk yet. They were weaponizing everything.

"GET DOWN!" someone yelled as the wood frame of her hotel room door exploded, splinters dodging and diving around her head like hummingbirds at the feeders at her mom's house. Caught up in the imagery of hummingbirds and the fact they are the only bird that can fly backward, Candace didn't react until the unknown voice yelled at her again

"YOU ARE GOING TO LOSE YOUR HEAD IF YOU DON'T KEEP IT DOWN".

She looked around and saw Javon crouching down near the ice and vending machine area on their floor that overlooked the open motel parking lot. From where the two of them were, they may as well have been royalty overlooking an arena as gladiators fought to the death.

Candace was much more exposed than Javon, and she knew it.

"Come here…wait…wait,….NOW!" Javon stood and from his hands exploded the cover fire of his Taurus 9mm. Candace didn't wait for a second invitation. Clarity had finally taken up rent in her unfocused and overwhelmed brain, and she was fully aware that she was in the middle of a life-or-death situation, so run to the friendly-looking guy with the gun.

"What's your name", Javon asked as she reached the safety of the vending machine.

"Candace", her name sounded foreign with a tremble in it.

"Do you have a car?"

"No, the military flew me in here and provided transportation right up until they dropped me off here."

"BALLS!", a favorite expression of Javon's. "Grand Theft Auto it is."

"You're going to steal a car"

With an understood "well, yeah" look on his face, Javon said, "Unless you think you can sweet-talk them into just handing us the keys."

"Not really my strong suit," she said

Surveying the motel parking lot, Javon found what he was looking for. An older Ford F150, something a bit easier to car jack than the newer models, something he was familiar with. Getting to it would be challenging, but not impossible, but he knew they had to go now. Hand on his backpack, he locked eyes with Candace with a look that said, "Shit's bout to get real" all he said was, "GO!"

They both grabbed their bags, Candace was half a step behind a man she just met, trusting him with her life and oddly not questioning anything. She couldn't put her finger on it, but Javon just gave off an air of …. shelter from the storm. They ran along the rail to the far end of the 2nd floor of the motel to the stairs in the corner of the building. Taking them two at a time, they were ground level and heading for the truck in no time. Javon thrust the gun into Candace's hands. She almost dropped it like it was a hot potato.

"Fire one before?" Javon questioned.

"Nope."

"Good, no bad habits to try and correct," he joked. "The safety is off; don't point it unless you plan to shoot it. If you have to shoot it, aim and squeeze the trigger."

Wide-eyed, Candace stiffened at his last instruction.

"I'm going to hotwire this truck. I need you to cover me. If anyone comes near us and tries to stop us, shoot them. Doesn't have to be a kill shot. Shoot them in the leg or shoulder, but shoot them. It's them or us, and I ain't fuckin' around."

"Clearly," she agreed. Nothing else needed to be said.

Candace had been in plenty of life-and-death situations before, but treating cancer patients and delivering the worst news or most hopeful news possible to family members was a whole different animal. This was like someone had cross-bread a Honey Badger with a Tasmanian Devil, put it in a bag and shaken it up, and then released it into a quiet library…an explosion of "HOLY SHIT!"

It seemed like forever as the world they knew disintegrated, replaced by a version ripped from the screen of a violent video game, the next few minutes were certainly not rated "E" for everyone. A stereo mash-up of screams of pain and terror mixed with pleading and begging and sorrow that blanketed a visual of destruction and blood….so much blood.

Javon was shielded from this. His sole focus was the wires, getting a spark, and getting the hell out of there. Candace, the gun trembling in her hand, witnessed it all. She never wanted to see anything like this again.

So much blood.

"HELL YEAH!" Javon screamed as the truck roared to life like an old dragon that had been wakened during some ancient battle.

"GET IN." He didn't have to tell her twice. She put their two over-stuffed packs on the bench seat between them. She jumped in the passenger side, the door shut, and tires let out a banshee-like squeal that distracted a few from their parking lot party of survival. Did the owner of the truck even realize it had been stolen? Were they still alive? It didn't matter; none of that mattered anymore. The two of them knew the world was never going to be the same again.

CHAPTER 20
A VIRUS BY ANY OTHER NAME

Pegamento – Spanish; Colle – French; Colla – Italian; Клей – Russian; 膠 – Chinese; Cola – Portuguese; غراء – Arabic. In just a little a week, what started with a couple of adventure influencers fighting over what was the best selfie to post, has now become a runaway train and the name of that train was GLU. The name had stuck, pun intended. It dominated every headline, every website, every newscast, radio broadcast, podcast, vlog, blog, Tiktok video – it was literally everywhere.

If the tone in the voices of those talking about it didn't indicate how serious the situation was, the images were there just to reinforce the "shut up and listen to every word I'm about to say" importance of it all. The larger cities looked like war zones. One really had to concentrate on the picture they were looking at to find the very blurry line of demarcation that created a border between people protesting their government and all the restrictions that were being put in place and the violence, the looting, the panic, the blood…

So much blood

Even with all that blood, some people were more concerned about their "God-given rights" than protecting themselves, believing the science, and caring about their friends, neighbors, and strangers. The 'Don't Tread on Me' crowd was hell-bent on doing the exact opposite of what the government was telling them needed to be done.

The popular rhetoric was, "We're not going to be sheep!" "Masks don't work, and they look ridiculous." "There is nothing you can tell us to take the vaccine you want to put in our bodies; we WILL NOT take the jab." Those were the hits, but the list of protests and disobedience was lengthy.

Travel by foot, bicycle, moped, motorcycle, horse – probably the best option. If you had a car, truck or van, you had a target on you back from people who wanted to separate you from said transportation. Commercial flights, forget it. If you had a private plane, you were popular, like that one guy in your neighborhood who owned a pick-up truck that everyone called on when they needed to move something.

The virus was slowly filling up hospitals across the country, with some hospitals in larger cities already having discussions about bringing in refrigerated trailers. A course of action that didn't seem nearly as impossible as when it was first used during Covid. With everything that had happened over the last 48 hours from Juneau to wherever the virus popped up next, there was still a portion of the population, with their tinfoil hats, that believed it was fake, like the moon landing.

With no known cure, the mortality rate was 100 percent. If you got it, you were going to die, short of being naturally immune. That part of the population hadn't been discovered yet, so the numbers continued to rise. Since the first infection in Juneau it was not only a health crisis, it was going to start affecting everything. As workforce numbers dwindled, so would productivity. Panic increased, and when the 1st responders, fire and rescue, healthcare workers, and law enforcement numbers began to shrink, crime increased.

At first, it was the opportunistic looters grabbing flatscreen TVs, toilet paper, and athletic shoes—at least the latter would have some practical use if the world came to an end and civilization had to rebuild in a post-apocalyptic new normal.

It didn't take long for people to reprioritize their smash-and-grabs: medicine, survival gear, non-perishable foods, weapons. If it was a weapon or could be made into a weapon, take it.

Still, there was a sliver of hope. Power grids and supply chains were still intact—for how long, no one knew. Scientists were working around the clock to find a cure. QR codes started popping up everywhere, asking those who weren't infected, those who appeared to be immune, to come forward and help, to be a part of the process, to offer a sample of their blood, which might hold some answers on how to stop this thing.

Of course, with that came the conspiracy theorists claiming all sorts of crazy things. Everything from a vaccine containing a microchip to the immune being put on a rocket to the dark side of the moon where world governments already had colonies built to repopulate the human race because they knew something like this was going to happen.

Humans are funny animals; even in the face of a possible extinction event, there will always be the grifters, those on the take, and those who want to make a quick buck by taking advantage of people. The price of water and gas shot up overnight in most places. If you need it, you better be ready to pay for it. Then there were the fake cures.

The promise of a life-saving regiment of shots or pills that would protect you from GLU. It wouldn't cure you if you got it, but if you didn't have it, this would keep you from getting it. The best part, the price was right. Expensive enough, so it seemed like for that price, it would work, but not too expensive to feel like price gouging. People paid, people got sick, people died, people got rich, all because fear sells.

Still, there was hope, but it was fading

CHAPTER 21
ALL EYES ON GLU

The chill of a late spring day in Vienna was a perfect reason to end a perfect day at Café Central. Kelly and Jill, journalism students and college roommates, had taken a semester off to travel. Vienna was the last stop of their European tour.

It's amazing how far your money can go staying in hostels, working a delivery job or waitress side hustle, and being smart with your money.

The morning had been full of social media posts and posing in the Volksgarten. From the roses to the Triton und Nymphe, they went on to enjoy lunch and shopping in the afternoon around the Stephansplatz, and as their energy and the air temperature dropped, the iconic Café' Central was a must.

I wish "Grimm" was still on tv", Kelly nostalgically mused over her Wiener Apfelstrudel and quite possibly the most amazing hot chocolate she had ever had. "I mean, there are only so many times you can rewatch the entire show."

"Says the girl who is on her 5th time through on "Grey's Anatomy," Jill said with a smirk on her face and heavy sarcasm font on her voice.

"Yeah, but this is the place, this is the café that was in so many of the scenes that were shot here in Vienna," Kelly said enthusiastically. "I can't believe we're actually here. It seems so impossible."

"Taking the semester off is the best decision ever." Jill said with an exhale that was a true sign of how far away she was from classes and text books and exams and papers. "I could just feel myself getting mentally; what's the word I'm looking for, THIN! Does that make sense?"

"100 percent! This really has been a great trip, I'm glad I got to share it with you," Kelly said with a smile.

As they drifted into a sea of café sounds and conversations that sailed on a scented breeze of pastries and savory delicacies, an intruder entered this perfect space. It was panic, loud voices, shouting, and then the screams. Kelly, who was unofficially the one tasked with documenting this whole trip was quick with her phone. Not as quick as the 20 other patrons who had been shooting video 30 seconds ahead of her.

Jill turned toward the epicenter of the screams, it was a scene of white linen tablecloths splattered and soiled with a combination of food and drink that was spilled in the disbelief of what was unfolding in the historic café, and blood that was egressing from this woman's body.

She looked to be about 60-something, there with family, possibly someone's grandmother. Words were almost impossible to separate from the German and English as a few poor souls tried to usher calm into this situation. Sadly, calm has stopped being a thing about three minutes earlier.

Bits and pieces of audio jumped out with clarity like a game of 'whack-a-mole'. "She said she was feeling tired". "Thought she ate something spoiled". "Rest", "Pain", "Fast". Whatever it was, Jill and Kelly soon realized this wasn't food poisoning.

While on their trip through Europe they had picked up a news story here and there about some infection at a hospital in Juneau, Alaska, but seriously, that was on the other side of the world. Surely, the two things weren't related. That seemed to be the case until…..

"Kelly…..KELLY!" Jill yelled in a way that was not frustration for not being heard, but in a way that said, "IT IS TIME TO FUCKIN GO!"

Jill pointed Kelly's line of sight to another table. This time, a young man about their age did the same thing. So much blood.

They ran. They were much more aware of how serious this was than most of the guests at Café Central, who thought it was just an isolated bit of excitement but were still not concerned enough to do the 'dine and dash'. That wasn't even a concern for the two college friends from the States. Luckily, their hotel was not far, so that negated any concern of clogged public transportation or a long wait for an Uber. They ran, got to their room, and started packing.

Jill was already scheduling an Uber on her phone while Kelly packed for both of them. This was not the kind of packing where you check two or three times to make sure you have everything. There would be no folding; clean clothes went with dirty, makeup, toothpaste, hair products, and lotions never made it into the TSA-required zip locks and clear plastic containers that were three ounces or less. Disarray by necessity was the name of the game.

They got to the lobby just as their Uber pulled up to get them to the airport. While they had planned for 2 more days in Vienna, getting home now, was paramount. A 35-minute car ride later, they were at the airport, bags in hand, through the turn style, and instantly, they knew getting out of Vienna was going to be more of a challenge than they anticipated. Every ticket counter, every line, every customer service agent in a blazer, was out numbered 8 to 1 like some teachers in U.S. classrooms.

The girls picked a line and committed. One hour later, it had barely moved, but it was forward progress. It was one small shuffle and suitcase slide closer to home. Just as that ounce of positivity was the only thing keeping hope alive, the military started pouring in through the turnstiles. Armed with assault rifles, riot gear, and not a lot of compromise, they were there for a purpose.

Once that became abundantly clear as Jill's gaze took her beyond the enforcers to the drop-off lane outside the terminal. Large military vehicles were filling all the empty space in her view. Barriers were going up, generators were growling to an angry start, flood lights popped on like some sort of sadistic paparazzi and that was it.
No one was coming or going. Arrivals, departures, and workers were all related by the word quarantine. Jill and Kelly were home, just not the home they wanted to be in.

The next morning, the video Kelly shot had 3 million views on TikTok. Also, at that time, tents, medical staff, and triage had been established. Make-shift surgical bays popped up overnight, and people were getting sick.

The news about GLU, the spread, the death toll, the panic - all of it seemed so hard to comprehend. As if the public didn't mistrust the mainstream media, this really didn't do any favors to mend that relationship.

As a child of divorce, Kelly recalled that place in time. Her parents tried to soften the blow of the harsh reality by distracting her with a new puppy, which would not be coming today.

That created an interesting shift—national and local news anchors, the so-called professionals, were losing credibility to the TikTok crowd and any other regular Joe with a video camera. No professional voices, shaky video, bad camera angles—none of that mattered to the viewer.

What mattered was that they trusted their friends and neighbors more because they believed they had less time, ability, and motivation to manipulate the truth. So, it was easier to believe that what the amateur was showing was 100% real and the truth.

YouTube, TikTok, Facebook, Snapchat—you name it. Every social media platform was now providing a bird' s-eye view of the end of the world, and that view was getting more and more horrific with every video. Long before GLU, social media creators were already comfortable oversharing stupid trends like eating detergent pods or a mouthful of cinnamon.

Making the leap to showing their friends and neighbors bleeding out wasn't as hard as you may think because, at the end of the day, the short-sighted creators were translating clicks and views into dollar signs, not realizing that there may not be a world to spend that money in before too long.

The idea of feeling guilty shooting a video of someone in the worst possible moment of their lives didn't even affect Kelly after a while. She got yelled at in several different languages, with some pretty colorful swear words. At least she assumed they were swearing based on tone, inflection, and facial expression. She didn't care.

She kept her phone charged and kept shooting and posting. She felt a journalistic obligation to share this with the world in hopes that it would alert the public and prevent them from getting caught off guard like the poor people in Café Central.

Soon, requests started landing in her inbox from the major networks: CNN, FOX, ABC, NBC, AP, Reuters, you name it. All looking for permission to use her footage. The cocktail of exhilaration, fear, pride, and adrenaline was fueling her every move.

Meanwhile, Jill tried desperately, while she still could, to connect with family and keep them looped into their level of progress and safety. Voicemail after voicemail did nothing to calm her fears of just how out of control and uncontained this situation was. It didn't stop her from trying.

She hit redial; gunfire exploded in the terminal, followed by a secondary blast of screams and crying and then silence. One of the soldiers was explaining that anyone who tries to leave runs the risk of being detained, and force will be used if necessary. That answered the girl's question about it; I wonder if we can make a run for it and drive to another city.

CHAPTER 22
HIT AND RUN

The hotel was in the rearview as they headed North on Route 7. Javon knew driving to the lower 48 wasn't going to be a thing.

"In the side pocket of my bag is my phone", he instructed Candace

Once she found it, he hit speed dial, it rang twice on speaker.

"I've been worried about you," the voice said on the other end. Javon had to wonder whether it was worry for him or worry for the reason all of this was happening – the artifact.

"Are you still in Juneau?", Spencer asked

"Hopefully not for much longer. I'm in a stolen truck with a Dr. Candace Stanton, who is clearly not in Kansas anymore,"

Candace made a face that was a physical equivalent of a groan in reaction to the failed attempt at humor

"The same Dr. Stanton the army brought to Alaska"

"Yes."

"Good, she'll come in handy."

"Excuse me!" she shouted, offended by the implication that she was just a piece to be used as anyone saw fit.

Realizing his misstep, Spencer quickly explained.

"What I mean is, my goal is to find a cure, and a mind like yours, Dr. Stanton is going to be a huge asset."

"I'm not sure what I can do to put this genie back in the bottle but…."

"Where are you?" Spencer interrupted.

About a mile away from the airport, what are our options?" he pleaded, knowing they didn't have many. With everything shut down, he was already thinking about a plan B.

"I can get you out of Juneau, but I need you to do something first," Spencer said with some urgency.

"You want me to stop at the gift shop and get you a "My friends visited Juneau, and all they brought me was this lousy t-shirt" shirt?".

"Thanks for thinking about me but no. I need you to go back to the hospital."

"WHAT! You do realize that place is full of infected and no one is getting in and out of there without authorization from the federal government at this point."

"What about Candace?"

"Sorry, Spencer," she said, "they basically told me to pack my things and go while I still could".

"Then you'll have to get creative. Tell them you lost your phone and just need to make sure you didn't leave it there."

"Really?", Javon asked with a "that's never gonna fly" tone to his voice.

"I don't know. You two will think of something, but I need you to get into the hospital. Once inside, I need you to copy and collect any and all data you can that has been curated so far in the battle against this virus."

"Oh, good, I thought breaking into the hospital was going to be the hard part. Glad to see I was wrong about that."

"Look, I know I'm asking a lot, but I need you to do this," Spencer pleaded. I think my company and all the researchers who work for me are the only ones qualified and focused enough on finding a cure for this thing. The world governments are so busy arguing among themselves on who should take the lead and the credit, they are losing ground to the spread by the minute."

Spencer continued, "I think if I can operate off the books and their radar, I ....we can be more successful. We can save the world while the politicians waste time posturing."

"The potential financial gain from all of this probably isn't a motivating factor in all this, I'm sure?" Javon asked with a healthy dose of sarcasm.

"Well, saving the world should have some rewards, should it not?" Spencer inquired.

"I see drug companies charging ridiculous prices for their miracle drugs when it comes to fighting cancer." Candace jumped in. "Way more than most people can afford with insurance, let alone without. I'll help, but you promise me right here, no price gouging bullshit. If you create a cure, keep your profit margins compassionate, you get me."

"Candace, you have my word," Spencer assured, "I have more money now than I could spend in 6 lifetimes; I can't spend it if I and most of the world are dead. Now get to the hospital. In the meantime, I have a private helicopter coming your way. It will be waiting for you at an outfit just south of the airport called "Coastal Helicopters", a tour company. With all the focus on airport security, you should be able to slip in there and board the helicopter before anyone is the wiser. Now the really hard part, you have 2 hours. That's the helicopter ETA and it can't be on the ground for more than 5 minutes."

"Two hours, got it," Javon confirmed while he reached for his watch and synced the timer. "Two hours, mark!"

"Good luck," Spencer said because it felt like the only appropriate thing to say at the time.

By the time the conversation was over, they had arrived at the hospital—not nearly enough time to formulate a plan.

"We're here", Javon announced as if there were 2 kids in the back seat who were over being in the car on a long road trip listening to dad jokes and bad music.

"What's the plan?" he asked. Hopeful the smart doctor would have one cause he had nothing.

"Follow my lead, and make it an Oscar worthy performance, got it?' Candace demanded.

"What's my motivation?"

"You're really sick" is all she said.

The two walked toward the front entrance of the hospital, which resembled the entry gate to a military base. Barriers, armed guards, and a makeshift check-in station led to lots of tarps and ventilation systems, providing one way in and one way out.

"STOP!" the soldier demanded, which was no surprise to either one of them.

"My name is Dr. Candace Stanton…."

"That's nice, ma'am, but I need you to turn around," he interrupted.

"You don't understand,"

"Ma'am, it is you who does not understand. This facility is no longer accessible to anyone. No one gets in; no one gets out. It is locked down and quarantined."

"As a doctor, I'm aware of the situation….."

Once again, the soldier steamrolled over her, "I don't think you are aware…."

Candace had had enough. "Soldier, you interrupt me one more time and I promise you, you will have a very bad day. I was practically kidnapped by Colonel Eugene Brighton less than a week ago while I was kayaking with my dog because he thought I would be of some value to this hot mess express. I really", emphasizing the word really," I REALLY miss my dog. I was on a river, nice and quiet, minding my own damn business, and the next thing I know, I'm on a Blackhawk helicopter, which did terrible things to my hair, and I'm headed for Alaska."

Candace continued and leveled up the hysteria for effect.

"I dreamed that one day when I was married to the man of my dreams, we would honeymoon on a cruise to Alaska, but thanks to the U.S. military, you have COMPLETELY ruined that for me."

Javon looked on, "was that a fake tear?" He thought to himself.

This man here is sick and his vitals are getting worse. My goal is to get him in here, and isolated before he becomes more part of the problem than the solution.

That was Javon's cue. Not missing a beat, a cough, a sniffle, a stumble, a hand to the head, "I think I need to lay down", he said weakly.

"Javon, stay with me, stay on your feet," she said with some panic in her voice and then turned her attention back to the one person standing in her way. "Right now, you are part of the problem.

So, you can let us in, and I can get him secure, or I can get Colonel Brighton on the horn; that's how you military types say it, right? I can get him on the horn and explain why you chose to be a hard ass about the rules at the expense of the human race."

"I'll just need to call the Colonel"

"I'm sure he won't mind," Candace said, dripping with a snarky tone.

"I can't imagine he's very busy. I'm sure he won't mind you possessing an inability to make smart choices for the good of the mission. I mean, that should do wonders for any hope of advancement you had."

"Proceed, head right to triage so he can be evaluated. If anyone stops you, tell them Corporal Jiminez okayed it."

"Thank you, Corporal. Your decisiveness may have saved this man's life and others."

With that, the two of them walked through the hospital entrance on their way to triage. Candace remembered that on the way to triage, it was a right and a couple of lefts to the conference room that was turned into command central.

Everyone in the hospital was either sick, dying or busy. Getting to the conference room was easy. On the way down the hall, she grabbed an extra lab coat from a chair, needing everything she could get her hands on to sell the story.

Lucky for the two of them, it was midday, and even with the world ending, doctors and researchers who weren't on duty were either at the cafeteria, recharging or grabbing some much-needed rest in any dark corner of the hospital they could find. Not getting caught while stealing all the research data was the hard part.

The monitors, dry-erase boards, laptops, and research notes were all there; they just needed to find a way to access them. Javon assumed his role as the muscle, standing just inside the conference room door, while Candace gathered documents and files and stuffed them in a bag. With the physical research trail in her possession, she needed to get the digital files. There was one laptop at far end of the large conference table, Candace flipped it open praying it wasn't password protected. Of course it was.

"One hour to go, and we still need to get to the helicopter," Javon announced just as the door swung open.

In walked a member of what was now a multi-national research team comprised of U.S., Canadian, and Japanese scientists. Javon recessed back against the wall, behind the door, and out of her peripheral vision.

"Is everything okay?" the 30-something Japanese woman asked with some concern but no suspicion. Candace didn't hesitate to say, "Ugh, this is so frustrating. With all this craziness going on, I've forgotten the password."

"You're not the first, we're all pretty tired," the scientist empathetically stated. "That's why someone got smart and taped it underneath." She paused for a moment, and Candace could tell the dots were connecting.

"But this laptop is for doctors here at the hospital; it's for the research team; why would you need it, and who are you?"

The woman was surprised how quickly Javon moved from the moment she caught sight of him out of the corner of her eye to when he had his one arm around her neck, cradling her throat in the bend of his muscular arm, and using the other arm to leverage pressure on the sides of her neck and cut the blood supply off to the brain. A move he had performed so many times, it was just a matter of muscle memory and timing and he laid the scientist gently on the floor.

"Tell me she's not dead."

"She's not, just a sleeper hold."

"I was hoping that's all it was. My many Monday Night Raw viewings with my dad growing up have finally paid of."

"Steve Austin," Javon asked out of curiosity.

"Puh-lease," Candace retorted. "The People's Champion-The Rock."

"Well, if you smell-l-l-l-l-l-l what the Rock…..is….cookin', you better hurry that up cause sleeping beauty is going to be missed before too long."

Candace rifled through a couple of bags, found a thumb drive, and downloaded everything. There was no time to be fussy; every document and image she could find went onto the drive and into her pocket. They exited the room, reversing the steps from earlier, and headed toward Corporal Jiminez. They exited through the tarps and fans, and the Corporal was still standing at his post. Seeing Candace and Javon, he quickly stiffened.

"I thought you said he was sick," Jiminez said with a 'what the fuck' tone in his voice.

"And I thought you were smarter than that," Candace replied. She was almost cocky at this point, knowing that they had fooled the poor Corporal.

Before he could react, Javon was on him and less gentle than he was with the scientist back in the conference room. This interaction required a bit more of a heavy hand. With the combination of his military training and his MMA hobby to stay in shape, Corporal Jiminez was no match. Javon closed the gap between him and Jiminez, close enough to kick downward with his boot to the knee, bringing the young soldier down on both knees. At that level, Javon grabbed the head of Jiminez, and drove it into his knee, hard. Lights out.

Candace, with this horrified look on her face, was frozen at the violence she just witnessed and the speed at which it was administered.

"Don't worry, he's not dead, but he's going to have the equivalent of the worst hangover he's ever had when he wakes up."
They got back in the truck and headed for the airport. The helicopter tour company was 10 minutes away. They had a total of 13 minutes before the pilot followed orders and bugged out.

"We're a minute out. Start gathering all our stuff; make sure we have everything. I'll grab our personal belongings; you are in charge of that bag of research, and the thumb drive." Javon's orders were necessary and firm for clarity, but not to be rude to someone who had never been yelled at by a drill instructor. Candace didn't take offense; the moment wouldn't have allowed for it even if she had.

Javon skidded to a stop 30 meters from the helicopter, rotors starting to spin. They bailed out of the truck like it was on fire and ran. Not looking over their shoulder, not wondering if they had been followed, they were singularly focused on getting on that chopper and out of Alaska. Hesitating is a luxury they could not afford.

The steps and door to the Leonardo AW189 were down and open. Javon and Candace stowed their gear and the stolen research closed the door and buckled in. They could already feel the machine groaning against gravity and lifting off as they put on the headsets lying on the seats.

"Glad you could make it," the voice washed in static said in their ears. "I'm Jeff."

"What's the plan, Jeff?" Javon asked, since for the last 2 hours, he hadn't had a chance to think about what would happen if they really did pull off their little heist.

"We're flying to Port Hardy, just north and west of Vancouver. I'll refuel there and then we'll continue on."

"To where, I mean, the world seems to be shutting down pretty quickly." For the first time, Candace could hear an ounce of panic start to weasel its way into her otherwise calm, composed doctor demeanor.

"Not sure yet, ma'am, but Spencer is working on it. You two and the research are my top and only priority,"

"and gas," she reminded him.

"Touché," Jeff replied.

CHAPTER 23
CARCHARODON CARCHARIAS

Dylan Kellett worked hard as a veterinarian in Streaky Bay. Ever since he was little, his love and fascination for animals – domestic and otherwise, was unrivaled by his friends and family. Anyone who knew Dylan knew he would grow up to work with animals in some capacity. At a zoo, a wildlife refuge, or an animal rescue organization. It was just a matter of where and when.

When he was 11, Dylan came across a koala that had fallen from a tree. Scared and making that awful, wailing noise, Dylan was drawn to helping it. With the help of his parents and a few phone calls, the little dude was soon in good hands, and Dylan was hooked on helping from there.

His other love was surfing. His talent with animals was only surpassed by his skills as a surfer. Before he could walk, he was on a board with his Nan and Granddad. The kid stuck to the board like his feet, and the board was made of Velcro. He could make it do his bidding like a magic carpet flying through the air.

His talents as a surfer earned him numerous school medals and trophies and a trip to the inevitable crossroads. Major sponsors were knocking on his door, blowing up his phone, and wanting to sign him to pro contracts. Some were even talking about the Summer Olympics since surfing had gone from an experimental sport to being a full-time part of the roster of games an athlete could medal in. As tempting as it was, Dylan's heart belonged to the animals.

He was like Steve Irwin reincarnated. In fact, his reputation preceded him so much that he was lucky enough to get a surprise visit from Bindi Irwin one day, who made a point of seeking him out after seeing some of his videos on social media.

As isolated as Australia seemed to some parts of the world, the island country was not immune to GLU. At first, it trickled into the recesses of people's minds and conversations. Then it was someone saying, "Well, I don't have it, but I know someone who does."

This was unlike tales of cow tipping. With cow tipping, you never did it but always knew someone who did. Cow tipping was a lie; Glu was not. Following the playbook provided by the rest of the world up until now, first came the mask, the looting, the disbelievers, the military, all of it.

As fast as GLU was spreading, when the day came that Dylan realized he was infected, it didn't come as any great surprise to him. Truth is, he had made peace with the inevitability of it months ago. He was a scientist, after all, and knew that statistically, there was a better chance he was going to get it than not. It seemed like overnight, he had seen dozens of people he knew – friends, relatives, the humans of the patients he treated – all get it, and he was aware survivability was extremely rare.

However, what he was not going to allow was for this virus to determine how he left this world. Even before GLU, Dylan had this altruistic wish to die while surfing, and that was exactly what he was going to do.

Once symptoms presented, and without the intervention of all the experimental medicines and procedures available, he knew he had about 9-10 hours. While he still had the energy and his wits about him, he loaded his favorite board into the bed of his truck and drove toward the water.

One of his favorite spots to surf was Sceale Bay, which is offshore from the Cape Blanche Conservation area. This is a Jekyll and Hyde area with some of the best surf around, and it is notorious for the number of lives that the Great White had claimed. The apex predator of the ocean, the thing that swam in your nightmares and lurked under your feet as you tread water in the swells.

Since records were kept, and an aboriginal woman was bitten in two near Port Jackson back in 1791 – the Great White Shark was nightmare fuel. The stories of parents told their naughty children to get them to behave, do as they were told, and go to bed on time. Whether it was bathing, swimming, an accidental fall overboard, spearfishing, or diving for Abalone, the Great White was to be respected as it lurked just on the other side of REM sleep, ready to strike like a viper.

Dylan, in all his years of surfing would never have been so careless as he was going to be today, but again – his time, his terms. He thought about nicking his arm a bit with his diving knife, but he could tell he was not far from the terrible stage of this virus where the "lights came on" inside his body and his red blood cells scattered like roaches at the first sign of light stealing the dark that concealed them.

He was calm as he paddled. There was no sense in wondering if the shark would come. It was a matter of when the monster would explode underneath his board with a violence unmatched in the animal kingdom. His drysuit held the icy cold of the water at bay. The middle of winter water temperature for late May was an icy 17 degrees Celsius. It was just cold enough that he didn't notice the blood running from his nose. The dinner bell was ringing.

Out far enough, he turned, looked over his shoulder at the building swell and paddled. Not his usual sleek hands like knives as he sliced through the surface to propel himself forward. No, open palm, lots of intentional splashing, almost as if he were more in distress or an amateur than the expert surfer he was. He was ringing the dinner bell. An action that caused a horripilation of the hair on the back of his neck to stand up and act as a lookout for what was to come.

His speed increased with the approach of the swell that was in pursuit of his feet, and just like when you feel the jet airliner start to leave the tarmac at takeoff, Dylan could feel the board slowly start to rise. Then in an instant, impact. From underneath his board, with the energy of a freight train striking a car stuck on the tracks, his board shattered. Dylan was launched into the air like the seal he was pretending to be, spinning and cartwheeling, with a disorientation that gave him no concept of how high he was or when he would hit the water next.

Hitting the surface of the water awkwardly from a height of about 8-10 feet was like landing on concrete. Head above water, tasting the blood from his nose in his mouth, fear crept in—not from dying but from the shark playing with its food. He wanted this to be quick and was hoping for the next ….

A pain seared into his nerve, originating from just below his right knee. He felt the force of one incredibly powerful tug, and then the shark was gone, and so was that part of his leg. Before he had time to think about the fact that between the cold water and the adrenaline, it really didn't hurt, his left side was turned inside out just under the armpit. Ribs, bone, punctured lung, seawater in places it didn't belong.

There was not enough adrenaline and cold water to mask the pain now; it was blinding. A blinding pain that robbed him of the definition of his surroundings, that calm he felt at the beginning was returning to help him float away for good.

BANG! BANG! BANG! Three loud explosions and all Dylan could think was, "Those don't belong in this nightmare; what are they doing here?" Then the sound of water slapping not what was left of his board but the side of a fiberglass hull.

"No!" he yelled, not knowing if the word left the inside of his head and made it to the audible outside world. "No, let me die, I'm sick, I want ……Dylan lost consciousness. It was the last thing he remembered.

CHAPTER 24
PEACH TREES AND PETRI DISHES

Refueled, awake from a combination of a "bird bath" washing in the restrooms at the airport diner, in a fresh (or as fresh as they could be after being stuffed in a duffle for some time) set of clothes – it was time to go. The obvious had been stated: the world was shutting down quickly, and they needed to get somewhere safe to begin studying the research they stole.

Leap-frogging from one small airport to another was going to be the only flight plan. It would require Spencer to call in numerous favors at airports he had flown into many times when remaining "under the radar" was a priority.

"Hey, you two, we're about to land", Jeff announced in their headsets. Startling both of them out of a thinly veiled slumber. "Welcome to Athens, Georgia."

At about the same time, Javon's phone vibrated. Bzzzzz Bzzzz Bzzzz—three short bursts, and then they repeated. He had put it on silent during the flight, worried about waking Candace. Truth is, with the noise from the helicopter, she wouldn't have heard it anyway.

"Hello Spencer." Javon answered in a Seinfeld "Helllooo Newman" sort of way.

"Nice to see you haven't your sense of humor"

"Not yet," Javon replied in a tone that suggested his humor tank was running low.

"You're landing at Athens- Ben Epps Municipal Airport. I arranged through my Turo account to have a car waiting for you. By now, authorities might be looking for you and checking all the traditional car rental sites. I figured since Turo was peer-to-peer, it might buy us a little more time. From here, drive about 7 minutes to the northeast to Athens Research and Technology. I did the CEO a favor and did an impromptu tech talk at a company outing a while back."

"Is there anyone who doesn't owe you?" Javon quizzed.

"Just the people I haven't met yet, Javon."

"Of course."

Spencer continued, "This is a small biotech company, but well-funded and well supplied with all state-of-the-art gear Candace should need to conduct the research."

"Why not just go to the CDC?" Candace joined in.

"Normally, that would have been my first choice, but since your necessary bending of the rules," she could hear the air quotes through the phone. The military, the FBI, and state authorities across the country have been sent information that requires you to be detained as "suspicious persons of interest."

"It's not like we killed anyone!" Candace exclaimed.

"And this isn't the top 10 most wanted list," Spencer assured her. However, they have a lot of questions for you as to why all the secrecy and why it was necessary to use force to achieve your objective."

"Okay, so when we get to this biotech place, are they expecting us or do we need to bend more rules?"

"Nothing quite so dramatic, Candace; the place is fully staffed, and they have all been instructed that you are the lead on this and to get you anything you need." Spencer informed her.

"As for you Javon, I need to play to your strengths as well. There is already a small security detail there. No one with your elevated skill set, mostly weekend warrior, Paul Blart types."

"Kevin James was so funny in that movie," Candace laughed. Her smile quickly faded as the memory of sitting on the couch on a Saturday night, curled up with Kahl, and a bowl of ice cream each flooded in. She missed her dog.

Kahl's face soon transitioned in a mental video edit to images of her parents. "God, I hope they're okay," she thought to herself. Did they heed her warning? Did they load up and head to the U.P.?

"Candace? Candace?" Javon interrupted the mind drift. He could tell she was elsewhere and wasn't listening. He didn't blame her; it was a lot for anyone, even him, someone programmed by the military to compartmentalize and prioritize everything in one's life.

"Sorry," she said with some embarrassment.

"No need. I asked how long it would be before you could be set up. We need to start testing as soon as possible."

"Realistically, give me half a day. I need to reacquaint myself with the research we 'borrowed,' find all the supplies I need; then there's the matter of finding enough mice to start tests on."

"No mice," Spencer interrupted on the phone. "As fast as GLU is moving (the irony of that statement wasn't lost on any of them), we need to jump right to human trials. Right to the infected."

Javon spoke first, "So are we going to add kidnapping charges to the list of things the authorities are mad at us about?"

"I'm hoping it doesn't come to that," Spencer replied. "However, it will require some creativity. You are about 2 hours from Atlanta. Javon, while Candace is getting things ready here, takes another one of the scientists from the building. A woman with a friendly, trusting face and head to Atlanta. Start with the city's homeless population.

Ask around and see if anyone knows someone who might be sicker than normal. It would be best if you could find half a dozen willing participants to avoid having to go back every day."

"Willing?" Javon asked with some uncertainty of the definition of that word. "Do we ask and offer them '3 hots and a cot' for their trouble and tell them they will put into a drawing for a free trip anywhere in the U.S.?"

"Look, Javon, I get it." Spencer's frustration was evident. "This is not ideal, but it's what we have to work with. You're a creative problem solver; that's why you are the head of my security. This is one of those times I need you to put your personal feelings aside and be a bit more mission-oriented. Can you do that, or should I find someone else to do it?"

There he is, the Spencer who was used to getting his way. He didn't always show his face, but Javon knew he was always lurking in the shadows of the "decent and fair" Spencer's personality.

"No sir, consider it done."

Candace looked on and for the first time she realized the people she was now aligned with. She wasn't sure who she was more afraid of. Spencer, the man with limitless resources and a gray area of ethics as wide as the Rio Grande, or Javon, the man Spencer knew was capable of delivering results when it came to the sketchy shit in Spencer's brain.

The helicopter touched down the Tahoe was parked right where Spencer said it would be. Throwing their gear in the back, they drove. For the next 7 short minutes to Athens Research and Technology, Candace contemplated jumping out of a moving vehicle and running. However, in the back of her mind, she knew what was at stake, and if she could be a part of the solution, she was going to have to get on board with continuing to do things that made her uncomfortable.

CHAPTER 25
JUNEAU NO MORE

The month of April and its showers and promise of May flowers were getting ready to come to an end. It had been almost 3 weeks since the artifact was pulled out of the glacier. A little over 2 weeks since GLU claimed its first victim….what was her name….Makayla? So much blood, so much death since then.

Now, on April 29th, the Juneau the world saw on postcards and cruise ship advertisements was no more. The city of Juneau was a shell of what it once was. There was no thriving tourism, no power, and no food (unless you were a lucky hunter remaining in the wasteland that once was).

The clear blue sky was still there, just beyond the smoke. Smoke from the wood stoves and fireplaces of the few that remained, the uninfected. Smoke, more so from the burn piles. With no power to cool the dead and infected bodies, burning them or mass graves were the only choices.

After some discussion, medical professionals and law enforcement came to the conclusion that since they didn't really know what they were dealing with yet, burning the bodies was the wiser of the two choices.

The idea was that the fire might stop this from spreading because buried bodies could simply leach whatever they were dealing with into the water table. At this point, no one even knew if this was transmissible to animals, so burning bodies it was.

A wilderness once so beautiful was now a landscape of black, putrid death. If there was any humanity left in this town, it was the prayers that were whispered by the volunteers in hazmat suits as they tossed another body on the fire. Isolation was survival at this point. Neighbors helping neighbors had turned into "It's all about me".

Doors and windows were shuttered and anyone with a brain in their head knew there was a pretty good chance if you knocked on a door, you'd hear the click of a magazine and safety on the other side of it.

The last of the surviving medical team was evacuated about 4 days ago. No power, no fresh supplies to try and do every futile thing possible to save lives – they felt helpless.

That was a terrible feeling, but not nearly as awful as the feeling they had watching Juneau get smaller out the window of the military helicopter they were leaving in.

It was a scene playing out all along the West Coast, across the country, and spreading globally. Of course, bigger cities with bigger infrastructure were better equipped to fight the losing battle longer, but it was a losing battle. As power grids in the smaller towns failed and law enforcement and first responder numbers fell, so did civility. When the threat of 80% of the people around you dying is a reality, it becomes much easier to go to that dark place in one's mind that allows the justification of "kill or be killed".

The only way you knew the world was ending was if you were lucky enough to hear rumors from the last remaining bits of pictures and video being shared on what was left of the internet and the depleted juices of a device here or there. What would happen when the internet went down completely?

Some clusters of survivors and gangs were placing more importance on keeping information flowing than water flowing. At this rate, both would be gone soon. Then what?

GLU had forced the world into a time machine, and those lucky enough to survive had to relearn survival. This isn't just about meme boomers posting about how confused young people would be if they had to use a stick shift or a landline; this was so much more. It was about starting a fire from scratch to boil water and cook food. It was about hunting and gathering while under the constant threat of infection or worse.

People were regressing into savagery, fueled by the fear of dying. Darwinism was alive and well, and no one wanted to be the weakest antelope in the back of the herd. Leaders rose from the ashes of burning bodies and buildings. Some more equipped to handle the power and responsibility than others. The world right now needed more "Peter Parkers", because with great power came great responsibility. Instead, the cities and towns far and wide were filling up with baseball bat-carrying "Neegans," demanding kissing of the ring in this new world order that had begun to develop at an alarming rate.

How has this all come to be in only about a month? Sure, there have always been those fictional shows, movies, and documentaries about how quickly things would devolve in a situation similar to this. Some showed the situation going from day one to critical in a few months, others in a few weeks, but nobody watching those shows ever thought it was really going to happen except a few doomsday preppers here and there.

The military was overtaxed and not immune to the assault of GLU. Thanks to better equipment and regulations, the progression of the virus was much slower than in unsupervised society, but soldiers were still dying. So, the advance to take on the enemy had turned into retreat, barricade, and preservation of power. While no one spoke it out loud, society was on its own.

CHAPTER 26
CINCO DE MAYO

Aside from St. Patrick's Day, Cinco De Mayo was probably the biggest drinking holiday in the United States. Okay, maybe only rivaled by Thanksgiving, because let's face it, get that many relatives in one room, there is bound to be a need to drink. I mean, we've all got that crazy uncle, married 5 times, a total pompous ass who thinks he knows it all.

Whatever you do, don't ask him what time it is because he'll tell you how the watch is made. He's loud, a terrible dresser, full of inappropriate jokes, and dysfunctional in every way, but yet every year, out of pity, you invite him.

If not for the cultural diversity in America, there would be no Cinco De Mayo. Even then, most Americans get it wrong. Many think it's all about a celebration of Mexico's independence. WRONG! It's a celebration annually on May 5 to mark Mexico's victory over the Second French Empire at the Battle of Puebla in 1862.

America was a young country then, less than 100 years old, and we were already fighting among ourselves in the Civil War all because the South wanted to keep slavery a thing, and the North saw African people as something other than chattel.

The really sad thing is that after Mexico won the Battle of Puebla under the leadership of General Ignacio Zargoza, the general died a few months later from illness. The French returned to the fight with the "big brother," a larger force, and ultimately defeated the Mexican army at the 2nd Battle of Puebla and proceeded with the occupation of Mexico City.

It was only then that America decided to get involved shortly after the Civil War by lending money and guns to Mexican liberals, forcing France and Mexican conservatives to the brink of defeat. Napoleon got involved, and it became this whole thing, kind of like that Uncle we all have, and now we drink.

So, just like Mexico in the first Battle of Puebla or the North in the Civil War, we are essentially celebrating a short-lived victory but mostly a defeat. At the very least, it was a situation in which nobody was really the winner. If that doesn't want to make you drink, I don't know what does.

This is important to think about because there will be no Cinco De Mayo celebrations this year. Not tacos, no tequila, no mariachi music. Instead, fear and distance were the two most popular guests at the party this year until a third guest crashed the fiesta – HOPE.

A rumor had started to spread out of Mexico City about a miracle drug. In the last week of April, there was a murmur paddling down the tiny creek of still viable internet information about the use of a native shrub, commonly known as Jatropha dioica Sesse or "Dragon's Blood."

A plant native to the arid, rocky climates of Mexico, it has been used for centuries because it shows a variety of benefits when fighting everything from strokes, small wounds, and acne to gastroenteritis and renal congestion. Parts of the plant were even used as antiseptics. Not the seeds, though; the seeds were well known to be toxic.

Some of the really important and beneficial properties of this plant involved using an extract derived from the shrub to fight cancer, asthma, and two of the most common viruses on the planet—simplex herpes virus and influenza type A. This was the win the world needed because, after a month of seeing the world reduced to a shell of its former self, Mother Earth needed a win.

Within a week of the first rumors, thousands of people had descended onto the U.S.–Mexico border. A border that, after 2 weeks of seeing what was happening in Juneau, had closed and barricaded itself from the outside world. The military was deployed to the physical borders and all ports of entry; Mexico had all but hermetically sealed the country off from the rest of the world.

That, as you can imagine, created all sorts of political misgivings and tensions.

Now, Americans were looking for hope of life from their neighbors to the south. It wasn't just American citizens; it was Canada, Central American, and South American countries, Cuba, Haiti, Dominion Republic, Bahamas, and other smaller island nations. Cruise ships were turned away daily, caravans were turned around daily, and airplanes were turned away by military aircraft daily.

With the shoe on the other foot, Mexico was quick to remind America and all the other countries about all the years and all the Mexican immigrants arrested and returned to Mexico who were attempting to flee the despair and corruptness of Mexico, looking for a better way of life in America and elsewhere.

Through all this, stories kept leaking and spreading about people not only living longer but also reversing symptoms. Once that news landed on the desperate thousands upon thousands wanting to get into Mexico, that's when things went from bad to worse.

What started as riots and fights breaking out with weapons of rocks and bottles and the occasional Molotov cocktail soon turned to people being shot on sight and even small aircraft being shot down by Mexico's Air Force. The message was clear: Mexico was going to do everything at its disposal to keep its country safe. No matter what.

It was on May 5th, that irony would have the last laugh. On the day people normally drank and celebrated an ephemeral victory in Mexico's history – Dragon's Blood proved to be an equally temporary solution. Rather than being a possible cure as the game of telephone between countries had suggested, it was more a means of hospice. Yes, it was slowing symptoms and even reversing some, but in the end, it was doing that only to provide comfort. A way to mask all the pain and let the victim slowly succumb to the virus rather than experience the rapid horrors like so many had. But in the end, mortality rates versus survivability rates were virtually unchanged. This was a cruel joke to be played on the Mexican people on the day of all days, a day the country was all too familiar with abbreviated celebrations.

News traveled fast about Dragon's Blood's failure. Cruise ships stopped coming, planes stopped coming, and migrant camps disbanded. Some stayed, but most didn't. All this really accomplished was to get thousands of people in close proximity to one another so the virus could spread some more—so the virus could live as it had intended all those eons ago.

CHAPTER 27
CLOSER

Athens Research and Technology not only had stores of things Candace needed to conduct her research, but it had become a storage bunker of sorts. Rations, water purification and filtration systems, waste incinerators, solar panels, and wind turbines for power—all these things were put in place long before GLU. It was as if the CEO, Spencer's friend, was a fortune teller. No judgment; Candace was happy the facility took the initiative.

Almost 2 weeks had gone by since they arrived, a little over a week since Cinco De Mayo. The news didn't travel quite as fast as it did B.G (before GLU), but it did travel. Candace heard all about Dragon's Blood and gave Mexico an "A for effort". She thought to herself she probably would have done something similar if she was in Mexico rather than Georgia.

Javon had done a masterful job with security and security details, putting people's lives in a handful of personnel that he took the time to vet himself. He needed to know he could trust them if they 'got in the shit'.

Javon was making runs to Atlanta about every 5th day. There was an abundance of sick, homeless subjects; he hated referring to them as that. He knew they were people, but in order for him to do his job, he had to emotionally detach.
He likened it to working in a slaughterhouse for cows or chickens. It was easier when the cows and chickens didn't have names, just numbers. For a brief moment, his mind wandered to a strange vision of a green pasture full of homeless people wandering and grazing. Every single one of them with a yellow, numbered tag in the same ear. Some were branded, but all accounted for and 'tagged'. Feeling the weighted blanket of inhumanity, he blinked the vision away.

Ignorance is bliss. This was easier if the homeless people he was promising better living conditions to, didn't have names.

From time to time, one would take the initiative and introduce themselves as a way to be polite and show Javon humanity and civility was still something they were clinging to. Javon did his best to forget the names as best he could.

It was harder for Candace because she was actually the one injecting them with a lie—at least that's what it felt like to her. After all, it had been almost two weeks and not one solid sign of progress. Anti-viral version #8 was the latest iteration of hope. To add some distracting levity to her work, in her head, she heard, "Homeless person number 8, COME ON DOOOOOWWWNN, you're the next contestant on THIS DRUG AIN'T RIGHT."

It was frustrating and stressful work, and it was bearing no fruit. It didn't help that Spencer required a daily meeting at 10 a.m. to discuss the research, the results, the progress (that was the shortest part of the conversation), and the plan for the future. Candace was in "rinse, lather, repeat" mode and not taking care of herself. Sleep was fleeting, headaches were frequent, and she had to be reminded to make time to eat and drink (and sometimes even shower).

"Hey Doc, I brought you a coffee", Javon offered with an outstretched hand and a gentle tone. He could see the toll this work was taking on her and assumed she was pretty fragile.

"Thanks," is all Candace could muster as she sipped her coffee and rubbed her neck with the other hand.

Javon and Candace had grown closer and more comfortable with one another. Nothing like the end of the world to bring 2 people closer together. Just the fact he had adopted "Doc" as her nickname and stopped calling her Candace and the fact she welcomed it showed the shift in their relationship dynamic.

They knew they needed one another if Spencer's research plan was going to have any chance of succeeding, but they also needed each other personally—as friends, listeners, confidants, shoulders to cry on….all of it.

Seeing Candance struggle to rub her own neck and chase away the tension, he put his coffee cup down.

"Here, let me help"

For a brief moment she thought about hitting an internal button that would launch the walls of emotional protection up fast as lightning, but at this point, she was too tired to fight the fear of being vulnerable. The moment his hands gently landed on her shoulders and the side of her neck, she unexpectedly responded to Javon's touch. Little, raised bumps of chicken skin shot upward to meet his surprisingly soft hands. She laughed.

"What's so funny," Javon asked as he applied a little more pressure to her tension.

"You're hands are REALLY soft, like weirdly soft for a man"

"Well, when Dr. Spencer Frankenstein raised me from the dead and put me back together, all he had to work with were the hands of an olive oil salesman who moisturized every day."

They both laughed out loud in a way that was so much more than a laugh. For the first time in over a month, it was a release of all the images, danger, close calls, and death being exorcised from their very core.

"O'keeffe's!" Javon exclaimed

"What?"

"O'Keeffe's Working Hands" lotion, daily, after every shower, now you know my secret. My Grandfather worked with his hands all his life, swore by the stuff. He and my grandmother were married 57 years."

"Maybe that was the secret," Candace said under her breath

"Huh?"

"If your grandfather's hands were this soft, I would have made sure they were on me every one of those days for 57 years," she said with a heavy coating of flirtatiousness. No sooner had the words left her mouth she realized how inappropriate they seemed. Sure, she and Javon were getting closer, but the flirting was new.

"Damn vulnerability," she thought to herself as she quickly changed the subject. "What happened to them? You said they were married 57 years ago."

"They were," Javon replied, trying to ignore the question in his mind. "Was Doc flirting with me?" My Grandmother died after an unfairly fast fight with melanoma; my Grandfather died of a broken heart 6 days later."

Javon stopped rubbing Candace's neck only because the conversation had clearly taken him to a place. Without turning around she could feel the tear in his eye and reached across her body, laying her right hand on his that was resting on her left shoulder. There, they just decided to 'be' for a minute.

After all the running, deceit, car chases, and helicopter rides, Javon and Candace had fallen into a place of consistency. Not necessarily comfort, because they still felt like they had to save the world, but there is something to be said for consistency.

It allowed them to be present for the first time in a long time, to notice one another, truly see them, and start to care as the walls that had quarantined their hearts for so long fell away. Hand in hand, they fell asleep.

PART III: WATER

CHAPTER 28
AWAKE

Beep......Beep.......Beep

The whirring of machines, the smell of sterility, the dull pain, the dryness of his mouth—Dylan's senses were slowly reacquiring their bearings and telemetry. Everything seemed to be waking up at once. His eyes slowly opened to a dimly lit room, which was a blessing. Even the lights from the machines making noise seemed as bright as the sun.

"Well, there you are," a gentle voice said with an Australian accent. "You gave all of us quite a scare." At the very least, Dylan knew he was still close to home, or so the friendly native tongue implied.

A hospital he was in a hospital. How could that be? The last thing he remembered was the shark, his leg, and the assault on his dying body. Then he remembered the very last thing, the gunshots and the boat. For all of his successes as a surfer, he realized he failed miserably at trying to end his life on his terms.

Dylan's throat felt like it had swallowed glass, so the nurse gave him some ice chips to help reacclimate him to swallowing and speaking.

"You're incredibly lucky mate. A little touch and go there for a few days."

Dylan was trying to keep up, but his head was swimming. He did hear, "A few days." How long had he been here?

The nurse continued, "I just took the tube out of your throat this morning, so that's why it's so irritated.

With an exertion equal to trying to lift a small car, or at least that's how it felt to Dylan, he managed to force one word past his lips, "How…."

The nurse knew what he meant. "How long have you been here? Today makes it 15 days since those fishermen brought you to shore. It's a good thing they radioed ahead, so there was an ambulance waiting at the boat launch. If they had to drive you, we may not be having this conversation."

"I'm Natalie by the way. Most people call me 'Nat' for short. I'll be your nurse for the next few hours until the night shift checks in at 7."

"Why?" Dylan asked.

"Why, What?"

"Why did they, you, the doctors…why did they have to save me."

Nat was caught off guard by the question, dumbfounded, actually. Here's a guy who should be fish food, but thanks to some good Samaritans, he gets to live another day. Despite the state of the world and the global threat of GLU, he was alive, which, in her mind, was a gift.

"We saved you because of that oath we medical types take to do no harm and all that." Nat continued cautiously, dialing the sarcasm back a bit. "Listen, mate, it's our job. We couldn't just stand by and do nothing."

As Dylan was becoming more lucid, he started to focus on that number of days, 15. He should be dead.
GLU should have ravaged his body. After all, to his knowledge, he didn't receive any special treatment, no experimental promised cure, but how would he know? He's been out for 15 days.

"I shouldn't be here; I shouldn't be alive," he started

"Well, admittedly, there is a little less of you here," Nat said, treading softly into Dylan's next journey of self-discovery. When she said that, was when he noticed where some of the pain was coming from. He looked down toward the foot of the hospital bed and saw one foot. The other leg stopped at a bandage at the knee.

To the nurse's surprise, Dylan seemed unphased by that part of his "new normal".

"I know it's a lot to process right now, but like I said, you had quite a go of it. Punctured lung, broken ribs, bones in your hand, significant damage, and some tissue loss at the thigh. You'll have quite a story to tell. Believe it or not, chicks dig scars," she smiled.

"At least the shark didn't go after that handsome face of yours", she added.

Was she flirting with him, Dylan wondered. Nah, maybe she was just being nice, doing her 'nurse thing'.

"Listen, Nat, I get it. The shark did a lot of damage, and I'm lucky; hell, anyone would be lucky to have survived that. What you don't understand is I didn't want to survive it."

Her smile faded, and concern swept into her eyes, "Dylan, we have some great specialists here if you want to talk to somebody."

"I'm good; I was never clearer on my purpose. I was dying anyway Nat. I had just been diagnosed with GLU. According to all the reports and research, I had half a day. I wanted to go out on my own terms, doing the one thing that really brought me close to God, Nirvana, Zion – whatever you might call it."

Dylan looked at the nurse, expecting to see a look of sadness, or maybe pity, that's not the look that greeted him when their eyes met. Nat's eyes were wide, in shock, unbelieving.

"Dylan, how do you know you had GLU? Did you receive a proper diagnosis?"

"Go find my medical records from my last doctor's visit; you can look that up, can't you? It was only yest.." He caught himself realizing he had forgotten his 15 days in the hospital.

"It was the morning of the attack. Like I said, from everything I read, I knew I didn't have a lot of time."

Hurriedly, the nurse left the room. So quick in fact, that Dylan was left wondering if he had somehow upset her. With the room now empty and the height of the daytime sun trying its best to infiltrate the room through the light-blocking curtains, He just lay there in his bed, becoming more acutely aware of the things that hurt, the parts that were bandaged, the parts of him there were never going to be the same.

Then he started questioning his own sanity. Did he hear the doctor wrong? Did he NOT have GLU? Either way, what kind of shitty, cowardly move was suicide, even if it was by surfing and shark?

"I'm better than that," he thought to himself. "I should have chosen to go out fighting, on my two feet, standing – now I can't even do that." Lamenting the decisions he made and the results they created, he shut his eyes, ashamed, grieving the physical and mental loss of himself that he'll never get back. He was soon asleep.

CHAPTER 29
ALL GOOD THINGS

Another 15 days had passed, and while the routine may have felt comfortable, the lack of progress was unsettling. Candace was trying

everything, and nothing was working. That, combined with a sheer number of 'walking dead,' Javon was rounding up.
Mentally, it was exacting a debt on their souls they could never make flush again.

It didn't help that Spencer, the guy funding this whole thing, was calling every day for progress reports. Candace and Javon were getting tired of saying the same old thing, and you could tell Spencer was tired of hearing it.

"WHAT am I missing?" Candace said like someone desperate to find their car keys or they were going to be late for an important meeting.

"So much of this is familiar. So much of this is acting like Polycythemia Vera. Yet, how in the hell do I stop it from forcing the blood from the body?"

"Spencer, have you called yet?" Javon asked as he handed Candace her third cup of coffee of the day and a protein bar.

"Not yet. At this point, I cringe every time the phone rings. What I'd give for a recording telling me my car warranty is about to expire."

They both chuckled. Candace continued, and Javon listened. He knew that's what she needed right now. Not a 'fixer', just someone to listen.

"I've done more pore-over than a Starbucks barista, as much as I have assessed, reassessed, and re-reassessed all the data. My data, the stuff we 'borrowed'," she said with air quotes. Nothing is leading to the answer to the question."

"Which is what?" Javon wondered out loud

"Which is," Candace exclaimed in a way that warranted a drum roll, "Why is the blood leaving the body, ultimately becoming the reason for the patient's death."

"It's like there is a mini Arnold Schwarzenegger in the bloodstream who yells "COME ON, GET IN THE CHOPPAH. COME WITH ME IF YOU WANT TO LIVE"."

Her poor Austrian accent aside, Javon was picking up what Candace was putting down.

"Then all the blood follows him blindly like the snakes following St. Patrick out of Ireland."

"You know that wasn't real, right?"

"What"

"Ireland, the snakes, St. Patrick….all just legend."

With a tone in her voice more reserved between a wife and her husband, Candace burst out, "IS THAT REALLY WHAT WE'RE GOING TO FOCUS ON RIGHT NOW?"

"Sorry, continue; I'll be over here shutting my mouth," Javon embarrassingly shifted his feet, looking down at them.

"Where was I?"

"Snakes," Javon said quietly, wincing, expecting another salvo of "fuck you and your poorly timed trivial facts" from Candace. It didn't come.

"'Right, snakes," she continued. But instead of living as little St. Arnold promised, the blood is bamboozled,"

"Does anyone really use that word anymore," Javon interrupted before he could stop himself. The look from Candace told him he would be wise not to do that again.

"Bamboozled, hoodwinked, deceived, lied to – pick whatever word or words you want to use. The facts are this part of GLU is deceptive. It's almost designed to get the body's natural immune system to stand down because it doesn't see it as a threat. It doesn't see what's coming. It's like a trojan horse, a phishing email, malware. The infection fighting white blood cells are promised great riches from a Nigerian prince, but only to be relieved of all their personal info and most of their life savings.

"Maybe you're looking at this all-wrong Candace." Javon treaded carefully as he spoke. He knew she was at a breaking point and the last thing he wanted to do was make her cry.

"How so?", she asked

"Look, you're the expert, but hear me out. From a tactical standpoint, when it comes to security, if the bad guy breaks in once, I don't keep on looking at the result; I eventually have to look at how the bad guy is getting in."

Javon continued, "When all that water was pouring into the Titanic, the captain didn't ask, 'Where is all this water coming from?'. In his case, the answer was obvious: it was the iceberg – but it was the cause, not the effect. That's what you need, find the iceberg, find the bad guy, and work backward from there."

Javon was so busy talking he didn't notice how Candace was looking at him until he did. She had a soft, knowing look of admiration and wonder on her face. Something that said, "Who is this guy, and what did he do with Javon? Because this think first and use brute force later, made the smart guy she was looking at kind of hot."

If Javon didn't know any better, he'd swear she was undressing him with her eyes, and it kind of made him feel like a piece of meat.

"Since when did you get so smart?", she asked with curiosity on her face.

"I've always been really smart, but if I showed you how smart, you would have had nothing to do for the last 5 weeks." He said with a shit-eating grin.

A sponge, wet with something, went whizzing by his head.

"Smart-Ass!!" Candace playfully yelled

"What would you do without me?"

"Let's hope I never have to find out." …..and the minute Candace said that, she could feel how incredibly awkward it made everything in an instant.

"Am I falling for this guy?" she wondered silently. She knew the answer, and so did Javon.

The satellite phone rang.

"Saved by the bell," Candace said under her breath with the relief of avoiding any more embarrassment.

"Spencer," she answered, I mean, who else was it going to be

Not giving him a chance to lead, Candace jumped in, "Okay, some promising news…."

He cut her off with a tone that was laser-focused.

"Not now. Do exactly as I say; we don't have much time."

Candace put him on speaker so Javon could hear.

"Grab as much of your research as you can, plus a week's worth of supplies if you can. Oh, and you'll need weapons."

"What's this all about, Spencer?" Javon asked

"It appears that all your road trips finally caught the attention of the wrong people," Spencer explained. "A militant group based just outside of Atlanta. Heavily armed thanks to how quickly things devolved, and they are looking to position themselves as the new rule of law in these parts – by any means necessary."

"So why attack us?" asked Candace.

"Rumors. Just like in Mexico with the Dragon's Blood, they think you have already developed a cure. Knowing that he who has the cure has the power." Spencer sounded concerned.

"But we don't," she said

"You and Javon know that I know that, but they don't believe it one bit. This group is made up of the same people who think the world is flat, we never landed on the moon, and that Pastor Bob Joyce of Household of Faith church in Benton, Arkansas was actually Elvis Presley in witness protection."

"Where do we go? Javon asked

"Listen, I'm not really sure at this point. My resources are running low as this thing perpetuates. I've called in just about all my favors.

You and Candace are going to have to survive on your own for a while."

Javon and Candace looked at each other, he could see the panic on her face. Up until now, she had felt comfortable with his ability to keep them safe. But now, with terrorists closing in on their position, she wasn't so sure. Regardless, she trusted him and had grown to be comfortable with the idea of following him anywhere – in battle or retreat, and this situation certainly warranted the latter.

"Now Go!" Spencer yelled. Check-in only when absolutely necessary. At this point, I'm not sure who is monitoring and what their intentions are. Trust no one unless they mention my name.

The phone went silent, the room was silent, and Candace and Javon were silent, but that soon changed.

Gunfire erupted on the outside of the lab. It sounded like the team Javon had pieced together was in over their heads. Just from listening, Javon had heard enough gunfire to know what was being shot by his team and the superior firepower coming at them from whoever it was who wanted into the facility.

"That's not good," Candace said nervously.

"Ya think!!" He retorted. "We're losing"

"How do you know"

"I just know. 5 minutes – that's all we have. Gather what you can. There is an old access hatch that connects with the wastewater tunnels. It's always been my "shit show" escape plan. This qualifies. I'm going to warn you, you won't like it."

"Listen, you had me at wastewater. I'm a lucky girl." Candance was doing her best to keep things light for her nerves, not Javon's. She knew he was at his best in situations like this.

The stolen Juneau laptop, her notes, anti-biotics, first aid, food rations, water, 9mm, ammo, and knife – in that 5 minutes, they both displayed a calm, deliberate efficiency. Exactly what they needed, nothing more, nothing less. A couple of packs, 30 pounds, just enough.

"Times up," Javon yelled over the gunfire that was getting closer.

Just then, their room shook like a truck drove into it.

"What the hell was that," Candace screamed. Startled and a little less calm than she was 5 minutes ago. She thought she was ready for what was coming. She wasn't.

"Grenade!"

"Who are these guys, and what are they doing with a grenade?" She yelled.

Just then another explosion

"Grenades," Javon calmly said, stating the obvious.

"I stand corrected," Candace replied, a little annoyed. Not so much at Javon but more at their current predicament, which was deteriorating by the second.

Javon took the lead; it was his escape plan after all. He grabbed Candace by the hand. There was another explosion, and the lights flickered. He pulled a small flashlight from his pocket and clicked it on without missing a step.

"Here", Javon motioned as he lifted the hatch.

Candace's nostrils were instantly met with an acrid, rotting smell of fluids, organic material, and who knows what else. She knew it was going to be bad, that smell exceeded her expectations.

"We have to?" She asked rhetorically.

Javon just looked at her and climbed down first. She tossed both bags down and then followed, closing the hatch behind. A dozen rungs later, they were standing in about 2 feet of water that made New York's Hudson River seem like spa water. Candace had kayaked in some pretty questionable waterways with Kahl before, but even he would have chosen to stay on shore if the water smelled like this. She missed Kahl, she missed her parents, were they okay?

"Let's go!' Javon ordered. His voice brought her back to reality. She wanted to hang on to that daydream a little longer, but she knew that was not a luxury their situation could afford.

Flashlight in his mouth, taking her hand again, they moved, putting distance between them and their attackers. They could only guess they had breached the room they once occupied and were busy digging through papers and pieces of a puzzle that wouldn't really help them. As long as they didn't know that and spent their time rummaging and not pursuing, their chances of escaping undetected were improving.

Candace searched the dimly lit tunnel, hoping her eyes would lock on light in the distance. Focusing on that, helped her not focus on the heart that was trying to break from of her chest. There, about 500 yards, give or take, an exit. Her pace quickened, surprising Javon who was no longer pulling her as much as trying to keep up with her.

Outside, they both looked around to get their bearings. The tunnel had spat them out on the other side of the razor wire fence, near a runoff pond and a tree line that was going to make perfect cover. Taking about 60 seconds to catch their breath, they ran. Not really knowing where they were going, just as long as it put them as far away from bad guys as possible.

"The bad guys," Candace's mind lingered on that term.

"That's it!"

"What's it?" Javon asked in between breaths

"Less talking, more running, but remind me about the bad guys when we stop.

CHAPTER 30
GLU GONE

In the days that followed, Dylan's injuries slowly healed. Thanks to the constant stream of antibiotics and nurses changing his bandages, he appeared to be one of the luckiest people in Australia, maybe the world.
Not just because he survived a suicide attempt by trying to serve himself up to a great white, but because, from what he could tell from

chatter going around the hospital, he no longer was showing any signs of GLU rampaging through his body. How was that possible?

Admittedly, he felt a little like a sideshow attraction at one of those parking lot carnivals. His Mum always told him not to trust those parking lot carnivals. If it can be set up in a day, how safe can it really be?

She also never missed a chance to tell the story of when she was younger, and she and a girlfriend were on a ride called "The Scrambler." A mechanical octopus-looking ride with a carriage at the end of each cold, steel tentacle. You would be whipped around and around, narrowly missing other carriages, all the while being shoved into the poor soul sitting on the bench closest to the outer gate. The centrifugal forces would smash the two people together, making it hard to breathe and laugh. Since this was a thrill ride, you always tried to do both with little success.

On this particular ride, his Mum was that outside rider who would have been fine if she hadn't noticed halfway through the ride, as it was ramping up to top speed, that part of the carriage, the lights, and the gate holding them in was being held together by duct tape and bundling wire. She told Dylan the laughter stopped at that point and she and her friend just hung on praying for the ride to end. It did, and so did their time at what they affectionately called "Duct Tape Carnivals."

There Dylan was, not going anywhere anytime soon, and a parade of people was streaming by his room. Doctors, nurses, people who were visiting family in other rooms, a couple of government looking officials – all hoping to catch a glimpse of what was the hospital equivalent of the 'werewolf boy'.
Nurse Nat was back on duty and greeted him with a smile as she walked in the room.

"You're the first familiar and prettiest face I've seen today," Dylan said and, in his head, immediately said, "Stupid, stop flirting with her; she's way out of your league."

"And you are the most handsome, one-legged surfer I've seen in some time."

They both awkwardly smiled, and Nat went about her business. She checked his vitals, the dressings on his wounds, and then..

A commotion in the hall near the nurse's station. Dylan couldn't see everything that was happening, but he did catch the light flashing off what appeared to be a TV camera lens. Reporters. Apparently, the rumor of the miracle surfer has spread about as fast as GLU when if first started burning like a wildfire through Juneau.

There was lots of shouting.

"You can't go in there?"

"How did you get in?"

Nat calmly walked to the door and started to close it. The shouting faded to a muffle

"I am not letting you go in there; the patient has privacy rights."

"I don't care if you're the bloody prime minister."

"Security!"

"Thanks!" Dylan said as he exhaled a sigh of relief

"'Sure thing. That's the closest they've gotten so far. Third try today. You, my friend, have become quite the celebrity."
"I would have let them in," she continued, "but it's time for your sponge bath."

"You're kidding right?"

"Yeah, I was never gonna let them in, but that part about the sponge bath, oh that's happening."

An instant flush of embarrassing heat washed over his face. Dylan hadn't felt this warm and feverish since his GLU diagnosis.

"Don't tell me you're shy," she teased. I've been doing this for 10 years now, and I've seen more man bits than I care to think about. I'm pretty sure yours are not going to be that dramatically different. Although, maybe THAT'S what helped you beat the virus."

Dylan could see she was having way too much fun with this. He knew she was just trying to get him to relax.

Nurse Nat could tell by the white-knuckle grip he had on the bed rail, that it wasn't working.

"Okay 'Modest Mike', tell ya what. I'll clean you up above and below your 'no-no square'…

"My WHAT??" Dylan shouted with curious surprise

"Your 'no-no square', your 'danger zone'," Nat could tell the references weren't landing.

"Haven't you ever watched 'Stuart' on 'Mad TV'?"

"It seems I have lived a meaningless existence and have been deprived of this Stuart."

"Okay mate, 1st thing we're doing when you get out of here is popping popcorn and I'm going to educate you on the comedic hilarity that is, 'Mad TV'."

"Did she just ask me out on a date?" Dylan thought to himself. It sure sounded like it. All the more reason to get better.

"Anyway," she interrupted his daydream, "I will wash your body, back, face and legs and then I'll leave the room so you can scrub the parts you don't want me to see, deal?"

"Deal!" Dylan sniffed indignantly, a little put out that he had to be subject to even the discussion of a sponge bath in front of nurse Natalie.

The sponge was cold across his chest, but that didn't bother him. His nostrils were filled with the aroma of Nat's body lotion. Resisting the urge to inhale enough to breathe all of her in, he took his mind off the intoxicating aroma but talking about GLU.

"How is it possible?" he asked

"How is what possible?"

"How is it possible that I had GLU? I was going to be just another statistic to die, and now here I am, free of this virus that, as far as the world knows, doesn't have a cure."

Nat paused for a second, searching for an answer that made sense; nothing did. Nothing at all in her medically rational mind could make sense of it.

"We're missing something, Dylan." She said, "Something that we're just not thinking about. All I know is your blood work is normal, and there's not a trace of anything extra-terrestrial trying to get you to bleed out"

"I know it sounds crazy, but do you think my body produced some sort of enzyme as a response to the shark taking my leg?" Dylan said, realizing that WebMD would have a better explanation than that.

"We could sit here all afternoon and give ourselves migraines trying to figure it out," she said as she wrapped up her part of the bath. "How about we just accept it as a combination of luck with a sprinkle of a miracle in there for good measure?" "Okay, I've done my part. You take care of your part of the deal and push the call button when you're done, and I'll come in and gather up the mess."

"Thank you," Dylan said with a softness of gratitude in his voice.

"No worries, mate, you're not the first to be a little shy with these things."

"No, I mean, thank you for being a friend to me in here. The world is falling apart, and a part of me is missing, yet you have found a way to distract me from all that, so thank you."

Nat smiled, "You can thank me by bringing the dinner before the popcorn on our 'Stuart Marathon' night."

"Deal," he said as she walked away and closed the door.

CHAPTER 31
THE BAD GUYS

It seemed like they ran 10 miles when in actuality, it was only about 1 and a half miles when Javon and Candace came out of the tree line near a Dairy Queen near Highway 29. The drive-thru should have been filled with cars full of people wanting to order blizzards, hot fudge sundaes, and banana splits. Instead, GLU appeared bad for business everywhere.

"Blueberry Cheese-Quake Blizzard," Candace moaned.

"I'm sorry, what?" Javon said, looking at her and grinning.

"No matter how stressful my day was, or how bad the date was, or how annoyed I was at Kahl for chewing up something he shouldn't have, it all magically disappeared at the end of my spoon when I was enjoying a blueberry cheese-quake blizzard."

I was more of a Dilly Bar guy myself. It had to be Cherry, which they discontinued for a time in 2023. You can bet your ass I was one of the crazy people who wrote a strongly worded letter to voice my displeasure."

"They had other flavors you know, like chocolate," Candace stated

"Nope, had to be cherry. I stopped eating them all together till they finally brought them back a short time later."

Candace wasn't going to let it go. "Not even '*car-mel*'.

Javon's head whipped around like he heard the bad guys, "WHAT did you just say?"

Looking puzzled, Candace repeated, "Car-mel."

"Oh good lord," Javon declared with his hand in the air like he was delivering a sermon. "For an educated woman, your English is not very good."

"What in the world are you talking about?" Candace said with a wrinkled brow and folded arms.

"It's CAR-A-MEL not *car-mel*. How would you like to be that second A in the word and get completely ignored by the savages who pronounce that delicious, sticky, gooey goodness as *car-mel*."

"Are we really having this conversation right now?" asked Candace.

"We sure are because I need to know that the person who's got my six can be trusted to say things correctly. Our lives could depend on it."

She rolled her eyes; Javon continued.

"Imagine if we got separated, and I was talking to you on a satellite phone, and you were giving me directions to where you were. If you were in a building on Caramel Street and you told me you were on Carmel Street, I may never be able to find you."

"Seriously?" was all Candace could muster for a verbal eye roll.

"Anyone ever tell you that you're high maintenance," Candace said with a smirk

"All the time, doc, all the time."

Done waxing nostalgically, Javon quickly brought reality front and center.

"We have to move," he said in a precise and urgent tone. There were 3 cars, a pickup and a van scattered around the parking lot.

"Let's start checking cars. We might get lucky and find a set of keys in the visor," he said.

Candace rolled her eyes, "That only works in the movies."

The van, the pick-up, car number one – all came up empty.

"I don't believe it." The words left Candace's mouth mixed with the sound of jingling keys.

"Despite your negativity," Javon smiled. "Looks like the odds are forever in our favor."

"Wait, did you just quote "The Hunger Games"?".

"Sure did," Javon said proudly. The books were so much better than the movies. Jennifer Lawrence was a bit too robotic for me to get emotionally attached to her as Katniss Everdeen.

The car started.

"Where do we go?" Candace had not forgotten the "bad guys" pursuing them, which again brought to the front of her mind the "bad guys" theory bouncing around in her head like a ping-pong ball, distracting her from the present moment from time to time.

"They would expect us to keep running. If I were them, whoever they're working with, I would have started setting up a perimeter and plans for pursuit. They wouldn't expect us to stay close by, so we're going to do just that." Javon clearly had a plan.

"Let's look for a place to sleep for the night. They don't know what we're driving; they never REALLY got a good look at us; we'll be better off staying out of sight than trying to keep running." Javon said calmly, his military training clearly helping him compartmentalize.

With a quarter tank of gas, they drove, not really sure of a destination.

It only took about 5 minutes on 29, and they came across The Knights Inn Motel.

"M'lady," Javon motioned, hoping his attempt at role-play would take Candace's mind off the fact the place looked pretty sketchy. He assumed she would consider the Hampton Inn with no free wi-fi roughing it, so he could only imagine what was going through her head.

"Thank you for guiding our trusty steed to such a fine inn for the night." Candace played along.

"Honestly, I've stayed in worse."

He tried not to let the stunned look on his face ruin the moment. Javon simply said, "M'lady, you dost continue to surprise me."

No surprise, it was empty, lobby and desk beckoning for a guest to welcome and a key to give.
Candace dropped behind the counter and found a few sets of keys starting with the number 2, she assumed for the second floor. Some odd, some even. The motel backed up to a tree line on one side and had a view of the road and the modest skyline of Athens on the other. That's the room she wanted. To be able to see and or hear trouble if it decided to find them.

They parked around back, unloaded the car, and headed in and up the stairs. After a 50/50 shot, it turns out the odds were street view. Room 243 it was.

Javon swung the door open and the awkwardness was the first to enter the room. One bed.

"I can go check the other rooms and see if there are 2 queens," Javon said in the most gentlemanly tone he could muster without making the moment weird.

"It's okay. It's a king, plenty of room for the both of us," Candace reassured him.

With that, they put the bags down. Javon was quick to draw the curtains.

"No lights!" he said as if Candace was 8 years old and reading under the covers past her bedtime. "We can't give away our position." As Javon was saying this, he was covering most of the flashlight lens with duct tape, letting only a sliver of light escape. Enough to make out features in the room. The physical features were more animated shadows. It was enough.

"A shower would feel great right now," Candace said as she grabbed the flashlight, a couple things out of one of the bags and headed to the bathroom. "I'll go first, you keep watch."

"Yes ma'am," Javon said obediently.

Javon heard the water and tried to focus more on the outside noises and potential threats rather than the idea of water and soap and skin. "Focus," he ordered the teenage boy inside of him.

Focus he did. Staring out the window through a slit in the curtain, the A/C unit gently blowing cool air against his chest. "Why do they always put these things right by the windows? Why not somewhere else in the room?" Javon wondered. He scanned the parking lot. Everything was so still.

For the first time in a few days, he thought about the number: As fast as GLU seemed to be spreading, how many in the country and around the world were infected? How many died or were in the process of dying? At last check, it was fast, and the mortality rate was unlike anything science had dealt with.

The saving grace was that while the initial outbreak in Juneau was so vigorous due to the artifact being compromised and going airborne, the majority of the infected seemed to have contracted the virus through touch or bodily fluid. He hoped, no, he prayed, it wasn't airborne.

It was advantageous that the population of Juneau was relatively small and not living on top of one another. Javon wasn't stupid; he knew if he and Candace could get away and stay ahead of the infection, how many got away who were infected. Maybe after the initial few weeks of infection and what the world knew versus what it didn't, people started to take precautions, and the spread slowed a little. Or, was GLU able to 'hopscotch' its way around the globe to expedite the spread? If that was the case, anything less than 100% containment was not going to work in their favor.

He was so lost in those numbers that he was startled when Candace touched his shoulder.

"You in there?" she asked.

"Yeah, just went down a pretty scary rabbit hole."

"I saved some hot water, and there's a fresh towel on the sink."

For one surreal moment, Javon felt like he was on some sort of vacation, a road trip, and not in a fight for their lives and the life of the planet. "Thanks. Your turn to keep an eye out; I'll only be a minute."

"Take your time, and enjoy a hot shower. Never know when we'll get another one." Candace was right. Each day that passed, what was normal the day before was not the next. The luxuries of running water, electricity, and food were all dwindling and would not last forever if GLU continued to spread unchecked.

Ten minutes later, Javon came out of the bathroom in shorts, no shirt, and a towel around his neck. As he sat down at the cliché round table that belonged in every roadside motel, Candace joined him. "God, she smells good," he thought, getting lost in that thought.

"Bad guys," Candace blurted out, jolting Javon from the intoxicating day dream he was drifting in.

"WHERE? GET DOWN!", Javon reacted.

"Easy big fella. We're safe. I mean bad guys. Remember me telling you I had a theory about bad guys when it came to our approach in trying to find a cure for GLU."

"Go On," Javon said, eager to see where this was going.

"Since the outbreak, we've been looking at and trying to attack this thing by studying the outcome. Think of the crime family. Now, think of the head of the crime family as the outcome. The worst of the worst. In any mobster movie, if you have a run in with the boss, it typically doesn't end well."

Candace continued on a runaway train loaded with thought and theory and there was no slowing it down.

"However, you at least always stood a chance of getting the upper hand when dealing with the lieutenants and the soldiers and the wise guys under the boss. You stood a better chance because, well, they were muscle, not the brains."

"I still don't get it." Javon admitted. "I'm usually pretty quick to put the pieces together, but I have to admit, I'm a little turned around on this one."

"It was something you said back in Atlanta, and as we were escaping, you used the word "bad guys" and it started to make sense to me. We need to stop trying to prevent blood loss and instead focus on the early symptoms. The fever, the heart rate, the blood pressure. This thing seems to advance in stages, like any virus. We need to try and slow the time between the stages. Long enough so that we can treat and attack the wise guys before it ever gets to the big boss. Get rid of all the 'men' under the command of the boss, and the boss eventually falls."

"Okay, I think I get it, but how do we slow the stage, the progression of this thing?" Javon asked.

"The canister was in ice for God knows how long. Hundreds, thousands of years, maybe more. Climate change has been melting glaciers for decades now. Exposed to the sun and warmer temperatures, who knows at what point the virus woke up. We need to put the genie back in the bottle. We need to put it back on ice.

What do we know? We know fatigue, headache, and fever all present rapidly and simultaneously.
Whenever we encounter a patient with those symptoms, we put them in an ice bath."

"Huh?" was all Javon could intelligently muster.

"Like the athletes and physical therapists use. Just throwing a patient in there isn't ideal; typically, you work up to about a 15-minute soak by pushing your body's limits. That's why we sedate the patient first, then put them in the ice bath.
While they're on the ice, we hit them with the same drugs and protocols we were using in Juneau; we're just administering them sooner and into a system that has a fighting chance because the virus has been made sluggish, slowed down, almost disoriented."

The excitement in her voice grew. Javon could tell that Candace believed she was truly on to something. Caught up in the possibility of turning the tide, Candace wrapped her arms around Javon and planted a playful smooch on the side of his cheek. At least it was supposed to be playful.

As she pulled back, in the dimly lit space where the definition was present thanks to the duct tape flashlight and the street lights outside, their eyes met. Eyes that, after all the theory, all the worry, all the potential, all the fear, all the running – eyes that simply wanted to forget about all of it for a while. Eyes that wanted to feel normal again, like things were before GLU.

Eyes met, hands touched, lips found purpose. Gentle and unsure at first until everything that was built up inside both of them found release. In an almost animalistic series of movements, clothes were shed, skin touched, bodies intertwined, spaces were explored, and bodies were bathed in sweat. Not knowing if this would ever be the last time, they felt so alive they did not waste the opportunity. Sometime later, they drifted off in their nakedness, Candace laying with her head on Javon's chest, drifting off to the sound of his heart, his breathing, and the sound of the air conditioning unit by the window.

Be a spark! Javon's mom said that a lot, when he was growing up. Javon never really got it. His mom's wisdom never really landed. He just thought it was some rote bit of advice 'old people' dished out.

"Be a spark," his mom said, as that light, that spark surrendered its hold on the light and the darkness overtook the last remaining evidence of who she used to be.

Javon couldn't sleep, not because of the nakedness, not because of what had been shared only a few hours ago. No, he couldn't sleep because it was quiet. The A/C wasn't running.
As soon as he noticed that, he also noticed the temperature in the room. It was warm. He pulled back the curtain, Bedlam greeting him. It was still early morning; the sun wouldn't be up for a couple more hours, but that didn't matter. Looking toward the Athens city center, smoke was rising from several burning fires. Their glow penetrated the room, the light finding its way to flicker in Candace's eyes, who was just waking up.

As much as she wanted to beckon him back to bed, she read the room, the look on Javon's face said it all.

"I think panic has officially set in." Javon said in a very matter-of-fact tone. "Power is out; stuff is on fire, I've heard a few gunshots. You know, that conversation about things devolving into darkness? Yeah, I think that's happening."

He then yelled, "THAT'S IT!!"

"That's it like – this is the end we're giving up?" she asked.

"No! THAT'S IT!! I get it now; It finally makes sense, the last thing my mom said.

Javon's excitement grew.

"Be a spark", he said.

"What?" Candace found the words very random.

"It's something my mother always used to say. 'Be a spark'. It was to remind me that when things seemed their darkest, all it took was one tiny spark to chase away the darkness.

"Be A Spark! Her message was hope. As long as there is a spark of light, there is hope. That idea you had, that's the spark. We are not done. We are not falling to our knees. Whatever this "GLU" is, where ever it came from, there has to be an answer, a solution, a cure.

As impossible and unavailing as that answer seems, you and I are going to find it."

On cue, the satellite phone rang. Spencer was short and to the point

"Get to the airport; you're going to Australia"

CHAPTER 32
BREACH OF CONTAINMENT

As the virus breached the walls of its prison, aided by the misfired bullet, so too did news of the miracle surfer in Australia.
Sure, the hospital tried its best to contain it. There were protocols and procedures implemented to prevent security leaks, but all it takes is one person. One person is overwhelmed by wanting to be the first to share this impossible truth with the world. That one person who thought they were doing it for the greater good. The one person who couldn't see the ramifications contained within the bigger picture. The bigger picture was the avalanche of press coverage, phone calls from foreign governments demanding answers and progress, and the impatient public wanting an anti-viral cure for GLU whipped up like one would make a bowl of cereal. Yeah, that's the kind of fallout the one selfish person who leaked the info about Dylan didn't think about.

As a result, the hospital was on complete lockdown. Triple the security checkpoints, triple the security. One family member gets in to see a loved one in the hospital, with no exceptions.

That said, hospital security wasn't enough. The Streaky Bay Police Department was called in. The mayor was watching the situation very closely. She didn't want to call in the military, but she wasn't opposed to it either.

Mayor Kathleen Southridge had been elected based on her "I'm not going to take anyone's bullshit" attitude. She was strong-willed, intelligent, intimidated by no one, and decisive in her actions. Granted, this was Streaky Bay and not Perth, but to her, it was, and she governed as such.

To show her support for the unraveling situation, she went to the hospital to talk to the hospital administration. If they needed something, they would have it as long as they could justify it in a way that made sense.

That was another good quality of the mayor, humility. She didn't claim to know everything; she trusted the people in their positions and what they knew and then made decisions based on the best facts possible and right now, all those facts said she didn't need the military, but she had a hair trigger dial finger and was ready to make the call at a moment's notice.

In a meeting room, appropriately socially distanced and masked and far away from the part of the hospital where cases of GLU continued to infiltrate the halls of the ER, the mayor sat.

"Is it true? Did this young man have GLU, and now he doesn't?" she asked.

Kami Rollins, the hospital's medical director, was quick to answer.

"It appears so. We've checked his records from his primary care physician before he went surfing."

"He went surfing after he found out he was sick?" the mayor asked curiously.

"Yes, his intent was to end his life by way of Great White. He almost succeeded, too. He lost a leg and will have a lot of scarring, but the one thing he no longer has is GLU."

"Well, it's not like it washed off," the mayor said. She did not intend for it to come across a little condescendingly, but how could it not.

"Correct, Ma'am, but something in the water is responsible; that's the working theory. That's the variable, the "x" factor that we can't identify yet, but we're working on it." Kami's tone was part offended and part things she really wanted to say. Thankfully, her filter had tamped that down.

"Report to my office as soon as you know more." The mayor ordered.

"At once," Kami replied.

The mayor stood up and smoothed her clothes, almost in a way that acted as a buffer between the last few minutes of wanting answers and not getting any and now having to go and think of what to say to her superiors who had arrived earlier in the day by military transport.

Kami left to go to the lab. The lab lived a double life. It was the most secure place in the hospital but at the same time the dangerous place. Nothing got in unnoticed, and nothing bad got out. She stood outside, donned the necessary PPE, and entered.

The interior space was as big as a closet with another door in front of her. The one behind her closed, and then for the next 20 seconds, it was like being in one of those big money machines you would see in the mall or at the fair. She only wished there was money flying around. No luck, just blasting off the outside world to make sure she didn't carry anything in that would taint the testing. The blast of air stopped, the other door opened, and she walked in.

Vikram Chatterjee was her lead researcher in the hospital. Born in Ahmedabad, India, he was one of the smartest people she knew. With a Master's in Virology from Harvard and a PhD in Virology from Johns Hopkins, Kami knew if anyone was going to crack the code; Vikram was her man.

"What do we know?" Kami asked

"I compared our patient's blood sample to that of a sample of someone in full blown GLU infection in the final hours of their life. I can confirm, there is no presence of GLU in his blood."

Vikram looked puzzled. "It's the best disappearing act since David Blaine."

"What about the water?" was Kami's next question. A lab tech had been sent back to the scene of the attack to gather samples of the water.

"Salinity was normal, microscopic organisms contained within were nothing out of the ordinary. Water temperature was within normal tolerance." We appear to be just chasing our tails.

"Well, anything you need, I'll make sure you have it," Kami reassured him. Test and retest as much as you need, the answer is around here somewhere.

She left the same way she came in, through the 'money machine'. The PPE came off, and she headed back to her office. As she walked the hallway of her little hospital, she felt the eyes of the world and all the weight that came with that, testing the strength of her resolve. She closed the door to her office, pulled the shades, grabbed a pillow off the couch, and screamed into it again and again. She knew time was running out.

CHAPTER 33
THE HARD WAY

"AUSTRALIA," they both shouted with surprise.

"Well, you two clearly have been spending a lot of time together. Soon you'll be completing each other's sentences." Spencer couldn't help but poke a little fun, maybe to take their mind off what was coming next.

"What's in Australia?" Javon asked.

"A surfer named Dylan."

"Seems like an inappropriate time for surfing lessons."

"Actually, I've always wanted to learn how to surf." Candace jumped in.

Javon shot her a look that said, "I do not have time for this." Message received; Candace reined in the levity.

Spencer continued, "About 4 weeks ago, Dylan received the news that GLU had found its way into his system. Rather than wait for GLU's gruesome end, he decided he was going to go out in a blaze of glory. He hopped on his surfboard, hoping to catch some gnarly waves and ring the dinner bell for a hungry, great white shark that might be swimming by.

Javon and Candace weren't speaking; Spencer had their undivided attention.

"He would have gotten away with it too if not for those pesky kids and their dog."

"What?" Candace asked.

"Sorry, I was a big Scooby Doo fan as a kid," Spencer admitted.

"Dylan did get his wish; a great white did attempt to make him a snack. Now, minus a leg and an inheritance of over 300 stitches, he is lying in a hospital in Streaky Bay, Australia. Other than losing parts of his anatomy, it seems our surfer also lost any trace of GLU."

Those last few words sucked the air out of the room. There was a look of astonishment on Candace's face.

"You're going to need to get there, and aid the researcher to get to the bottom of this." Spencer then took a deep breath that shifted the invisible focus of the phone call squarely on Javon.

"I'm not going to like this, am I?" Javon asked. He was smart and experienced enough to know that his skill set was not going to be used in the research lab.

"You have a vehicle, yes?"

"We do"

"As I told you when I got you to Athens, I was pretty much out of favors. Flying from Atlanta to Australia isn't an option; too far. So, you two are taking a road trip to Los Angeles."

"Ooh ooh, can we stop at Buc-ee's," Clearly Candace was becoming hysterical.

Javon looked at her annoyed. "Sure. Hey, while we are at it, we're going by Memphis. Do you want to stop into Graceland? Maybe hit Beale Street?"

Spencer didn't encourage her. "Once you are there, you will need to borrow,"

Javon could hear the air quotes in his voice

"A plane big enough to make the flight from LAX to Streaky Bay Airport. As you can imagine, this won't be easy as LAX is, like every other airport around the world, locked down in an attempt to slow down the spread of our little alien invader. You've always been incredibly resourceful, Javon; that's one of the reasons I hired you."

"Won't be easy," Javon barked. Let's entertain for a moment the multiverse timeline that has us safely driving cross country through a landscape of power grid failures, panic, and lawlessness. Then, in that same timeline, I am able to use my resourcefulness, as you put it, to procure a plane – How about a 787 Dreamliner, go big or go home, right?"

Spencer could sense Javon's lack of faith in the plan

"There is one important piece to this plan that I think we are going to have trouble with; who is going to fly the damn plane?"

Javon's lack of faith in the plan showed as he continued. "It's not like I can call Tank and have him download all the schematics and knowledge I need to fly the play, like he did for Trinity and that helicopter in The Matrix."

Spencer paused a few seconds to make sure Javon was done; it was best to just listen and let him finish.

"You're going to have to convince a couple of pilots who might be stuck at LAX in the lockdown that they are needed to help save the world, and they, like you two, need to risk getting shot at by the military as you borrow a plane to fly halfway around the world."

"You hear how crazy that sounds right?" Javon didn't wait for a response. He took a deep breath.

"Is there any other way?"

"I'm afraid not. I know it's kind of a Hail Mary at this point, but it's all we have. We need to get there before the military. That hospital in Streaky Bay has the puzzle piece, and I believe Candace will find the answer to where it goes to complete the puzzle. If the military gets down there, we'll never see that kid again. They'll take him to some Area 51, black site and test him in every way imaginable. I fear our surfer won't survive it."

"Well, Buc-ee's it is," Javon said with a resigned tone. Looking at Candace he said, "Okay, make sure you go potty before we leave because I'm not stopping till we need gas."

"Okay Dad," Candace played along.

"Javon"

"Yeah Boss"

"Time and options are running low; this has to work."

"No pressure." Javon said with a bit of resignation

"No pressure," said Spencer, knowing it couldn't be further from the truth.

"I'm going to kick myself hard when we realize the solution was right under our noses

CHAPTER 34
FLIGHT LESSONS

Bags, supplies, and belongings were all in the car. Leaving the Knights Inn parking lot, Javon noticed the first order of business was gas. With the power grid failing, this could be their first challenge before even getting a mile down the road.

"Ok, we have enough gas to at least get heading in the right direction. Rather than be caught out in the open here looking for a gas station where the pumps work, let's drive for a little bit and see if we can find something a little less exposed on the way to Alabama."

Candace heard every word, but she knew he was sharing just so she knew what the plan was. This wasn't going to be up for discussion. That would be like Javon questioning her science. Getting to LAX was his show, his expertise and she 100 percent knew she didn't want to be anywhere else with anyone else than Javon.

On a good day, traveling from Athens to Atlanta took 80 minutes with light traffic. Most of the route was state route 78 to 138, then I-20 just outside the city. Small towns like Monroe and Walnut Grove, which once thrived with their festivals, parades, and Friday night football games, were quiet, eerily quiet. A few small fires burned, and storefronts showed signs of the smash-and-grab panic that comes with a growing pandemic.

"Ever hijacked a plane before?" Candace was once again trying to lighten the mood.

"Funny you ask, just the other day on my way to lunch…..NO! This will be a first. Something to tell our grandkids about."

Realizing how that sounded, he quickly pivoted, "I mean, your kids and my kids will have kids, not kids we'll have together. Kids with other people and…."

She put her hand on his knee and laughed, "Relax Romeo, I'm not counting that and what happened last night as a marriage proposal, I know what you mean."

"That laugh," he thought. "Kind of makes all the bad shit melt away for a moment." He smiled back

"Technically, we're not hijacking the plane," getting back on topic. "We just need to get to the airport, past whatever checkpoints and security they have set up, and strongly persuade two experienced pilots that they need to fly us to Australia and help us save the world. Easy, peasy, lemon squeezy."

"If you say so."

"How hard could it be? I'll just ask really nice." Javon smirked as they approached Conyers.

"This would be a good time to look for a working gas station and fill up before we pick up I-20 to Atlanta. We'll be on that highway for a while. The less we stop, the better." It wasn't a sound of worry in Javon's voice, just a healthy dose of caution and respect for the situation.

The rolling blackouts seemed less prevalent in Conyers, maybe because of the close proximity to Atlanta. Regardless, that was a bit of good news.

As Candace scanned side roads, road signs, streets, for any indication of gas,

"Don't look," Javon startled her.

Now, any parent will tell you that when you tell the kids in the car, "Don't look!" They are going to do the exact opposite of that and look for whatever it is you don't want them to look at. Clearly, Candace had not outgrown her inner child's curiosity because she instantly stopped looking for gas stations and started twisting and contorting her neck and head to get a glimpse of the forbidden fruit. The second she found it she regretted it. There was so much to unpack from what she was seeing.

A small camper had hit a tree opposite a small ice cream store. Broken glass made the ground glitter, as if the camper was not a camper at all but a small boat on a sparkling lake. A couple of benches used to reside under that tree, benches where a young couple, friends, or Mom, Dad, and the kids would stop to eat their ice cream in the shade of that tree.

Those benches were now a twisted pile of wood and metal underneath the front wheels of the camper. Interwoven amidst the textile nightmare was flesh and bone and blood. One maybe two bodies, hard to tell. The camper had hit with a force, that didn't leave much chance for survival.

Smoke seeped from the hood; the driver's side door was open, and the driver spilled out of the seat toward the ground, following the torrent of blood that had left his body in a hurry.

"So much blood," Candace whispered, unsure of how long she had been holding her breath before speaking.

The back of the camper was open and tossed like an inmate's cell during a surprise search. However, instead of looking for "toilet hooch" or a shiv, whoever explored the contents of the camper was looking for supplies. This was clearly a sign of the continued devolution of civility and politeness. Survival was paramount—the line between right and wrong was blurring, and time was running out.

It wasn't until 5 minutes past the camper's nightmarish scene that they came upon a Circle K gas station.

Javon parked behind the dumpster.

"Wait here," Javon demanded as he grabbed a handgun from the bag, checked the clip, and stored a couple extra in his pocket.

"That seems excessive," Candace remarked.

"Better to have and not need than to need and not have," Javon replied. "Something my mother always told me when I would argue about needing to wear a jacket to school in winter."

Candace thought it was sweet that he had such love for his mom.

"I just want to do a quick look around to make sure it's safe. If it is, I'll come around the corner and signal you. When I do, pull the car up, hit 'pay inside', and start putting in gas. I'll go inside, authorize the pump, and grab some snacks, drinks, and other things we may need. I'm not sure when the next time will be when we get this chance." No restroom break, sorry, leaving too much to chance being out of each other's line of site for that long. We'll make a stop roadside when we need to.

"Just don't get me a hot dog off the hot dog roller; who knows how long those have been there."

Looking at Candace, shaking his head, "Got it, no mystery meat, check!"

She watched him walk around the back corner of the building and then the front corner, presumably heading toward the front door. Candace was no dummy. She stayed alert, making sure there were no surprises. She always brought her point of view back to the corner of the building, waiting for Javon's signal.

It seemed as if he had been gone for hours; adrenaline would do that. With every nerve and sense on alert, seconds seem like hours. 5 minutes later, the signal. She started the car and rolled toward the pump. Looking at the gas gauge for the little sideways triangle to see what side the gas tank was on, she pulled up to the pump. Candace didn't need to get out to realize that despite the inside of the store having power, the pumps did not. The screens were blank. No price per gallon, no tiny LED screen with an ad about what tasty snacks were inside, nothing. She waved at Javon, got his attention, and then gave him a combination of thumbs down and a cutting gesture across her neck. She wanted to make sure he understood they wouldn't be getting gas at this station.

Javon quickly walked back to the vehicle, dropped his bags in the backseat, and they left on the hunt for a gas station with power and gas. They repeated this process two more times before finally coming upon a Quik Trip oasis. Like an old friend, you could always rely on, which was one of the reasons Quik Trip was ranked 2nd best convenience store chain in the country.

Javon repeated his recon process, and moments later, the pump came to life, and gas was flowing. Still looking around, she saw Javon busy stuffing bags with power bars, sports drinks, and so much jerky. Sure, he also picked up the occasional sugary snack, bag of chips, and candy bar, but the name of the game was good calories equals good energy.

Javon hurried to the car, putting the loot in the back seat. A couple of bottles caught her eye.

"Wine and bourbon?" She gave him a look. "Is that in the survivalist handbook," Candace quizzed him, knowing it wasn't.

"No need to live like savages, right?" he said with a smile on his face

She smiled back just as the pump handle clicked. "Want me to drive?" she asked.

"Maybe later, I'm good for now."

They both climbed in, the car started, the needle on the fuel gauge was on F, there was plenty of daylight, and signs for I-20 were visible in the distance. Stop one, a success.

CHAPTER 35
FISH BOWL

The awkward embarrassment of yesterday's sponge bath seemed so far removed from the lunch on the hospital tray that sat before him. After almost a month in the hospital, Dylan had a list in his head of what was good coming out of the hospital cafeteria and what was not.

"You don't suppose I could just have these fruit parfaits for the rest of my stay here, do you?"

Natalie smiled, "Sorry dude, doc has you on a pretty straightforward dietary plan while they try to figure out how you escaped the jaws of a shark and GLU."

Natalie had been spending a lot of time at the hospital. Dylan wondered if she had picked up extra shifts. She seemed intent on being the one caring for him the most. He was okay with that.

"Okay, just no more chicken, if that's what it really is," scrunching up his nose as he said it. "It's like chewing on a tire."

"I will be sure to let the chef know," she said with a tone that Dylan picked up on in an instant.

"Sorry, I'll try not to be so picky. I really do appreciate you." He blushed a little when he said it.

"But c'mon, how long is the hospital going to keep me here?"

"I'm afraid it's gone above hospital administration at this point. Mayor Southridge and the people who tell her what to do have given us strict instructions to keep you here while they try to figure out how your body rid itself of something that is killing a lot of people. You want to help, right? The answer to this whole thing is somewhere in your blood. I don't know why, but it is, and we need you to understand how important that is."
Dylan knew Nat wasn't exactly pleading as she was very honest and upfront with her answer; it was more a tone of "I know this sucks, but please understand it's for the best."

"I do want to help," he said looking her in the eyes, "But if we could find some balance when it comes to how many people come in this room. It's just a lot somedays."

"Funny you say that," she said nervously.

"Oh lord, what?"

"Well, you have to admit you've become a bit of a celebrity. There have been a ton of requests for interviews. So far, we have turned them all away but kept all their contact info for when you feel ready."
Nat could tell he didn't like the way this conversation was going.

She continued, "My bosses aren't oblivious to the relationship you and I have developed. They were hoping I could use that and ask you to consider one interview. One that could then be shared with other news outlets. People need hope, Dylan. There is some horrific suffering going on around the world. GLU continues to spread, society is panicking, and people need to have something that will help them hang on to their humanity."

"What about my humanity? I feel like one of the sideshow freaks that used to come to town with the circus." There was resentment in his voice. "Come one, come all, see the monkey boy with the magical blood."

"I get it, Dylan, I really do," Natalie said. "There isn't a day that goes by in this job where my patients and their families aren't asked to set aside their modesty, their privacy and sometimes a little of their humanity – all in the name of hoping for a positive, best case scenario outcome. Sometimes, they don't get a choice."

The volume of her voice came down to a loud, forced whisper as she leaned in. "Listen, you don't see what I see outside this room. People are watching their loved ones die on the other side of a barrier, unable to hold their hand in their last moments. Yesterday, parents had to watch their 9-year-old suffer the final, worst parts of GLU."

Tears filled her eyes; she sobbed the next words, "They stood there, looking on in horror as every ounce of life-giving blood that fueled that child's future left her body, and as their nurse, I had stand there in the absence of words, and just be with them."

The flood gates that Natalie had kept locked up were breached, she continued.

"Dylan, we are using rooms in this hospital to keep GLU patients that were never designed to be patient rooms. Still, we are better off than some hospitals in the bigger cities. Refrigerator trucks are being parked outside those hospitals like trailers outside middle schools that have run out of class space. Except, instead of students, these trailers are holding the dead because there is no more room in their morgues."

The look on his face was a blend of shame and horror. "I'm sorry Nat, I…I had no idea."

"I know, how could you? But now you see this is much bigger than just you. We….I…everyone here at the hospital needs you to tell your story."

As she dried her tears Dylan asked. "Will it be on video, audio, or print?"

"Well, I suppose that's up to you, why?" She asked curiously.

"I need to know if I have to have another sponge bath or not."

With a smile on her face and a broken filter, Natalie said, "You can have those anytime you want."

She blushed, not believing what came out of her mouth. She was pretty confident and straightforward, but even that seemed a bit overboard.

"Sorry…..I…" she stammered, trying to think of a way to shift the weird vibe she had created. Her face was on fire with embarrassment.

"Natalie," Dylan took her hand. "Relax."

For the first time, his touch was different. It was void of the clinical, sterile touch that came with hospital procedures. It was soothing, calming, and welcoming.

"Let's see that list of news outlets. Let your bosses know I'll have an answer by tomorrow."

With a gentle, knowing look all she said was "Thank you" as she left the room. Dylan was smart enough to know she wasn't thanking him because he agreed to do the interview. He shut his eyes for an afternoon nap.

CHAPTER 36
TUPELO

On January 8th, 1935, a boy was born in Tupelo, Mississippi, who would change the world. Little did his parents, Vernon and Gladys, know that some would view their child as nothing short of the anti-Christ. Something wretched was being spat forth from the speakers of their radios, twisting, tempting, and deceiving the minds of the children.

He transfigured the entire landscape of the music world in a way unlike any other artist. Some thought Elvis Aaron Presley was a plague on society. His devil music and what he did with his hips, well, they were downright obscene.

It seemed fitting that Tupelo was on the way. Javon and Candace needed more gas, so they pulled off I-22 and headed toward the center of town, which had a couple of hotels, restaurants, bingo, and a Travelers truck stop.

"Did you know you don't have to be a trucker to shower at truck stops?" Javon's random and prideful matter-of-factness left Candace unsure of what to say.

"Reeaaallllyyy" as she dragged out the word to boost his male ego, "I had no idea."

"Yeah, one day on an unexpected and long road trip,"

"You mean like this one," she interrupted

"Yes, minus the whole end-of-the-world vibe. Anyway, it had been a long day, I was tired and as I was paying for my stuff at the counter, curiosity got the best of me and I asked." Javon continued as he drifted into the memory.

"The clerk told me anyone could use them, so you know what, I did. Lord, that was the best shower I had in a long time. Completely changed the way I did road trips after that. Like, I would intentionally plan and block off an hour for a shower and a little R&R."

"Too bad we don't have time for one of those great showers now," Candace teased

"Yeah, too bad. Anyway, the place looks quiet; same drill. I'll do a sweep of the area, outside and then in. If it seems safe, I'll motion you toward the pumps. Don't deviate – another quick gas and grab and back on the road.

Just like before, Javon parked out back, away from what would have been considered the path of traffic if this truck stop was alive with all means of wayward travelers and modes of transportation. Just a mini ghost town now. Cars that had been picked over like someone had gone through the bag of Halloween candy and taken all the good stuff out. The only things left around this travel center were circus peanuts and wax lips.

Just like before, gun, clips, corner and corner, and he was gone around the building, once again leaving Candace to wait. This place was bigger than the last time they gassed up. She expected it would take a little longer before she got the 'all clear'.

As before, she was doing her own sweep of the area. Doing her best not to be caught off guard by someone trying to sneak up on her. Still, she couldn't help but get a little distracted.

"Love me tender, love me sweet, and never let me go." Her impersonation felt like very bad karaoke, but she was an audience of one. She continued.

"You have made my life complete, and I love you so."

There it was, the all clear, and right before the chorus. Slightly disappointed she didn't get to finish, she rolled up to the pump. She flashed two hands of 5 fingers, then one hand of 1. Pump 11

Javon ran back inside, turned on the pump and they were once again in business. This resupply mission for Javon was a little different. They still had plenty of food. So, a couple more cold drinks and then anything and everything that was left in the medicine aisle. Then he went out back to what would have been the employee lounge. He explored the employee lockers; a knife was the only score. He grabbed the first aid kit off the wall and headed back toward the pumps. He had already been out of sight longer than he felt comfortable.

Candace was wrapping up, putting the pump back in the cradle, and heading toward the passenger side of the car when the rear window exploded in a hailstorm of glass, followed instantly by the loud report of a large caliber weapon.

"JAVON," she screamed, doing her best to locate him and still keep herself from being an easy target. She looked toward the front door of the store to see Javon giving her hand signals to stay down.

"Thanks 'Captain Obvious'," she thought to herself.

The rear of the car took two more bullets. The upside was that it was opposite the gas tank side; the bad news was that the shooter was dialing in his aim. Everything happened so quickly that she couldn't really tell what direction the gunfire was coming from. Regardless, this was not good.

Javon needed some cover to get to the car and Candace. He ran back inside and grabbed a bottle of vodka off the shelf. Tearing off a piece of his shirt, he stuffed it in the neck of the bottle. One Molotov cocktail was coming right up.

"Matches, matches," talking to himself to help him think. Of course, by the register. A treasure trove of Bic lighters and matchbooks. Trying not to be seen and staying away from windows that weren't obscured by sunglass racks or ice machines, he waited and watched.

Two more bullets pierced the rear passenger door, punching through the metal as easily as a hand of a contestant on The Price Is Right playing the punch game. That's all he needed, though; the sound and trajectory gave away the position of their enemy. He lit the strip cloth, leaned out the door, and tossed it in the general direction of the gunshots.

The bottle hit the ground, exploding like mini napalm on the asphalt of the truck stop. No sooner had the improvised incendiary device left his hand than he was running as fast as he could toward the car. Empty-handed, leaving all of his spoils inside the store. Going around wasn't an option, and Candace knew it. Javon came diving toward her through the passenger side. It wasn't ideal and not exactly as graceful as the movies made it look, but it's amazing what you can do when you're being shot at.

Another hole punched through the passenger door, missing Javon and creating an exit wound on the other side of the door the size of a dinner plate. The door heaved on its hinges as shrapnel launched in every direction.

"GET IN," Javon yelled. Candace moved quick. As her butt hit the seat, the car was started and rocketing away from the pump.

"WHAP! WHAP! WHAP!" Three more shots into the trunk of the car. At this point, distance and the padding of the backseat was the only thing that saved them.

The on ramp to westbound I-22 was just up ahead. Javon looked in his rearview mirror.

"Well, nuts!" he blurted out, much calmer than Candace was.

"Are you hit?" was her first thought.

Looking over at her, "No, but you are." He pointed at the right temple of his head. Candace touched the right temple of hers. She drew back a hand wet from blood in her hair. Touching it again, she felt what she assumed was part of the car door.

The adrenaline had clearly masked the pain, but now that her brain connected the dots between the physical wound and the nerves, her head throbbed.

She touched it again, this time in a triage sort of way. Assessing her situation, she quickly realized it wasn't as serious as all the blood suggested. The 2-inch piece of metal had travelled a trajectory that buried it under the surface of the hair and skin, but it didn't penetrate bone.

"Wish I had that first aid kit right about now," Javon stated. Candace was already a step ahead of him. Tearing off a piece of the shirt she was wearing, she put it in her lap and then reached for the jagged metal invader. Like ripping a band-aid off, she pulled hard and fast.

"Son-of-a-bitch," she strained through gritted teeth. Somehow that made it hurt just a little less.
Once removed, she pressed the cloth to her head and applied pressure to stop the bleeding.
"Why are head wounds such bleeders?" Javon wondered out loud.

"Capillaries, veins, and other fancy medical stuff I'll tell you about later." She explained.

"We've got company," Javon alerted her as he stayed on target for that on-ramp.

Behind them, their shooter was in pursuit. Javon could see a person holding the assault rifle leaning out of the top of a Jeep Wrangler. Face wrapped in a bandana to hide their identity. With anonymity came empowerment to do things you normally wouldn't do.

Two motorcycles flanked the Jeep. Each rider's identity was hidden by the helmet. Each rider held what looked like 9 mm-style handguns. A hail of gunfire was being sent in their general direction. Lucky for

Javon, he could tell by their aim that these were not trained professionals. They were just some scared, good-ole boys who were going to do what it took to survive.

"Almost there; the on-ramp is just on the other side of the overpass." Javon's confidence level when it came to outrunning and outmaneuvering them was pretty high until....

On the other side of the overpass, coming straight toward them, was a truck, 3 more gunmen in the bed of the truck, plus the driver. That's 7 now, and they are all armed. Javon had clearly underestimated their resourcefulness. They were a lot more organized than he gave them credit for.

Options were limited. Making the on-ramp wasn't going to be a thing right now.

"What are we going to do," Candace trembled. It was the first time Javon had seen Candace worried and scared.

"Look, it's going to be okay. I need you to load and reload anything and everything in that bag. I still have the 9mm on me. I think there is a .38 in the bag and a shotgun behind my seat."

Candace didn't argue. She knew that after all his training, he was the much better shot. Put a gun in her hand, and she would miss her intended target like a storm trooper. "Pew Pew" was all that came to mind in her head.

Compartmentalizing the situation, Javon had a plan, not a great one, but the only one. Up ahead was an abandoned delivery truck from a local florist. Just enough cover to get to the high ground.

"See that van up ahead? I'm sliding in there; it could be a bit of a bumpy stop. As soon as we can get out, we evacuate and head up the side of the slope under the overpass. That flat part at the top where they say you shouldn't go if this were a tornado, that's going to give us our best chance of cover and best chance to take these guys out one at a time."

Candace nodded; she knew this wasn't good. Her head was pounding, and all of a sudden, GLU was the farthest thing from her mind. Her mom and dad, Kahl, Wichita, that's all she could think of right now, what she wouldn't give to be back in that kayak right about now.

The daydream was cut short by the car slamming into the florist van. Grabbing the bags with the guns and ammo, she bolted from the car and up the embankment. Javon was right behind her. They dug in and waited.

The shadows of their spot helped conceal them a little, enough to maybe give them a fighting chance. The Jeep, the truck, the two motorcycles all came to a stop about 20 feet from their car. When the engines cut off, it was unnervingly quiet. Minus the occasional 'coo' of a pigeon, there was just the wind until one of the party crashers yelled up to them.

"Hey, you two, we don't get many visitors to Tupelo this day. The world has kind of gone to shit."

"Just let us be on our way, we're trying to get by just like you." Javon continued, "We don't want any trouble…" he was cut off

"Oh, you won't be any trouble. The way I see it, we have you in quite a pickle. Outnumbered, outgunned, I'd say you're out of options."

The snarky tone in his voice made Javon all the more determined to see this though. He hated arrogance, and this hillbilly had plenty of it.

The group's lead negotiator motioned one of the motorcycle riders toward their car. Clearly, they were getting ready to help themselves.

"The research," Candace whispered

"I know"

"We can't let them take it," Candace knew she didn't need to say it, but she did anyway.

"I know," Javon whispered louder. Then he took aim and fired. For untrained marksmen, that shot would have been tough. Javon put the bullet right at the feet of the motorcycle rider.

"We don't want to hurt you; we just want to be on our way, but we are not going to let you take our stuff." Javon's tone was loud, defiant, and uncompromising.

"I'm not sure from where I'm standing that you have much of a say so in the matter." The hillbilly gestured for the motorcycle rider to continue forward. Javon didn't hesitate. In an instant, the shot from his gun rang out at about the same time the knee of the motorcycle rider was rendered useless by the impact of the bullet, right where Javon had intended for it to go.

Shouting over the wounded rider who was screaming from the hot pain that was washing over his leg, "I told you two things: we don't want any trouble, and hands off our stuff. The next person who steps any closer than your guy on the ground gets one to the chest or head, I haven't decided yet." Javon's confidence was part bluff, but it seemed to be working.

"That's fine, son; we got all the time in the world. We can wait." The hillbilly sounded so sure of himself. A radio squelched in the hillbilly's pocket; he took it out. Neither Javon nor Candace could make out what he was saying. They didn't need to. This meant there were more, and it was a pretty good bet it wouldn't be long before they joined the party.

Candace was smart and could read faces, but Javon's expression did not instill much confidence in her at the moment.

"Javon, I'm scared," was all she could say.

"I know, me too, but I've been in tighter spots. We'll figure it out. Let me think, weigh our options." He looked at her trying to quiet her fears.

"How much ammo do we have?"

She took a quick inventory. "6 more full clips for the handguns, about 8 shells for the shotgun, and we are armed to the teeth with witty banter and bluffs."

"An unlimited supply of that, and that might just be what saves us." He was bluffing.

As expected, there were more hillbillies. 2 more cars, 2 more trucks, 6 more, and heavily armed. They began to scatter just on the opposite side of the overpass, what seemed like a safe distance. They had rifles; Javon had pistols and a shotgun. This was a heavyweight boxing match, and the opponent had a much longer reach. He could see what was getting ready to go down.

"Remember what you learned in school about the Revolutionary War?" he asked Candace.

"You're going to have to be a bit more specific."

Javon continued, "The way the British fought in a line. They just marched forward, fired, and then another line. It's really one of the reasons they lost because the colonists used more unconventional, almost guerilla-like tactics."

"Go on," Candace said with more than an ounce of curiosity.

"You're going to take the shotgun, and we're going to spread out. They won't expect it, and it's our only chance."

"But I only have 8 shots, and well, my aim is not that great."

"Doesn't matter," Javon stated. "The most important thing is they need to hear the gunfire. We need to keep them off balance."

He took a breath.

"You won't like this next part. I need to get closer. My guns aren't effective up here. I need to get between our car and the van. I'll have cover and should be able to make things really problematic for them."

"You're right, I really hate that part." He could hear the concern in her voice.

"Take your position and fire one shot. The buckshot will ricochet and put them off balance just enough for me to get down there."

He looked her in the eyes, those eyes that had a spark of light, and cupping her face in his hands, kissed her deep on the lips.

"You can do this. WE can do this."

All Candace could do was nod, before she belly-crawled toward her position. Once there, she made eye contact with Javon, he gave her the thumbs up, and she fired.

As expected, all the party crashers ducked for cover. Just enough time for Javon to get to his position before bullets kicked up the gravel at his feet and found purchase in the van behind him.

Gunfire thundered all around. The acoustics under the overpass amplified the noise. It was deafening, it was violent, it was overpowering. Javon knew he was going to have to 'pick his spot'. He didn't have the rounds his enemies had. So, strategy number 2.

Javon loved the Rocky movies, all of them, and the Creed movies too. In this situation, he was focused on Rocky III. Balboa was up against a force in Mr. T's character, "Clubber Lang". Clubber was bigger, stronger, faster, more powerful but the one thing he wasn't was a fan of cardio. Rocky started darting in and out, landing a punch here and there, enticing the enraged Clubber, getting him to swing wildly and throw a lot more punches than Rocky did. Taking an impossible beating, Apollo yells from the corner, "He's getting' killed", and Pauly replies, "No, no…he's getting mad."

"Make 'em mad, make them shoot more than they need to, make them miss, buy some time." Those were thoughts running through his head. So, he did just that.

With each shot he fired, there was reason. It was close enough to scare its intended target but not wound them. He wanted them to fire back, and they fired back a lot. He was confident in his cover and in Candace.

Another shotgun blast from above only made the hillbillies see more red. For each shot he and Candace sent down range, 20 came back. This went on for a few minutes and as good of a plan that it was, it just wasn't a match for the firepower they were up against.

"Jesus Christ, did these guys knock over Cabela's right before they found us? When are they going to run out of ammo?"

Number 8. Javon heard the last shotgun blast. He knew Candace was out, rendered ineffective. He checked his ammo. 1 in the chamber, one magazine left.

For the first time in Javon's life, he felt a tinge of hopelessness that was the harbinger of failure. It was a very unfamiliar feeling. He didn't like how it tasted. He looked up at Candace, and even from that distance, she could see the "I'm sorry" on his face.

The look she gave back was pleading for him to wait, to hold on just a little longer. He remembered telling her that he had been in worse situations; well, that was dumb. He might as well have said, "What could possibly go wrong" and invited the universe to kick him square in the 'yam bags'.

Instead, from under his breath came "Hold my beer and watch this." It seemed the end of the world was going to come sooner than they had planned.

CHAPTER 37
HOPE

"Reuters, AP, Al Jazeera, Washington Post, all the major networks in America – crikey, the only one who doesn't want to speak to me is the Pope." Dylan was clearly overwhelmed, needing to make a choice of who to grant the interview to. Who was going to tell his story?

"Actually, the Pope just called,"

"Really??" Dylan blurted out.

Natalie couldn't fake her amusement, "No, not really."

She shifted the discussion to the serious side, "All kidding aside, I told everyone you'd have a decision by 7p tonight. You have 15 minutes."

"Allen Reston!" he said definitively.

"Sorry, who?" Natalie was clearly confused.

"Allen Reston, he writes for the Erye Peninsula Advocate."

"You want to give quite possibly the most sought-after interview in the world to a guy at our local paper?" Natalie said with surprise.

"Who better?" Dylan argued. "GLU may be happening to the world, but THIS, this potential turning point, is happening here. Streaky Bay, Australia."

Dylan pulled himself up in bed, body language that suggested how serious he was. "When the world thinks of our country, when tourists want to plan a trip here, where do they think of? Brisbane, Perth, Melbourne? Why not Streaky Bay? I'll tell you why. What are we famous for? The Streaky Bay Jail and rock pools. His will remember Streaky Bay from this day forward as the place that saved the world."

"I get all that, and that's commendable," Natalie responded, "But do you think Allen is up for this?"

Dylan smiled and touched the top of her hand resting on the rail of his hospital bed. "Nat, journalists like Allen have waited all their lives for a story like this. All the stories he has told here in Streaky Bay have been told with as much heart and passion as any journalist anywhere. I've read much of what he's written. Any news outlet or publication would be lucky to have him. He's my choice."

"Allen, it is," Natalie said with a smile. "I'll set it up for tomorrow at 2pm."

For the interview, Dylan was freshly bathed and dressed in a clean robe and taken to the small room where Allen was waiting. Ironically, the room, where families received the worst news of their lives, was clean and sterile. There were minimal chances for anything stopping Allen from getting this story to the world. Both men were wearing N95 masks.

"Hello," Allen said, Dylan could tell he was nervous. No handshake, not in these times.

"Allen, Hi, thanks for coming."

"Are you kidding? I haven't stopped hyperventilating since I got the news last night."

"You're not going to pass out on me, are you?" Dylan joked.

"Well, if I do, what better place to do it than a hospital?" Allen laughed; Dylan did, too. With the ice broken and rapport established, Allen placed a digital recorder on the table between them and hit record on the camera sitting on a tripod. "Shall we get started?"

The first few minutes of the interview were standard. It was the "let's get to know Dylan" portion, so the person watching or reading could enjoy a little character development.

Then, the hard question. "Why?" Allen asked.

"Why, what?"

"Why try and end your life?"

Dylan paused for a moment. "Allen, have you ever read the book "The Road" by Cormac McCarthy?

"I have heard of it but never had a chance to spend any time with it," Allen said honestly.

"The book is about a father and son in a post-apocalyptic world who realize that they can't survive up north in the United States, so they have to journey south to a rumored 'better' place. All industrialized civilization is gone, and there are really bad people along the way. I was watching this movie adaptation with a girlfriend at the time. While movies are never as good as the books, Viggo Mortensen, Charlize Theron, and Kodi Smit-McPhee did it justice."

A little off track, he continued.

"Anyway, watching the movie with my girlfriend made me realize there are two types of people in the world, 'dreamers,' aka optimists, and 'realists,' aka pessimists.
After the movie we talked about how I would have simply just stopped that long, arduous journey and gone out on my own terms because it was hopeless. There was literally nothing to live for. I would have ended it for myself and my son rather than condemn him to a life of hardship and loneliness. She, on the other hand, could not accept that. There was a rumor, whispers of help, a better place, maybe more people. She would have kept going believing it to be true until it wasn't."

Dylan paused, clearly a little emotional

"Up until now, most of the world outside of the medical community believed GLU to be a death sentence. Not just a death sentence but one of the most awful ways to die. Then, after you die, there is no funeral, celebration of life, and closure for all who knew you. You are burned and discarded like you never even existed. I couldn't accept that. I lived on my own terms and choices, and I was going to die that way. I wanted to die doing something I loved. Was I looking forward to the vicious attack? Of course not, but I kept telling myself it would be less of a suffering than painfully bleeding out of every hole in my body."

Allen, who had been hanging on Dylan's every word, shifted the interview to the here and now.

"How's the PT coming after the loss of you leg?"

"Bonzer!" Dylan said excitedly. "As soon as I get out of here, I'm going to apply for a job at IHOP."

Allen who had chosen that moment to take a drink of ice water, nearly spat it all over the table. Their robust and unexpected laughter filed out of the room and down the halls, catching the attention of doctors and nurses who were not really curious about what they were talking about.

"Honestly," Dylan said, "It's going to be an obvious adjustment, but a new chapter, a new beginning. A chance for me to reinvent myself I guess."

"I know you're not a scientist that studies viruses and things of that sort, but what do YOU think is the reason for GLU being in your body one day and gone the next after your suicide attempt?" Allen, leaned in a little with anticipation.

"I've asked myself that question so many times. I've gone over it in my head over and over and over again. It has to be environmental. Something in the conditions of the surroundings I was in that didn't exist anywhere else. Something in the water being secreted from the ocean floor or the nearby rocks, or the coral. For all we know, where I was attacked could be a secret dumping ground for radioactive waste, and now, I'm going to turn into some sort of mutant superhero. I wonder if the X-men need a new member?"

"Have you ever considered it's something in your genetic makeup?" Allen pondered.

"Sure, for a brief moment, but if that were the case, I would have never gotten GLU in the first place, right? Nah, it has to be environmental, but what? And do those conditions still exist now, weeks later?"

"Many who are learning of your story are using your name with the word 'savior' in the same sentence. They believe it's a 'God thing', a miracle, divine intervention. They say the people who died were part of God's plan to reset an overcrowded, ungrateful, and faithless world. Do you see yourself as a 'Christ-like' savior of this world?"

"Not at all, mate." Dylan was quick to reply. "I was never really the church-going type, although I do accept that there are powerful things at play in this universe beyond our comprehension that have a great influence on us. This, I think, is one of them. I'm not going to begrudge them of their beliefs if that's what keeps them going, but if not me, it would have happened to someone else eventually. Some other person would have to bear the weight of this burden."

Allen didn't miss a beat on that last thought, "Why a burden?"

Dylan's face drew pensive and a little serious. "Allen, I have succeeded at many things, sure I've had my failures too, and drawn learning opportunities from those. This is different. Potentially, something in me, about me, could prevent millions, maybe billions, from dying. What if it was a one-off?" Dylan's rhetorical pause was only to give Allen a moment to connect the dots.

"Right now, I represent hope. This is the most encouraging news the world has received since GLU took its first life. The doctors, nurses, and scientists are working around the clock to crack the code to this mystery. I guess I'm just asking anyone listening, watching, or reading – to be like the girl who I watched "The Road" with. Believe with all your heart that what cured me will cure all, but don't stop doing all the things you're currently doing to keep you and your loved ones safe. And remember, it will all work out in the end, and if it doesn't, it's not the end."

There was silence in the room, Allen knew there was nothing else to ask or say after that. It was a perfect ending to what would be the biggest interview of his career.

CHAPTER 38
THE CAVALRY

"Hold My Beer, really?" Javon thought to himself. "This life-defining moment, and that's what you're going out on. If this were a movie, you would have said something much cooler than 'Hold my beer.'" The thought that delayed his actions continued.

"Think of the Thing from the Fantastic Four, 'It's Clobberin' Time,' or the Incredible Hulk, 'Hulk Smash.' Even some of the cheesy lines that Arnold Schwarzenegger delivered were better, like 'stick around'. Nope, I come up with 'hold my beer'.

Javon sighed; it was time. He stood up behind the car, locked on the closest target and fired. At the exact moment he pulled the trigger, the underpass area exploded. Everything that was once the hillbillies, the cars, the motorcycles, all of it was coming apart and being shredded by a swarm of really big rounds.

While Javon had been so caught up in finding the right words for the moment, and the hillbillies were locked on him and Candace, no one had noticed the approaching Black Hawk helicopter coming in hot, sound and sight greatly shielded by the highway infrastructure and all the commotion under the highway bridge.

In an instant, what was once a giant blender of smoke and metal and body parts, was once again quiet. The air was still, the dust and smoke being pushed out as the imposing 4 blade, twin-engine killing machine touched down. Javon motioned for Candace to stay in her position, he wasn't sure if these were the good guys or something worse than the hillbillies.

From the whir of the helicopter stepped a familiar face, Colonel Eugene Brighton. Candace started down the slope toward Javon and ground level, all converging on Javon's position about the same time.

"Looks like you two were having trouble making friends," the colonel quipped.

"They offered us some sweet tea and we said we wanted unsweet. Who knew the people in the South were that sensitive about the subject."

Candace snorted, a sign she was no longer the 'I'm going to die' ball of nerves she was just moments ago.

"I don't get it," Javon said, looking puzzled, how did you find us?"

"Pegasus," the colonel said as if Javon should have instantly known what he was talking about. Being a former military, he had heard about it.

Pegasus was spy software developed to help world governments fight crime and terrorism. Of course, it was also used to monitor journalists, lawyers, political dissidents, human rights activists, and others. The program is capable of reading texts, monitoring calls, collecting passwords, tracking locations, and more.

The colonel furthered his explanation. "When you two left Alaska on 'Pee Wee's Big Adventure'," looking right at Dr. Stanton as he said it, "We were a few days behind while I asked my superiors really nicely if I could play with Pegasus to find you two. I knew better than to think you were merely running for safety. Both of you aren't built like that."

Wiping the sweat from his face and dust from his glasses, he continued.
"I knew how smart Dr. Stanton was and how resourceful you are. The two of you together were a formidable team. You were on to something, and I just needed to know what. I figured if left alone for a little while, you would work better that way. We've been keeping an eye on you since Athens. Those satellite phones were your downfall."

Javon and Candace looked shocked.

"Yeah, we can track those too," the colonel confirmed.

"Now that we're all up to the present-day dumpster fire that is the planet we call earth, there has been a development. You both need to grab your gear and come with us."

"But," was all the protest Candace could manage

"Yes, we know all about the crazy idea of convincing the crew of the plane to fly you to Australia. We're going to save you the trouble. Ms. Stanton (he remembered her preference from their first interaction when she was kayaking), we are taking you home to Wichita. There, we will all get on a KC-46 and start the long flight to Streaky Bay, Australia. With some refueling assistance and favorable weather, we should be on the ground in about 22 hours. I have teams waiting to take us to the local hospital."

The Colonel continued, "While some of my superiors view this as an enormous waste of resources when, as they put it, you could just zoom your way to a cure, I feel you and the other scientists already on site will be able to work more efficiently when you are all in the same room. I also didn't want to take the risk of losing power and or internet on this end or on that end.

Your research, Dr. Stanton, along with the work that is already being done, is our best shot at providing some answers as to why that surfer who once had GLU no longer does after being attacked by a great white shark.

Javon looked at Candace, "I was so looking forward to going all 'Mr. and Mrs. Smith' to get a flight crew together.

"I'm sure there will be time for that later," Candace flirted in a way that Javon instantly knew she wasn't talking about covert, save-the-world stuff. She then turned toward the colonel.

"Okay, give us a couple of minutes to grab the stuff out of the car and tell your team to (in a really bad Australian accent) *put another shrimp on the Barbie because we're bringing our talents down under.*

Javon cringed, and so did the Colonel; the hillbillies said nothing.

PART IV: FIRE

CHAPTER 39
WILDFIRE

It has been a few weeks since the horrors of Vienna played out on social media and the major news networks. Up until that point, no one had really connected the dots that this was not just a 'you problem,' but it was an 'US problem,' and something was terribly wrong. In the weeks since, the death toll was rising fast.

Despite best efforts from world governments to mandate isolation, travel restrictions, and mandatory rationing of essentials, the wildfire that was GLU was incredibly hard to contain. With not everyone on board because of the 'we know better and you can't tell us what to do' mentality, GLU was winning, and people were dying. That was about to change.

In Washington, D.C., President Arlington was about to once again let America lead the way and set the example, this time in an effort to take the fight to GLU. His special State of the Union address was two hours away.

"Sir," the President's Chief of Staff started. "I've looked over your speech, and this is some pretty strong language. Are you sure you don't want to soften the ask a little?"

The President looked at Chief of Staff Greenwell and said, "Sally, I'm done asking. I tried asking, and sadly, it fell on deaf ears of a large percentage of the population. No one ever thinks it's going to happen to them until it does, and then there are all sorts of regrets and remorse and 'oh, I should have listened.' I'm done with that."

The look on his face told Sally Greenwell this was not the President she knew before GLU started killing.

"This speech tonight is intended to scare and at the same time be a show of force, not just against GLU but against anyone watching or listening who still thinks this is no big deal." He could tell his Chief of Staff still wasn't fully on board.

"What is it, Sally?" he asked

"Well, it's just.... I don't think any sitting President has ever used the term "fuck around and find out" in a speech.

"Well, it certainly would have changed the tone of Roosevelt's 'Day of Infamy' speech. Imagine him saying, 'Today is a day that will live in infamy. A day when Japan decided to fuck around and find out.'" He smiled.

"I see your point," Chief of Staff Greenwell said. "Except, you're not addressing an attacking nation. You're addressing the people.

"Yes," he cut her off, "but when those people start acting recklessly and jeopardizing the lives of their fellow citizens, they need to realize they are no better than an attacking enemy, and I intend to make that abundantly clear in two hours."

With that, the President excused himself to the Oval Office, shut the door, removed his mask, and placed his head in the palm of his hands. In front of his Chief of Staff, he was strong and imposing, but in the solitude of the most important office in the land, he understood tonight's speech was going to solidify his place in the history books, for better or worse. Career-defining or career suicide, history would be the judge.

Two hours later, in the Oval Office, with just one camera operated robotically, the President was ready.

"My fellow Americans, thank you for letting me join you, wherever you are, from the Oval Office. I have delivered hundreds of speeches in my political career, and I can honestly say I never, ever imagined a need to write and deliver the speech I'm about to deliver to you now."

President Arlington took a breath before history verbally unfolded

"In the spring of this year, a couple of travel bloggers in Canada stumbled across an artifact in a glacier. At the time, they believed it to be something, maybe military or belonging to a space agency. It did not. The events that then unfolded accidentally unleashed a virus contained within that artifact that this planet had never seen before. It is believed to be the first concrete proof of alien life.

Chances are you have seen the stories on the news and seen some pretty shocking images online. Ever since this virus began to spread, the United States, in cooperation with other governments, has been working very hard to stop its spread. We took all the necessary precautions: restricted entry into the country and other travel restrictions, social distancing, and the encouragement of extra diligence when it came to daily health and sanitation habits.

We asked these things of you because we did not have a cure for this virus. Through our own ignorance and superiority complex, we threw all of our top science and research at it and felt there was a high probability we could get it under control."

He paused like he was about to admit to his wife he had an affair

"We were wrong, we were painfully wrong. We were also wrong about not demanding enough of you, the American people.
We were our own worst enemy and hence, created an environment that made it seem like it was no big deal, we were wrong.

Here is what we now know all these weeks later. FIRST AND MOST IMPORTANTLY THERE IS NO CURE AT THIS TIME. The GLU virus is spread through touch, bodily fluids, and particulates in the air. If there is any good news, it needs to be in close proximity to be transmitted, and it doesn't seem to be able to penetrate the N95 masks and other PPE precautions that we take in labs and hospitals. However, to those who haven't taken this situation seriously and have refused to mask or maintain social distancing, you are in grave danger.

If you contract GLU, you have 1800 seconds, 30 minutes before the first symptoms start. What starts as a bad headache and fatigue has a 100% mortality rate and ends in every drop of your blood leaving your body by any means necessary because it is being replaced by a thick, GLU-like substance that pushes it out. Obviously, the human body was not designed to survive this replacement, and death is very painful.

You must do everything possible to avoid becoming infected. So, from here forward, I am implementing new, stricter measures that will hopefully help us achieve a greater level of protection and slow and possibly prevent the further spread of GLU.

Starting today, I am requiring mandatory N95 masking and the wearing of latex or nitrile gloves that are meant to be used for a day and then disposed of. I have authorized local and state authorities to arrest anyone caught outdoors not taking these measures.

You may think this could cause an overcrowding problem in our jails, prisons, and detention centers. I have compensated for that by setting up temporary holding centers using churches, warehouses, empty malls, football stadiums and arenas, basically anything at our disposal. There you will be quarantined for 3 hours to make damn sure you do not have any signs of infection.

Unless you have good reason to be out after 10 p.m., there will also be a curfew from 10 a.m. to 6 p.m. If you are caught out between 10 p.m. and 6 a.m., it best be for employment reasons or you are on your way to the hospital. Not much else will be tolerated.

Finally, I do not want to involve the military and impose martial law. I think we are all scared enough, and tensions are high, but make no mistake, This is no longer a suggestion. This is a demand, an executive order, and it will be enforced for the sake of our country and the world. Do not test me on this, FUCK AROUND AND FIND OUT how quickly I deploy the full might of the United States Military in every corner of our country if I have to treat you like children and send you to your rooms for behaving badly. The time for being selfish is over; the time to think of your friends, neighbors, and all the citizens of our planet is now.

Thank you for doing your part and with any luck this will all be over soon.

God bless you, and God Bless America.

The camera faded to black

It would not be long before the President's new measures would be tested. The 'Don't Tread on Me" crowd was the first to "Fuck Around and Find Out," as the President so eloquently put it. Really, that was a surprise to no one because nothing says all I care about is me than a flag that wants to protect THAT person's right without concern for anyone else.

Within an hour of the speech, towns and cities across the country had their first arrests. What the President had hoped would be a serious threat was more of a "Don't make me turn this car around" statement kids would hear from dad while they were beating the snot out of one another in the back seat.

As reports started coming across the President's desk, he put his head in his hands, realizing he may have made matters worse. For the first time in his first term in office, President Arlington didn't want to be President of the United States.

CHAPTER 40
WICHITA

The Blackhawk helicopter carrying Candace, Javon, and the Colonel touched down close to midnight. Up until this point, they had gotten very little sleep.
The ride was bumpy and loud, certainly not the abandoned hotel they left back in Athens, Georgia.

Candace's mind drifted for a brief moment to that night, she looked at Javon and smiled.

"What?' he asked

"It's nice to be home, that's all. I would show you around town, given different circumstances, but I'm not sure that's an option."

"Rain check it is," he said in a way that said, 'Wild horses couldn't keep him away'.

"Okay, you two, jump in this jeep; it will take you to quarters to get freshened up and a bite to eat; you even have time for a few moments of sleep if you're able. Set your alarms; we leave at 0500 sharp, which means I need you right back here at 0445, clear?" The Colonel was in mission mode and not in a mood to joke around.
Something told them both he had slept less than they had in the last 48 hours, and his tolerance for sarcasm bailed out of the Blackhawk somewhere over Louisiana.

"Yes sir, Colonel," Javon answered for both of them in quick, military fashion. "0445 hours, sir!"

They climbed into the jeep, which sped away on the wide-open tarmac toward a series of hangers and buildings. Two minutes later, they were walking through doors, escorted to separate quarters, and given instructions on where they could find everything from showers to food and a change of clothes.

Candace couldn't wait to peel herself out of what she was wearing. The situation under the Tupelo underpass was less than ideal to not keeping your cool and not sweating no matter how much those television commercials told her that her specially formulated, just-for-women deodorant could handle it. "Lies," she thought, "All lies."

The steam from the shower enclosed Javon in a foggy blind. He knew he was alone, but he still didn't want anyone to see him. Over the last couple of months, he had been what Candace and Spencer needed with complete disregard for his own physical and emotional needs. Now, in this shower, he was being selfish, letting his guard down.

He began to shake, and his knees buckled; he slid down the wall of the shower and just sat while the water washed away that hardened layer of toughness, revealing the scared, vulnerable, unsure, less confident skin he wore underneath. That version of Javon was trembling from the idea of how close he had come to dying. That version of Javon spent a lot of time on the "what ifs".

"What if the cavalry arrived at that underpass just a couple of seconds later?" Javon reflected in his mind. He shook it quickly out of his head. That vulnerable layer had seen enough daylight; time to stow it. Time to stop worrying about the what-ifs, the things that didn't happen and haven't happened. The things out of his control. The armor Javon had been wearing the last couple months was back on.

Javon dried off, went back to his room, and sacked out for a couple of hours. Time was short, sleep was a precious commodity, and Javon didn't waste a moment of either.

At 0400, his alarm went off. Down the hall, he could hear the alarm in Candace's room. Ten minutes later, they met in the cafeteria for a couple of breakfast MREs, some really strong coffee, and the last couple of minutes of quiet before they were swallowed whole by the monster that was GLU.

Sipping on her coffee, Candace looked around. She noticed a sign above the door that led outside.

"No One Kicks Ass Without Tanker Gas." This was the proud motto of the 22nd Air Refueling Wing at McConnel AFB in Wichita, KS. That gas was delivered in flight by the mighty KC-46 Pegasus. This was the plane that would breathe life back into the Air Force, and its less than youthful tanker fleet.

The KC-46 was, first and foremost, a flying gas station, able to refuel most receiver-capable aircraft. However, it can also be trimmed out to accommodate a mix of passengers and cargo in a variety of configurations. The United States Air Force, Navy, and Marine Corps, along with partner nations, were lucky to have such a plane at their disposal.

That same KC-46 was going to get her and Javon to Australia. It felt very 'Custer's last stand'. Candace knew this would be their best and possibly last chance to turn the tide on this virus before humanity faced the real threat of extinction.

Moments later, they were right where the Colonel needed them to be.

"0440!" The Colonel said with a tone of surprise. Maybe he figured that Candace being a civilian and a woman, she might struggle with the more rigid expectations of the military.

"If you're not early, you're late." She said with an ounce of pride. "It's something my dad always told me. Plus, as you were running down instructions earlier, in my head, I went to the days of my residency. In my head, I finished your words with 'STAT'.

"What does that even mean?" Javon jumped in.

"No one really wants to agree on that, I've always believed it to mean, 'Sooner Than Already There'.

Javon had this look of surprise on his face that said, "I was today years old when I learned what STAT meant." Whether Candace's definition was true or not, to Javon it was rock solid.

"Alright, the crew transferred everything from the Blackhawk shortly after we landed. Get yourself on board and secure your duffels. Wheels up in 10 minutes." The Colonel stepped away to talk to a couple of airmen. Javon couldn't read lips, but the expressions on the faces filled him with an uneasiness.

"I love that show," Candace's randomness left Javon a little perplexed.

"I'm sorry," he said with a curious tone

"Criminal Minds! The Colonel said 'Wheels Up', that's what they always used to say on the show before flying of somewhere to go look for the unsub. I must have watched every season at least a dozen times. Mostly, I kept it on in the background when I cleaned house."

"Got it," Javon confessed. "You know, you are incredibly hard to keep up with sometimes."

"That sounds like a 'YOU' problem, not a 'ME' problem." She smiled.

Strong, beautiful, confident, quirky – Candace had a lot of layers. Javon knew he was in trouble. He smiled back as they entered the plane.

CHAPTER 41
THE MAGNIFICENT 7

Founded in 1779, Harrisonburg, Virginia, is now a big little town
nestled in the Shenandoah Valley. It is home to James Madison
University, Farmland, and all the modern-day conveniences anyone
wanting small-town living without the small-town feel could want.
Situated about two hours southwest of Washington, D.C., and two
hours northwest of Richmond, 'big city' luxuries like major airports
and amusement parks are a short drive away.

Being south of the Mason-Dixon line also gave the city a typical
'southern' persona. Sweet tea, conservative, pockets of racism bigger
than other parts of the country, and not a lot of trust in the federal
government.

So, it only stood to reason that when President Arlington delivered
his State of the Union, a town like Harrisonburg would be one of
those first reports that came across the President's desk.

From the college kids breaking the curfew, because classes were
canceled to the lack of cooperation in wearing the n95 masks, the
local police started handing out citations and arresting people. As
promised, the newly renovated football stadium on the campus of
JMU became the detention center for the uncooperative. It did not
take long for the police to realize how undermanned they were and
how fragile the situation was. If they couldn't manage a small city of
around 51,000 people, what hope did larger populations have?

It only took hours for Harrisonburg to fall to civil unrest. Cars were
being set on fire and buildings were being looted like back in the
good ole days when the closest professional sports team won a
national championship. Not in this case.

People were mad, and with their "it won't happen to me" mentality,
they thought the President's measures were more than a little
excessive.

As soon as the first few arrests were made and curfews were broken, support was on its way from the Stanton-based 116th Infantry Brigade Combat Team south of Harrisonburg. The martial law the President had threatened was not an empty threat.

It was just after midnight when the convoy of trucks rolled in. Followed by Humvees mounted with intimidating-looking weaponry and a couple of gunships landing in empty parking lots. From the trucks spilled dozens of soldiers, in full gear, fully armed, fully capable, and ready to implement the orders of their Commander in Chief. Harrisonburg had 'fucked around', and they were about to find out.

Some of the trucks spilled barricades, barbed wire, tents, and every other iteration of temporary structure and housing. With great military proficiency, in a matter of a couple of hours, Harrisonburg, Virginia, was on lockdown. A perimeter was set up a mile outside the city in every direction.

If you were traveling on I-81 northbound or southbound, you were met at checkpoints and grilled about your reason for being on the road. East heading toward Elkton and west toward the West Virginia state line, on route 33, the same thing. At this point, you had to have a very good reason to be anywhere near Harrisonburg. Most everyone, didn't have that reason. In a city full of college kids, expecting life to stop at 10pm was more than a little unrealistic.

Harrisonburg was just one of many growing examples of towns and cities not complying as President Arlington had hoped. Fort Wayne, however, will go down in history as the first to push things a little too far.

The Indiana National Guard from Warsaw, Indiana, had been deployed to the city. With a population of over 260,000, Fort Wayne had indigenous people roots that went back 10,000 years, had ties to the French, and was now another example of a 'typical' midwestern town filled with the hardworking middle class. A middle class that was not going to go quietly in accepting these new rules and regulations from the President.

It was 10:20 p.m., and a group of seven twenty-somethings were walking down Main Street after a night of pounding a case of PBR in the parking lot of a closed 7-11. They had migrated across the street to the Courthouse Green to smoke, laugh, and share their mutual discourse with the President.

There were two problems with this scenario. First and most obviously, it was past curfew, and two, with Indiana's concealed carry laws, some within this group were carrying. After all, as the world was ending, it seemed the appropriate response.

A truck with three soldiers from the Indiana National Guard pulled up first alongside and then in front of the group to impede their progress. The two in the cab got out, along with their easily visible sidearms. The third remained in the truck bed, standing, shouldering an AR-15.

"STOP!" One of the soldiers demanded in a way that made no mistake who he was addressing.

"We're on our way home now, so we'll just be on our way," Stuart Randolph said authoritatively, thanks to the liquid courage still on board.

Stuart had always been that guy in high school. Popular because he pushed limits and railed against authority, feeling like the soldier was not addressing him came naturally.

"I won't ask again," the soldier announced with agitation in his voice as the one standing in the truck bed moved her AR-15 into a more ready position.

"Oh, I bet you will because we're just gonna keep on heading home like I said.

Unsnapping their holsters both soldiers outside the truck drew their pistols, pointed them at the group and added some clarity to the situation.

"You WILL stop and tell me why you are out after the curfew put in place by the President."

"We just lost track of time, we're sorry for the trouble, just let us get home and we'll be more careful." Stuart's tone had clearly softened and become more reasonable. Sadly, Russell Krantz was part of this 'magnificent 7' and that was going to be a problem.

Russell, a mix of outcast and abusive home, was not a fan of being told what to do by anyone, and he drew the Glock 43 he had tucked in his waistband.

"He said we were just on our way home," defending his friend but setting fire to the situation at the same time. Both soldiers trained their pistols on Russell as they clicked off the safeties. The AR-15 in the truck bed was also trained on Russell.

The yelling was deafening. "DROP YOUR WEAPON, NOW!" This was not a suggestion. Sadly, Russell did not comply. Stuart and the other 5 were also yelling at Russell, "WOAH, WOAH, WOAH...Russell, seriously, dude, it's good; just put down the gun, and we'll see if we can fix all this."

Russell had already tuned out his friends; his focus was on the three barrels pointed at him.

The soldier in the truck bed reached for the radio on her belt, a move that proved costly. Catching just that hint of movement, Russell reacted, firing four rounds at the soldier. As she fell in a heap, the other two opened fire on Russell.

At the same time, two other members of the 'magnificent 7', in a panic, pulled their weapons, and in less than 30 seconds, it was over. The two, better-trained members of the National Guard fired with precision and without prejudice, one taking a bullet to the shoulder but not before the 'magnificent 7' fell.

The 48 hours that followed in Fort Wayne were fraught with civil unrest, so many arrests, and a greater level of compliance from almost everyone else.

News traveled fast, even with the limited resources that GLU had left the world with. Those protest in Fort Wayne soon multiplied like barn mice, cropping up all over the country. Protests led to pockets of resistance; resistance led to more violence and destruction of public and private property, and more death that was NOT a result of GLU.

Candace's parents and Khal had just arrived in Warsaw right before the National Guard arrived, right before the 'Magnificent 7' fell. Another day or two in Fort Wayne, hitting Walmart and Costco for supplies would have proved disastrous.

The curtain had been lifted on life's theater, and it was as if the movie "RED DAWN" (the original, not the remake) was playing out before the country's eyes. Patrick Swayze, Charlie Sheen, and C. Thomas Howell were yelling "Wolverines", but instead of U.S. citizens fighting the invading force from Russia, the invading force was their own government. Things were going from bad to much worse. GLU was spreading, GLU was winning, and all thanks to help from the exact humans who were trying to survive it. Time was running out.

CHAPTER 42
REFUEL AND EMERGENCY LANDING

About 4 hours southeast of the Hawaiian Islands, the KC-46 Pegasus carrying humanity's Hail Mary needed to be refueled. It would be another KC-46 that would do the honors.

With about 6 hours left in the flight, the call sign "Quik Trip" pulled into formation above "Hail Mary", and the telescopic boom began to inch downward and backward. With great accuracy, it approached the valve, ready to unload fuel. The upside is that "Hail Mary" didn't need a full complement of fuel. One, because distance didn't require it, and two, because what Javon and Candance weren't being told is the Streaky Bay Airport runway is about 5,500 feet long. The problem is a KC-46 needed at a bare minimum of 8,000 feet. The math was easy, there was not a scenario that presented itself that wasn't going to involve some form a crash landing.

Candace had seen the KC-46 circle in the sky of Wichita a hundred times a day but had never had a bird's eye view of the refueling process till now. The boom retracted, and "Quik Trip" pulled away. "That was fast. I didn't expect it to be that fast." Javon heard this in his headset and immediately sought out the colonel. He had enough experience to know that when his 'spider senses' tingled like that, to trust them.

"What aren't you telling us?" he asked, almost demanding.

"I was going to wait until about an hour out from the airport to say anything. No need to put the two of you under any extra stress." The colonel explained.

"I think that ship has sailed," Javon stated.

"I suppose you're right," the colonel continued. "Streaky Bay Airport is small. The runway is about 5,500 feet long."

Javon cut him off, "Let me guess, we need a little more than that to land."

"A lot more," the colonel didn't even try to lie about it.

"How short are we?"

"About 2,500 feet."

"BALLS!" Javon's one word statement said it all. There was no scenario where even the most experienced pilot keeps that on the runway.

"Do me a favor," Javon asked, "Let me tell Candace.

"I was hoping you'd say that." The colonel managed a smile, placed his hand on Javon's shoulder, and walked off toward the cockpit.

The colonel and Candace essentially switched places as she left the cockpit after watching the refueling. Walking toward Javon, she could see the look on his face and could tell something was on his mind.

"You in there?" she asked

"Yeah, sorry. I was just thinking about something the colonel just shared with me," he admitted, and he continued without hesitation.

"I have to tell you something." Candace started getting a sickening feeling in her stomach. "We are going to have to crash land the plane."

"WHAT!!" Candace was not one to panic but she had also never been in a plane crash before. "Why? Are the engines failing? I mean, we just took on fuel, I haven't …"

"Candace," Javon cut her off. "The place we're flying to, Streaky Bay, the runway is way too short for us to safely land. The pilot is incredibly good at what he does and he's going to use all of his training to put us down as safely as possible with the best chance to walk away. That being said, it's going to bumpy, it's going to be loud and it's going to be dangerous."

Candace sat stunned for a few seconds, processing what he had just told her. "We will walk away from this, right?" The flicker of fear danced across her eyes as she asked that question. All Javon could say was, "We SHOULD walk away. It will be chaotic, there will more than likely be smoke and dust, and you'll need to be sharp. Can you do that? Can you be the most hyper-focused you've ever been?"

"I can, I mean I will, I just need some time to get in the right headspace," she responded

"You have five hours." Candace had now spent enough time with Javon to understand that when he was that blunt, he was serious, and there was no room for humor, not even a little.

They say, "Time flies when you're having fun." This was not fun at all, yet five hours went by in a flash. "Time to buckle in," the pilot announced to everyone aboard the KC-46. A symphony of clicks and zips filled the cabin as everyone prepared themselves. Hearts were racing, just some faster than others. Sitting next to Javon, he grabbed her hand. She managed a sheepish smile—the best one she could manage considering the circumstances.

"Streaky Bay Airport, this is Hail Mary requesting permission to land." 5 hours were up, and the pilot had gone over the scenario a hundred times in his head, trying to plan for every eventuality he could think of.
The pilot had apprised the airport tower of the situation at the same time. That gave them time to call in all the necessary personnel and prepare the emergency equipment, hoping for the best but planning for the worst.

The tower answered back, "Hail Mary—tower, you are clear to land on runway 2-6. All other air traffic in the area has been diverted to Ceduna. Our airport is all yours."

"Roger tower, Hail Mary starting approach." The pilot took a breath, he'd only get one shot at this. "Altitude 5000 feet, beginning fuel dump." With the flick of a switch, fuel left the plane making it appear for a moment as the world's largest crop duster. The less fuel onboard at the time of the crash, the better.

At the end of runway 2-6 was a tundra of dirt and gravel and brush that stretched beyond the tarmac about 1000 feet right up to the border of Finders Highway.

On the other side of the road there were trees, lots of trees. There was no question the KC-46 was going in the trees, the pilot just had to try and do it as gently as possible.

"Hail Mary - Tower. Crews on site to perform containment and remediation of fuel, emergency vehicles standing by at landing site." The tower was referring to the dozen or so fire trucks, ambulances, and other emergency vehicles flanking both sides of the dusty tundra, just prior to Finders Highway.

"Tower – Hail Mary, 1500 feet," the pilot informed as the landing gear was coming down and locking into position.

"Roger Hail Mary, the tower will stay out of your ears and let you concentrate. God speed Hail Mary, tower out," and with that, the radio silence preyed on every last bit of nervousness and anxiety the pilot had left. It was time for the pilot to compartmentalize everything, and his singular mission now was to get this plane to a stop and ensure all souls in his care walked away.

"PULL UP! PULL UP!" The plane alerted the pilot in a tone that was cold and robotic yet still seemed to have some concern about his approach. The pilot had a plan and knew the plane would protest. His goal was to not touch down like a typical landing. Instead, he was coming in low, very low, and just as the tarmac of the runway was underneath the plane, he would apply full flaps and aggressively decelerate, cutting power to all the engines. The theory was the plane would then 'stall' and drop like a sack of potatoes downward. In order for this to work, he couldn't be too high off the ground because the stress of that drop would be too much for the plane to bear.

"PULL UP! PULL UP!" The altitude was 500 feet, and the runway still seemed impossibly far away. 400 feet, 300 feet. The KC-46 Pegasus approach could be likened to that of American Airlines flight 77 that slammed into the Pentagon on September 11th. Unlike that ill-fated flight that slammed nose first into and through several fortified walls of one of the most secure buildings on the planet, "Hail Mary" was going to hit the ground below harder than any plane should. 200 feet. 100 feet. The plane was now the height of a rooftop off the ground, and thankfully, there were no houses to be found. Just a little lower, a little further. There, the runway just passed under the cockpit, the pilot slammed any lever down that was sending power to the engines, and the plane dropped.

Candace's stomach reacted to the drop, and she was instantly thrust into a teenage memory. Summers in Indiana on Goose Lake and nights out with friends riding around, making the occasional bad choice or two. There was this stretch of State Road 14 near South Whitley with a hill the kids (and some adults) called "Thrill Hill." It was one of those hills that had such a steep drop on the other side that if you were going fast enough, every once in a while, you could feel the tires leave the ground. Most times that dramatic drop on the other side simply just tickled your insides with a sensation you could only get on that stretch of road or a roller coaster. Candace thought, "Who knew?" You could also experience "Thrill Hill" in the middle of a plane crash. If Candace lived through all of this, and her best from those days in Indiana was still alive, she would tell her all about it.

That sensation lasted for only a brief moment, followed by a teeth-rattling thud. The behemoth flying machine protested to the non-conventional landing, creaking and groaning like an old Spanish galleon. For a moment, she swore the plane was going to come apart.

As soon as the plane hit the ground, the pilot was on the brakes hard. The plane didn't like that either. Normally, the pilot would be concerned about the brakes getting too hot and catching fire. That was the least of his concerns.

He was on the brakes hard, like he hated them. The growling sound they made in return revealed the feeling was mutual. Imagine a dog on a chain that's been on that chain for a cruel amount of time, and its owner comes out for the first time in a week to throw a scrap of food in its direction. The dog growls as if to say, "There is a special place in Hell for people like you."
The brakes were making that kind of noise. The smoke, the sparks, and a river of asphalt and tundra and trees rushed toward him as if the levee broke and no wall of sandbags was going to slow it down.

Candace's eyes slammed shut when the plane slammed down, and she decided she wasn't going to open them until this was all over. Sadly, her body betrayed her with its feedback of what was happening, painting a vivid image in her mind's eye that she didn't like.

3000, 2500, and 2000 feet, the runway was vanishing, and the brakes were now on fire. "C'mon, C'MON," the pilot screamed, willing the plane to slow down and come to a stop. 1000 feet, 500 feet. "Damn it," he resigned under his breath then pushed the button to the intercom. "BRACE! BRACE! BRACE!"

When the KC-46 left the runway and was introduced to the dirt, the gravel, and the brush, the pilot was still applying the brakes, but at this point, the only thing that was going to stop the plane were the trees that were getting bigger by the second. With little purchase left for the tires, the plane began to drift sideways. Everyone on board could feel it, a sickening misdirection that clearly wasn't normal. Just as the plane went across Finders Highway, it was parallel to the tree line, certainly not a best-case scenario.

Most of the trees were no real threat to the plane. Most! However, the one that stood the tallest was up to the challenge to wreak as much havoc as possible. The plane fuselage and that tree met right where Colonel Eugene Brighton was sitting. The skin and the skeleton buckled; the colonel's buckles failed as the plane was coming apart at that point of impact. Everything after that happened so quickly. An amalgamation of metal, earth, and hydraulic fluids and the colonel spun around those still strapped in. Like a tornado, the debris completely missed some; others weren't so lucky.

Slowing, but still sliding the wing planted in the ground like a vaulting pole. Javon could feel the plane start to lift, and he knew if it began to barrel roll, the chances of walking away would decrease dramatically. Candace squeezed his hand so tight he thought she would break it.
Just when it felt like the plane would tumble over, it collapsed back down in a heap, the slide slowed, and then it was over. The only thing moving was the smoke and dust in the air that had been trailing behind the plane as it crashed and was now washing over the scene of twisted metal and trees.

Javon was aware of two things. He could hear the sirens of in the distance. Help was on the way. That was good. He could also smell smoke, lots of it. It was burning his nostrils, and he started to cough. He opened his eyes to see pockets of fire breaking out.

He looked over at Candace, who was visibly shaken and disoriented. "You good? Hey, hey, look at me. Are you good? We need to move; I need to know how bad you're hurt."

"I'm okay," she said as she reached for her buckle.

"Get off the plane and to a safe distance. I just need to check on the rest of the crew. I'll be right behind you."

As much as she wanted to argue and say, "You know I'm a doctor, right?" She also knew this was not the time or place to have a pissing contest. Javon pointed her toward a safe opening, and she crawled out. He then turned toward the direction of the cockpit, nothing but daylight. Spinning 180 degrees, he saw the rest of the crew in the section that had torn away had already freed themselves and were getting as far away from the plane as they could. Some on their own two feet, others being carried. From what Javon could tell, injuries, not casualties.

Colonel Brighton? Javon looked around for the colonel. Looked to where he should have been. He wasn't there. Nothing was there except the negative space of what was once part of the plane. Javon was smart enough to know that no one could have survived that. Javon was the last off the plane

A cacophony of sirens whirred in his ears as first responders arrived. Fire trucks were attacking the small fires scattered in and around the plane. Paramedics began the process of treating the wounded. Javon and Candace were both cut up pretty badly. Most wounds just needed to be cleaned and dressed. A couple required a few stitches, but the important thing was, they were alive.

Looking at Javon, Candace asked, "Colonel?" Javon shook his head. They didn't speak of it again.

"You two okay?" an unfamiliar voice yelled behind them. They spun around to see a soldier approaching, behind him, a jeep. "I have my orders to get you to Streaky Bay Hospital, can you move?"

"We're good," Javon assured him. They both slowly got up and made their way toward the vehicle. There would be time to process the horror of what just happened later. Right now, they had to put it in a box, dig a hole, and bury it in the ground. A grim time capsule that would be opened later. For now, they had a job to do, and they had a virus to kill.

CHAPTER 43

THE HOSPITAL

Javon and Candace arrived at Streaky Bay Hospital an hour removed from their near-death experience. As they pulled up, they were shocked to see an ocean of media mixed with the military outside the hospital. Sure, everyone was wearing their N95 masks and trying to keep as much distance as possible from one another (and failing miserably at that); Candance couldn't help but wonder how many had fallen ill while either trying to report on GLU or provide security to the hospital.

The vehicle pulled through the crowd and up to the emergency room. The soldier, armed and intent on delivering 'the packages,' had no issue with ordering people to "Get out of the way" in a very loud and authoritative voice. For those who did not listen the first time, they were given the gift of profanities for emphasis.

Moments later, they were on the "GLU" floor of the hospital. A nurse gave Javon further attention to redress his wounds and get him cleaned up. Candace was greeted by Kami Rollins, who ushered her toward the lab. Shown where to dress in the necessary biohazard PPE, a short time later, Candace was inside and introduced to Vikram Chatterjee.

The two got acquainted very quickly, sharing a brief summary of their course of study and field of expertise. What seemed like a nerdy, biomedical first date was simply a way to let the other know their strengths and shortcomings so they could put all their pride and ego aside and focus on saving the world.

Vikram ran down a progress report similar to what Kami had received days ago. He explained that Dylan's blood, which once had a full-blown GLU infection, is now healthy and GLU-free. He shared with Candace how the water samples from the scene of the attack showed normal levels of salinity, no out-of-the-ordinary microscopic organisms, and a temperature that was normal for that time of year.

"Before you arrived, I had run a series of tests yesterday and you are just in time for the results," Vikram announced. '

"What sort of tests?" Candace asked

"After all those other tests, my next course of action was to test Dylan's blood against the blood of another infected patient. This would at least let us know if Dylan's blood could be used to cure other patients." Dr. Vikram continued, "If it does, I know it's unrealistic to think we could mass-produce Dylan's blood to save the planet, but it will put us a step closer. I waited 36 hours after the start of the experiment, which was about the length of time from when Dylan was attacked to when it was officially confirmed he was GLU-free."

Candace could see Vikram was on a roll and was in no way going to stop the momentum. She nodded, stood back a little, and watched as Vikram retrieved the samples from a small rack of test tubes. Walking over to a table with a microscope, a sample of blood was dropped on the slide. Kami, Candace, and Vikram held their collective breath, hoping for progress.

"I just don't understand," Vikram said exacerbated. "What am I missing?"

For the next several hours, Vikram and Candace read and re-read notes, lab reports, and lab results. From what Candace could tell, he had done everything by the book. With a level of security surrounding what Vikram and Candace, they didn't have the luxury of consulting with their peers. The fewer people that knew about what was going on in Streaky Bay, the better. All they needed was the distraction of having to answer a lot of questions about what they were working on. For now, the world would have to focus on surviving and just believe someone was working on finding a cure.

What the two research doctors did have, at least for now, was the internet and AI like ChatGPT. They would put in a variety of prompts, and AI would point out what they were doing wrong as opposed to proving they were getting closer to an answer.

In between the 3rd and 4th cup of coffee, Candace had a thought. "I have a silly thought, but did you test the shark?" Candace asked, trying not to sound like that should have been an obvious step.

"What," Vikram either didn't quite hear her or realized how he had missed what was right in front of him. "At this time, I have not."

"Why not?" was Candace's next question, while it sounded accusatory, Dr. Vikram knew there was no room to be 'butt-hurt'. So, he answered honestly.

"It never dawned on me to test the shark." Dr. Vikram's embarrassment was enough, and Candace didn't need to pile on. Instead, she enthusiastically fostered the idea to get Dr. Vikram excited about it.

"There is so much we don't know about the Great White Shark, even today. We're talking about an animal that is 70 million years old with an ancestry of predecessors that can be tracked back between 200 and 500 million years. Yet, in all this time it is rather shocking how little we still know. In fact, recently, scientists have recently discovered special cells called melanocytes in great white sharks' skin that appear to allow the predator's coloration to lighten or darken. It's thought this ability may lend even more control over their cloaking ability as they sneak up on prey from below.

"I thought you were a cancer doctor?" Kami questioned.

"I am. I've always been a scientist at heart, and when I find time and things interesting, I study them. From the very first shark week on the Discovery Channel, I was fascinated by sharks and how ancient and unknown they were. So, I read a few books, attended a couple of TED Talks, and now I know enough to be dangerous."
"I need to get out more," Kami admitted with a bit of embarrassment. Candace's enthusiasm and lust for learning made her feel a bit like a slacker.

"So, who do we get to go on this fishing trip for us?" Dr. Vikram asked bluntly. "I get sea sick, so I'm not your guy."

"I know just the guy," Candace smiled, "He's right down the hall." With that, she stripped out of her PPE and ran to where Javon was.

"Do you like to fish?" She asked with excitement.

"Not really. Never went much as a kid." Javon said. "Plus, I'm an okay swimmer in a pool but not a real fan of being in the ocean; that's a whole different animal."

"Well, it's time to cowboy up, I need a favor," Candace said.

Instantly, Javon knew he wasn't going to like what Candace was scheming.

"I need you to catch me a Great White Shark." The request rolled so easily off her tongue, like it was something Javon gets asked all the time.

"A WHAT!!!" To say Javon was a little surprised would have been an understatement.

"Listen, before you say no, it's the only thing that hasn't been tested in the research so far. There has to be something about the shark that contributed to this surfer Dylan shaking GLU out of his system."

"Can't you find anyone else to do it? I mean, it's Australia, for Christ's sake; these people live for this kind of stuff." Javon's protests were not landing on receptive ears.

"There's no time to audition people for the part, I need you to be the guy." Candace pleaded. "It doesn't have to be a huge shark, just a great white from the area where Dylan was attacked."

Javon was warming up to the idea until…

"Oh, and I need it alive," Candace said in a way, someone would order a venti iced brown sugar shaken espresso from Starbucks.

"Anything else? Should I dress it like Woody from 'Toy Story' and give it a name while I'm at it?"

Candace had a blank look on her face. At this point, Javon's sarcasm was meant more as a coping mechanism for his own fear rather than a frustrated attack on Candace. He knew there was no getting out of this.

"Okay, when do I leave?" Candace squealed with joy and gave him a peck on the cheek. "Thanks, Captain Ahab." She smirked.

"No! That is NOT going to be a thing." Javon squashed that nickname before it had time to stick.

"Argghhh matey!" Candace couldn't resist.

"I said no," Javon said, having completely lost his sense of humor.

Candace giggled knowing that if they survived the end of the world, she'd probably pay for her teasing. Somehow, she knew she'd be okay with that.

CHAPTER 44
GONE FISHING

The next morning, Javon was on the "Wakey Wakey," a 36-foot fishing vessel headed for Sceale Bay Conservation Park. It was stocked with top-of-the-line fishing gear and a harness so that once the shark was caught, it could be sedated and secured alongside the boat to be kept alive for the ride home.

Around Speeds Point and past Yanerbie Beach, it was almost time. To get in the mood, Javon was recreating that scene in Jaws where Quint was singing, "Farewell and adieu to you Spanish ladies, farewell and adieu you ladies of Spain. For we have received orders for to sail to England, but we hope in a short time to see you again."

Singing it did little to make Javon feel like Quint, who was a rugged, salty, scared of nothing, took shit from no one, called it how he saw it, straight shooter. Nope, Javon felt more like the naked girl in the opening scene, just blindly swimming to her death. Well, at least if he was going to die, he'd die with his pants on.

One of the crew started to string the largest fishing pole Javon had ever seen. This was no closed reel, Zebco with 4-pound test monofilament. The reel was the size of a 48-ounce can of stewed tomatoes; the rod looked like someone had just pulled a 20-foot maple sapling out of the ground at the landscaping place before getting on the boat.

"Where you gonna put a tree that big?" he asked the guy diligently going about his work. All he got was a blank look back with a one-word question, "Tree?"

Clearly, "National Lampoon's Christmas Vacation" isn't nearly the national holiday treasure in Australia as it is in the States.

"Never mind," he said a little defeated, "but really, do we need a fishing pole that big?"

"Ever gone fishing for a Great White before bro?" the crewman asked.

"First time. Bass, bluegills and catfish all day long." Javon answered boastfully. Then he saw the hook attached to a length of steel wire. The hook was massive, like the ones farmers use to pick up hay bales.

"Candyman, Candyman, Candyman," he said at the sight of it. Another movie reference completely wasted his new fishing buddy.

"Did you steal that hook from a crane before we left the mainland?"

"Nah, have to have a big hook to catch a big fish. Did you know that the Great White will bite with a force of 4,000 pounds per square inch. That's 25 times greater than you and me." The crewman continued, "Plus, I needed a big enough hook to put a raw turkey on." Said in a way that it just seemed normal to fish with the centerpiece to any Thanksgiving meal.

"We're going to drift with this line out and the turkey on the hook while we send the chum into the current at just the right depth so when it reaches the turkey, it will be too much for the shark to resist." Javon hung on every word at this point. It was time to stop messing around and quoting movies and time to put his game face on.

"When we hook up, and we will hook up, I want you to calmly get in the fighting chair, buckle up, and nod when you're ready. Do that, and I will set the pole in the holder, make sure it's secure, and then you do everything I tell you. Reel when I say reel, lift when I say lift, let it run when I say let it run, you get me."

Javon nodded, and now they wait.

About an hour had gone by, and the sun was climbing toward the midday sky. It was late fall in the southern hemisphere, and even a partly cloudy day welcomed as much sun as possible to take the chill out of the air.

"CLICK," the noise from the reel made everyone stop talking and, it seemed, even breathing. Was it just the motion of the boat in the swells?

"CLICK, CLICK, CLICK".

"Is it supposed to do that?" Javon asked, "I would have thought it would be more agress……"

When Javon was a little boy, about 7, he was hanging with a friend out behind his house. His friend Trey had this little 50cc Honda dirt bike. Javon had never ridden anything like that before and didn't really want to. If not for the teasing of Trey, he wouldn't have. Javon climbed on, got some brief "how to ride a dirt bike" basics, which he forgot immediately, and twisted the throttle. That little dirt bike shot off like a rocket. Javon had forgotten about the noise it made in that moment until now.

The reel and line exploded, with that exact noise from his childhood, as the 485lb test wire braided cable, the 600lb Roscoe swivel, the rest of the line, and turkey rocketed in the opposite direction from the stern of the boat. Initially, Javon was mesmerized by it all. He quickly snapped out of it, remembering his instructions.

He sat in the chair, buckled in, took a deep breath, and nodded. The pole was placed in the holder between his legs, which was securely bolted to the boat's deck.

"When I say click that lever and pull back like you were trying to stop a plane from crashing, you do it."

"Of all the analogies he could have used, that's the one he landed on?" Javon thought.

"One, two, three, NOW!"

Javon pulled back as hard as he could, and the resistance he was met with surprised him. It felt like he had a school bus on the other end.

"Good, the hook is set, let him run for about 30 seconds than the real work begins." The crewman warned.

It was quite possibly the longest 30 seconds of his life till then next command came in.

"Lift up and reel down, lift up and reel down. When you reel down, don't put any slack in the line. Do that till I tell you to stop."

Javon considered himself to be in pretty good shape, but after about five minutes of 'lift up and reel down,' he was humbled by the shark's sheer power.

"Stop reeling," that command came as he heard the boat engine go into gear. The boat started to back up, the stern slapping against the waves, shooting a fountain of sea water into the air and over the stern onto the deck. The late fall water was cold and penetrating, but Javon was already sweaty and welcomed the sensation.

"Reel, as fast as you can to keep up with the boat backing down, we need to make up some ground on the shark." The authoritative instructions were never questioned. Javon could tell this guy has caught a lot of sharks.

"C'mon you bludger, don't let it get the best of you," the crewman yelled about 20 minutes into the battle.

"Wait, what did you just call me? This isn't Quidditch."

"Never mind, mate, focus on what you're doing."

The boat kicked out of gear, and break time was over.

"LIFT, REEL, LIFT, REEL," two words being shouted over the sound of boat and surf that Javon was certain he would hear in his sleep for the foreseeable future.

45 minutes in and now it was just a battle of will. The Great White was the perfect killing machine, a swimming Abrams tank made of muscle and teeth. Javon, if nothing else, was determined and also focused on Candace as he cursed her under his breath for putting him in this situation in the first place.

"You're going to be good and buggered when this is all said and done, mate. You land this beauty and drinks on me back at shore." The crewman said with a smile that suggested he might be enjoying watching Javon struggle just a little much.

"Free beer, well why didn't you say so," Javon quipped. With that, he seemed to find another gear.

"You're doing great," the crewman said as Javon was praying for a break from the 'lift – reel – lift – reel'.

And then the first sign that his prey was close at hand: Everyone on the boat got their first look at the shark. It shot out of the water like an ICBM just left the tubes of a nuclear attack sub. Twenty yards off the stern, it was massive and for a brief moment while in the air, it eclipsed the sun.

"Sick," Javon's fishing buddy yelled, "She's gotta be 18 feet.

"We're going to need a bigger boat." Nope, Javon didn't stick the landing on that reference either.

"C'mon, NOTHING?" He said in shock. "You really need to watch the movie "Jaws" when you have time.

The shark was a monster with a mouthful of teeth, and it was not going to go quietly. However, the fact that it was this close to the surface was a good sign, Javon thought. Between that and the promise of free beer, he was ready to see this through.

The battle lasted another 20 minutes, and the shark was close enough to put a tranquilizer dart in it. Loaded with just enough sedative to calm the agitated shark down but not too much so that it put him to sleep, and they ran the risk of killing it.

Javon saw a second crew member pass his chair on the way to the stern, carrying what kind of looked like a .22 rifle. He pointed, pulled the trigger, and a dart shot out and took up squatter's rights on the back of the shark near the dorsal fin.

"Not long now mate, the hard part is over with," the crewman assured Javon. Confident that the shark would start to calm down, they prepped the 'shark hammock', securing it to the side of the boat. Next, a rope around the tail and another around the body of the shark resting just behind the dorsal fin, and the two men were able to pull and guide the shark into place along the side of the boat.

Cheers rang out, Javon was too tired. His arms felt like rubber, and he couldn't lift them in a celebration of victory if he wanted to. Tied to the side of the "Wakey Wakey" was an equally tired shark. Water was flowing through its gills as the weary crew began the slow crawl back to Streaky Bay.

With no aquarium, zoo, or holding tank big enough in Streaky Bay, the plan was to get the shark into the harbor and deliver it to a sectioned-off portion of water. A crudely fashioned but formidable holding tank where the shark would be monitored and kept safely sedated. Candace was at the dock to meet Javon and the shark; she was thrilled at Javon's success.

"My hero!" She said in her best damsel in distress voice.

"Funny," was all the verbal eye-roll Javon could muster.

"When you have your strength back, I'll thank you properly sailor." Candace smiled.

It took all of Javon's energy to smile back.

Candace began snapping pics; her plan was to take as many pictures from every angle as she could. She would take those back to the lab so that she and Dr. Vikram could develop a plan on what to test and harvest from the shark. What would the first few experiments be

CHAPTER 45
ANSWERS

"Let's start with the mouth," Candace suggested. All the pictures were splayed out in front of her and Dr. Chatterjee. "Since Dylan was attacked straight on, maybe it's something in or on the tooth or the gums. Maybe it's something released when the shark loses a tooth or something. A chemical or hormone that tells the shark's brain to tell the shark's mouth to produce more teeth.

Vikram chimed in, "Or maybe it's a stomach enzyme or something in the saliva. Do sharks even have saliva?" Feeling slightly out of his depth, he continued, "I think we need a shark expert.

We are strong in our respective fields, but we can't possibly do this without someone who has a more intimate knowledge of sharks. If we don't, I'm afraid we'll miss something."

"You're right," Candace agreed, "Let's ask around and make some phone calls."

A couple of hours passed when Kora Bandjin's phone buzzed on her nightstand. With travel restrictions what they were, traveling for work and attending research conferences and speaking engagements were non-existent. She spent much of her time locally, on boats, day and night, continuing to study the Great White.

That much time in the water is hard on even the most conditioned diver, so afternoon naps were her friend. Not recognizing the number, she answered anyway.

"Hello," forced its way out breaking the bonds of fatigue that still wanted her eyes to be closed.

"Doctor Bandjin?" the voice asked

Doctor Kora Bandjin received her PhD from Nova Southeastern University in Florida. Known for its multiple departments of study, including biology, marine biology, chemistry, and physics, it was always her first choice to further her education. As a graduate student, she had access to a range of researchers and topics that focused on movement patterns, shark physiology, and more. Lucky for Candace and Dr. Vikram, Kora called Streaky Bay home and had not been out of the country as the world began to shut down.

"Dr. Bandjin, my name is Candace Stanton. I'm here in Streaky Bay, and my colleague and I could really use your help."

"What's this all about then?"

"I am working with Dr. Vikram Chatterjee, the lead research scientist here at Streaky Bay Hospital. I'm a hematological oncologist, and the U.S. military and other global governments have tasked us with figuring out how one patient here in this hospital had GLU one day, and it was gone after a great white shark attacked him." Candace tried to be as thorough as possible.

Kora jumped in, "Right, the surfer, yeah, I heard about him. A nasty bit of business that was. But, I'm still unclear on how I can be of any assistance."

"We have tested everything. Run every possible, hypothetical experiment from the rational to shooting in the dark. We have exhausted all possibilities so that now the 'why' and the 'how' is landing squarely on one thing, it has to be something about the shark.

There was a brief pause, "I see," Kora said, "Even if that's the case, we're going to need time to get a shark…."

"Already have one," Candace interrupted.

"WHAT!!" Kora was clearly caught off guard.

"We have an 18-foot great white in a holding area in Streaky Bay Harbor. It's being closely monitored and safely sedated. I need the shark alive as we run tests." Candace didn't get to finish

"I'm putting my clothes on now. I'll meet you at the harbor in an hour. Don't touch that shark till I get there."

Kora hung up the phone. Over the years, she, like any biologist, had developed a bond, a love with the animals she studied. Their well-being and conservation are paramount to her world, and she didn't need just anyone prodding and poking in places they had no business.

As promised, an hour later, she was on site in the harbor. Walking up to Candace and Dr. Vikram, Kora said, "Hi, you had some questions about sharks?" Kora said with some light energy to break the ice.

Masked up and not shaking hands Candace politely and quickly moved through the introductions and got down to business. "We brought a copy of our research with us," handing Kora a tablet, "to show you how we arrived at the shark being the answer."

Kora handed it back quickly, "I appreciate that, but just as you don't know a lot about sharks, which is the reason I'm here, I don't know enough about human blood diseases and human anatomy. Sure, I took those classes we all had to take, but this is your focus; sharks are mine."

Candace appreciated her straightforward humility, "Excellent, so let's start. Dr. Chatterjee and I were going to focus on the mouth first, speculating there might be something in the gums or saliva that could be the key. Maybe the shark's mouth releases some sort of enzyme that tells the brain it's lost a tooth."

Kora raised a hand slightly to signal she needed to slow Candace down. "Look, you're asking all the right questions; that's how we're going to figure this out. Let me address the first couple of things."

She took a breath and began her mini-TED talk on sharks, "Let me address the teeth first; no, there is not an enzyme that is released or a chemical reaction that takes place when a shark loses a tooth or, in some cases, a row of teeth. The tooth either falls to the ocean floor, gets stuck in what it bites into or it is swallowed, which sucks because then they get nothing from the tooth fairy." She smiled and continued. It's not as much of a mystery as you might think. The shark has rows of teeth already formed and ready to go. When a tooth or teeth fall out, more rotate into place. Think of it as a bullet in the chamber gets fired and the next bullet is moved into the chamber. It can be fast, too. Some sharks can replace a lost tooth in less than 24 hours.

At this point, Candace and Vikram were hanging on Kora's every word, fascinated by the "Everything you wanted to know about sharks but was afraid to ask" lesson they were getting from Kora, who moved on to the next part of the lesson.

"Secondly, a shark doesn't have saliva like you're thinking of when it comes to saliva and salivary glands in some animals, including humans. A shark's mouth is all teeth and tongue, and they will more times than not take large bites and swallow large chunks of food."

"God, it sounds like some of the first dates I've been on." Candace couldn't help but share that trip down memory lane.

"You too?" Kora commiserated, "I'm surprised my date didn't just eat with his hands." The two women laughed.

Vikram being the only man in this trio, felt a little attacked. The ladies stopped poking fun and moved on.

"Anyway," Kora rolled on, "It's all very mechanical so much of the digestion process happens in the shark stomach. Since sharks are always moving, most of the digestion process for energy is efficient, unless they swallow something they are not supposed to eat like a license plate." She saw the look on their faces, "Joking, joking, really that only happens in the movies."

Sharks instead have salivary cells that are dispersed among epithelial cells. The number of mucin-secreting cells varies greatly between the esophageal, gastric, and intestinal sections of the shark's anatomy, as does the flow of mucus, from low concentrations in the mouth to higher amounts in the intestinal region. So, if we are going to start anywhere, I would take a sample of fluid from the shark's stomach and test that. We'll start in the most obvious place and work our way to the mouth if we have to."

Vikram wasn't afraid to ask the obvious questions, "Can we do it without hurting the shark, and if so, how?"

"Easy mate," Kora said with a bounce in her voice. I get in the water, poke the old gal, and extract it. My gear is in the car; I'll be ready to go in 20 minutes."

With that, she was heading back to the parking lot to fetch what she needed to get in the water. Candace and Dr. Chatterjee looked at each other, hopeful that they might finally get some answers.

In no time, Kora was back, pulling on a wetsuit and strapping a tank to her back, and ready to get in the water. Before putting on her mask, she asked, "When was the last time the patient was given some sleepy juice? I would hate for her to wake up and find me sticking a really large needle in her."

"She was given a dose about 2 hours ago," the veterinarian on site answered.

"Let's give her about half a dose more, just to be safe," Kora said. They did, and waited about 10 minutes, and Kora entered the water. Kora never got tired of the feeling of smallness she got when swimming next to such a massive, ancient animal. She took a few beats to drink that feeling in, then got to work. In no time, she was back out of the water, several samples in a mesh bag that she handed to Candace and was starting to get out of her wetsuit.

"You two mind if I tag along. I'd love to be in the lab to help if you needed it." Kora asked

"We were hoping you'd say that, a third set of eyes is always better than two," Candace responded. "Not sure if you need any caffeine along the way, but you may want to pick something up, something tells me it's going to be a long night.

CHAPTER 46
TRIAL AND ERROR

In the 1950's, Dr. Curt Richter of Harvard asked an important question. Can hope be measured? Can it be quantified? Can it be more than just this invisible force that some of us have more of than others? In an effort to answer that question, Dr. Richter used rats as test subjects. In a brutal and, some might argue, cruel experiment,

Dr. Richter placed rats in a pool of water to see how long they could tread water. On average, the rats gave up and sank after 15 minutes. But, right before they were completely exhausted and ready to succumb to the swear release of death, Dr. Richter and his team would rescue the rats.

The rats were saved. They were dried off and allowed to rest for a bit, and then, much to their displeasure, they were put back in the water a second time. Surely, the rats must have believed they were going to be rescued, just like the first time.

The story of this experiment has been told hundreds of times, and each time, the audience was asked how long they thought the rats tread water the second time. All sorts of guesses were given, from 5 minutes to maybe as much as an hour. The result: The rats swam for 60 hours!! 60 HOURS!

The conclusion was simple. The rats believed they were going to be rescued a second time and pushed their bodies well beyond their physical limits as they clung to that belief. It turns out hope actually does float.

With the three doctors back at the lab, mission-critical energy was in the room. All three focused, knew what was at stake, and knew time was not their ally. Beakers, test tubes, microscopes, and centrifuges were all being used. Even the microwave was getting a workout because as soon as one person heated up their coffee, it would set and get cold as they got caught up in the work. Only 30 minutes later, they microwaved it again.

"Okay, I'm going to drink it hot this time, I promise," Vikram said before going on a tangent. "Let's be honest, whoever invented the microwave and the subsequent marketing was a genius. All those promises of it being the appliance of the future. All anyone really uses a microwave for is reheating things, defrosting things and popcorn. Try and think of a single person who has actually prepared a 4-pound roast chicken in a microwave. I'll wait!" Dr. Chatterjee had made his point. Ill-timed or not, it seemed to be a welcome diversion and mental break from the research.

Enzymes, compounds, and cells were all separated into individual test tubes, representing possible solutions in the fight against GLU. They had created six possible cures, and it was time to test each one. Six Petrie dishes with a sample of an infected patient's blood and each one given a sample of the possible cure created in the lab. Just like other tests in the past, they waited, but not as long. The all agreed if cures were going to work, they would have to start showing signs of working within an hour. If GLU couldn't be slowed down in that time, it wasn't going to be.

It was the longest hour the three of them had ever experienced. At the end of it, they looked at one sample after another, each one failing to slow the progression of the virus.

"Back to the drawing board," Vikram said. He thought about giving a peptalk, or words of encouragement, but they were past that. So, he kept it simple and stated the obvious without stating the obvious result of failure.

Frustrated, Candace asked, "So, where to now?" As if the three of them were lost on some road trip in the outback. "The stomach was a bust. Do you think there is something in the esophageal area?"

"We can try it," Kora answered, "but the stomach would have contained everything we need from the mouth down to the stomach. I think you two were right, it has to be something in the mouth, but what? What are we missing?"

Candace spread the thumbnails of the pictures she had taken of the shark across the desktop of her laptop. Opening them one by one and studying them. The teeth were ruled out, the water, the micro-organisms, the digestive cells, and enzymes, it seemed she was running out of parts of the shark to blame it on. She looked at image after image till her eyes blurred, and kept coming back to the close up of the teeth in the upper jawline and the skin around the mouth.

"Dr. Bandjin, what are all these tiny little holes around the mouth of the shark," Candace inquired. "They look similar to pores."

"Ampullae of Lorenzini," Kora quickly responded.

"I think I ordered that at an Italian restaurant once," Candace joked

"Ampullae of Lorenzini are believed to have evolved from the lateral lines of early vertebrates like fish, eventually presenting in sharks, rays, paddlefish, and a multitude of other species. Most bony fish have lost their Ampullae of Lorenzini and seem to have evolved to rely solely on their lateral lines to basically do the same thing.

These little pores are electro receptors, little sensory organs that can detect everything from changes in electrical fields, water temperature, mechanical pressure and possibly even the salinity of the water. Think of them like cat whiskers or a snake tongue. The shark can tell a lot about their environment thanks to them."

Kora didn't realize how much she had missed the teaching aspect of her job until she paused in the middle of her explanation about the Ampullae of Lorenzini. She kept going.

"The really cool thing is that this network of hundreds, sometimes thousands of little holes is filled with jelly-like substance, almost like a mucus, to help these little receptors do their job."

Dr. Chatterjee knew where Candace was going with her line of questioning, "Could that jelly, that mucus, could that have gotten into the wound when Dylan was attacked?"

Kora stopped, stared into a corner of the room in deep thought, and turned back to the other two, "I mean, it's possible, but we're talking really tiny amounts. Even if several dozen of them discharged on impact and entered the wound, it might amount to 5cc, and even then, it would be watered down."

"Yes, but we know these receptors evolved from early bony fish," Candace interjected, "We also know there is still so much we don't know about the shark; maybe this is one of those things that has never been studied in the way we are right now."

Any remnants of fatigue were decaying away as Candace was trying hard to temper her enthusiasm. "Can it be harvested? Can we extract it from our shark so we can test it?"

"I suppose," Kora sounded a little skeptical as she said it. "But again, we're talking a minuscule amount."

"Maybe that's all we need Kora," Candace was dispensing with all the formalities at this point. "Vikram and I have tested everything, I mean everything, except this. If this is what beat GLU in Dylan's body, it didn't take a lot of it to do it. Let's imagine for a moment that the artifact that the virus was in came to earth shortly after humans popped up about 6 million years ago. Whoever or whatever sent it wanted to test the effects it would have on us.

Just like a dud grenade or an old-World War II mine, some guy named Harry Biggles finds in his backyard in the English countryside while planting his cucumbers and peas for the season. The canister never opened."

Candace explained further. "We know sharks have been on this planet, conservatively for 60 million years, with some of their evolutionary ancestors dating back over 200 million years. That jelly substance was here long before that canister. Isn't it possible that the virus wasn't engineered with that substance in mind?"

And there it was, in the quiet of the room, the three scientists looked at each other, not with a look of more questions, not with a look of doubt. What they saw on each of their faces was hope. A blind hope that said what didn't have to be said out loud. "This has to work, please God, let this work." A hope they no longer had to keep swimming for because it was right there in front of them. A hope that would hopefully put an end to the 600,000 people dying each day in the most horrific way possible. With the global death toll closing in on 100,000,000, they needed this.

CHAPTER 47
I DON'T THINK YOU'RE READY FOR THIS JELLY

At first light, Kora, Vikram, and Candace were back at the harbor. After checking on the shark and the level of sedation, Kora was back in the water.
In their excitement and rush to get started, they hadn't really thought of an easy way to extract the substance. So, with two dozen small syringes in her mesh dive bag and a special magnifying lens on her dive mask, she spent pore by tedious pore taking tiny sample after tiny sample.

An hour later, it was done. The samples were in a padded metal case, and the doctors were on their way back to the lab. Kora, Vikram, and Candace didn't really say much on the drive back to the lab. No one really wanted to raise their hopes any higher than they already were. They sat in outward silence, but in their heads, they were already working hard on building an antiviral that would work.

Candace had done a lot of really important work in her lifetime, but the weight of what she needed to accomplish now was crushing her like a tin can at the bottom of the Mariana Trench.

In theory, recreating the conditions that were present during the attack would only consist of a few ingredients: saltwater, a minuscule amount of jelly, and blood from a patient infected with GLU. Nothing more, nothing less. The fate of the world now sat in a dish for the most significant 60 minutes in human history.

Like Big Ben, the 'ding' of the timer filled the lab because no other sound existed. Such a tiny little death nell, that would spell the end for one of two parties. GLU or the human race. The three doctors looked at one another, each hesitant to be the one to go get the sample and look at it under the microscope. Candace was sick to her stomach.

As a doctor who battles cancer, she was all too accustomed to delivering devastating news to one family at a time. News that typically started with, "I'm sorry, we tried everything we could." Now, the thought of having to deliver that news to over 8 billion people on the planet was enormously overwhelming. However, she's the one the military trusted. The one Spencer trusted. She had been from the beginning when they plucked her from her kayak, she knew she had to be the one to see it through.

Candace walked over to where the sample was kept, all the while in her head, repeating, "Don't puke, don't puke, don't puke." She really wanted to puke. Sliding the dish under the microscope she peered in while the other two watched. She looked for about 20 seconds. Adjusting focus, lifting her head back to blink and rub her eyes. She leaned forward again, more focus adjustment, more moving the dish to look at other areas of the sample.

Vikram and Kora wanted to yell out, "WELL!!!!" They did not. They let Candace work. Whatever the outcome, they wanted to make damn sure it was accurate what she was seeing. Regardless of the answer, there would be no room for someone asking, "Are you sure."

Candace lifted her head from the microscope and turned to the other two doctors. Tears were streaming down her face. Vikram and Kora, assuming the worst, not knowing what to say. They just stood there, and then Candace smiled.

CHAPTER 48
THE CURE

As soon as Vikram and Kora saw Candace's smile, they knew. There was no loud celebration, no screaming, yelling, or jumping up and down.

With all the death that GLU had caused up to this point, there was no celebration that would justify that sort of reaction to the people who had suffered such monumental loss. Their grief would always surmount this kind of joy. Instead, Vikram and Kora walked over to Candace and the three doctors just held each other. Soon, similar to when a yawn becomes contagious in a group of people, all three were crying. Hope was winning the day.

In the hours that followed they tested more samples. They had enough for 5 more tests. They wanted to make damn sure it worked before the next step, human trial.

Success in a dish at the bottom of a microscope is one thing, testing in the human body with its crazy immune system was not a guarantee, but this was closer than they had ever been before.

One after another, the next 5 tests came back with the same result. The blood that was infected with GLU was not. Before GLU had a chance to replace it, it did not; it was gone.

"Vikram, please go get Kami, have her come in here. I would rather tell her our findings in this controlled environment than run the risk of word getting out before we are really, 100% sure it works."

Candace knew she had to be cautious; if news of a cure spread too early, the ramifications of people demanding it and who was going to get it first could be just as devastating as the virus itself. She had to do this right.

During Vikram's absence, Kora and Candace removed themselves from their PPE and were waiting outside the lab when he returned with Dr. Kami Rollins to share their encouraging findings.

Kami's job was to ask that question, "Are you sure?"

"Yes. 6 tests, 6 negatives," Candace explained. "GLU was completely gone from the blood of their test subjects. It's all thanks to Ampullae of Lorenzini." She said like she was now an expert on something she only knew existed a couple of days ago.

"Lorenzini what?" Kami asked.

"Ampullae of Lorenzini," Kora jumped in. "It will all be in our report. You'll have to excuse my unwillingness to share at this moment, but we're still not out of the woods yet."

"What do you mean," Kami asked. In her excitement, she didn't stop to think about the steps needed to get from 'point A' of working in a dish to 'point B' of having something to mass produce to save the world.

"Normally, there would be more tests, just to be even more sure than we already are." It was Dr. Chatterjee's turn to talk. "However, to quote that woman who went viral some years ago, "Ain't nobody got time for that!" By the look on Kami's face, that viral sensation hadn't made its way to her social media algorithm.

"Human trials need to start right away," Vikram announced.

"I don't know," Kami hesitated. I have to clear this with the board, maybe at least loop the Mayor in, and what about your government Dr. Stanton? Shouldn't we at least get those people who brought you here looped in?'

"No offense," Candace said, which is always something someone says right before they offend, "In the history of terrible ideas, that one is pretty high on the list. We just don't have that sort of time. Every hour we waste, more people are getting infected. More people are dying. More civil unrest is tearing towns apart."

Candace could hear the words in her head, and yes, they sounded a bit dramatic, but she was right. "Look, we do this under the radar; if human trials are a success, then yes, we can tell high-ranking officials and the board. If it doesn't work, it won't matter, and we'll simply tell them we tried, at which point we will be out of time because, honestly, the three of us are out of ideas."

The space was silent. Kora, Candace, and Vikram could see the wheels turning behind Kami's eyes. No one had to say it, but honestly, they were ready to proceed regardless of whether they were given permission.

"Okay, what's your plan?" Kami asked, much to their relief.

"So far, the tests we've run have been on blood that was in the early stages of the disease," Vikram took the lead since it was his hospital,

Kora and Candace deferred to his seniority. "To recap, as GLU progresses it doesn't change the blood so much as it replaces it. The volume of blood that is there gets pushed out, replaced by the much thicker and viscous GLU."

The faces of the four of them clearly showed they had all seen way too much of what GLU can do and those visuals were rushing back. "We believe that the amount of blood needed in a transfusion to put the volume of human blood back in the body after GLU moves out will all depend on how far along the infection is. Now that we're talking blood, I want Dr. Stanton to walk you through the next part." Dr. Chatterjee stepped aside.

"Dr. Rollins, what is the blood supply like in the hospital?" Candace asked.

"Not great, all things considered."

"Can you find me 12 units of O negative? We will test on 6 patients who are only a couple of hours into the infection. Once GLU is out, 2 units for each patient should be enough to get them stable and allow their bodies to start to heal." Candace continued, "If you don't have 12 units of O negative on hand, I need you to as discreetly as possible get it. I don't care how you do, but you need to. We can't put a call out for blood drives yet, it will raise too much suspicion."

Kami was making a note in her phone. She usually had a pretty reliable memory, but considering the gravity of the situation, she wanted to make sure she didn't forget anything. This wasn't like forgetting a loaf of bread at the store. This mattered.

"When I find the 6 patients, should I move them?"

"No, that also will make even the most passive observer more than a little curious," Candace said. "I hate to be so sneaky about this, but the fewer people who know, the better. I'm not even going to be the one administering the anti-viral. By now, most of your employees know who I am and what my role is to some degree. If I start shooting stuff into a patient's line.."

"More questions," Kami interrupted.

"Yes, more questions. However, at this point, I don't trust anyone on your staff not to talk. News of a cure is just too tempting for someone to want to be the first to break it to the world. In journalism, the old saying used to be, 'You don't' have to be right; you just have to be first.'. I don't buy that. Then, it was more about being right and not necessarily first. I want to be first and right on this. It's that or nothing.

"Well, we better crack on," Kora said, suddenly reminding everyone she was a part of this process, too. There's not much I can do at the moment, but if all of this works, I am ready to put the call out for blood drives. I will also reach out to all my friends who have boats and oversee the catching, wellbeing, harvesting, and eventual release of sharks."

"The substance in the Ampullae of Lorenzini, can the shark regenerate, much like humans do red blood cells?" Dr. Vikram asked.

"Great question; the short answer is yes; however, in the early stage of manufacturing this anti-virus, if it works, we're going to need a lot of it. The more sharks, the better to allow for the supply to catch up with demand."

Kora then proceeded to her next thought: "I'm also going to need to chat with the mayor when this is all in the open. In order to accommodate that many sharks, we'll need a lot of room. Like, shut the harbor down to anyone who doesn't have a shark attached to their boat."

"Well," Kami said, "Doctors, we've got some work to do. We better get to it."

While Dr. Rollins was rounding up patients and blood, Candace, Kora, and Vikram took advantage of a little downtime to sleep. Easier said than done. This was one of those, "Who can sleep at a time like this" kind of times. However, exhaustion won out over-excitement, and all three were able to get a few hours of solid sleep.

It took about 6 hours total for Dr. Rollins to get everything needed. It would have been sooner, but some of the O negative had to come from donors. In order to find donors on her staff, she may have broken a few privacy laws by going through employee files. Once she found them, she had to make sure they weren't infected and then asked them to donate under the disguise that the supply of O-negative for patients was uncomfortably low. Technically, that part wasn't a lie. To avoid the "how did you know what blood type I was" question, she simply approached those staff members as if she was simply asking everyone. She asked, they told her and that was that.

While she was doing her part, Candace and Vikram had manufactured 6 more doses. When Kami was ready, she took the syringes as inconspicuously as possible, went to each patient, and administered the antiviral into the line. If they were awake and asked what she was putting in their line, she gave the standard "Something to make you more comfortable" line.

All in all, it went smoother than expected, and in 30 minutes, Candace and Vikram had their human test subject. Once again, another painstaking wait.

This time, the hour went by fast. Maybe it was the affirmation of "this has to work" rolling around on the tip of their tongues.

Again, so as not to raise any more suspicion necessary, Dr. Rollins made the rounds, checking in with the charge nurses and asking about the patient, whether they were stable, anything unusual, that sort of thing.

Right on cue, she was met with inexplicable shock and surprise when the nurses and doctors, who were none the wiser, reported that a few of the patients had made a remarkable recovery. They didn't know how; they checked the records, and there should be no reason for it. Since the anti-viral was administered and not recorded, that reason would be kept under wraps for a little while longer.

Dr. Rollins excused herself and headed toward the lab where the other three doctors we anxiously waiting.

"It worked, HOLY HELL, it worked." Kami could barely contain her excitement.

"Okay, now the important part. We need to roll this news out in stages. Starting with the mayor. I need you to call her to one of your meeting rooms. I will have Javon round up the 'need to know' military officials and get them to that room, too. It will be easier to answer any of their questions and formulate a plan with them all in the same room."

At this point, Candace was triaging the situation as she would in any trauma unit, but instead of medical emergencies, she was dealing with protocol, multiple people in charge, and not much tolerance for a power struggle. She had taken charge, and the others were going to let her take that ball and run with it.

"The three of us will also be there," looking at Kora and Vikram. "Kora, I'm not looking for the mayor to deputize you or something like that, but I am going to ask her to give you a lot of authority when overseeing everything harbor and shark-related. I'm talking about local law enforcement. They will answer to you. Are you okay with that?"

Kora nodded. This was all new to her, but she knew what was at stake. A lot had happened in a short amount of time since her phone buzzed on her nightstand; this was not unexpected.

Candace was on her way to find Javon as everyone left the room. She still couldn't believe it had worked. Like any average person with an ounce of pessimism, part of her was waiting for the other shoe to drop. Trying to keep that negativity out of her head, she focused on being present and enjoying the win instead. She also decided that if there weren't an Italian dish called Ampullae of Lorenzini, she would indeed invent one when all this was over.

CHAPTER 49
WE'RE GOING TO NEED A BIGGER BOAT

There was a buzz in the meeting room from only the people who needed to be there. The colonel's replacement was Lieutenant Colonel Bradford, Mayor Kathleen Southridge, her chief of police, a couple of senior doctors and nurses, and Javon.

In the days Candace had been a slave to finding a cure, Javon had done what Javon does best. He assisted hospital security in conjunction with the military to maintain order in all facets of the operation—family visitation, security, media, logistics—and it hadn't taken long for him to integrate himself into the folds. He had also been keeping Spencer apprised of the situation.

Candace was no dummy. She knew Spencer hadn't been helping all this time out of the kindness of his heart. Spencer had an agenda. Spencer had A LOT to gain from a cure. Having Javon in the room made sense because security would play a vital role.

His sharing everything he hears with Spencer is just an acceptable byproduct she would have to deal with later.

"Take your seats, please," Candace announced to signal the beginning of the meeting. She had become the United States government's expert and face in the fight against Glu. She was to Glu as Doctor Fauci was to COVID-19. After all this time in the trenches, she had quickly earned the respect she deserved from the people in the room and no one was about to ask the question, "Why are we taking orders from this lady?"

"Thank you for gathering on such short notice. I'll get right to the reason you are here. We have a cure." Candace let those words hang in the air for several seconds just to let them sink in.

"How can you be sure?" Candace expected that question and expected the military or the mayor to ask it. It was Lt. Col. Bradford.

"The research is sound, we have tested in the lab and human trials, and the anti-virus has a 100 percent success rate."

"Human trials!!" Now it was the mayor's turn to play politician in case she needed to cover her ass. "You really should have looped me in at that point."

"With all due respect, ma'am," Kami chimed in since her report with the mayor was a bit more familiar than what Candace had established, "Time was not an ally for my team, and having to explain our actions would have just wasted valuable seconds."

Before the mayor could protest, Kami continued, "Frankly, there was nothing to lose because if it didn't work, this was our 'Hail Mary'. If it didn't work, the human race would have run out of options."

"That being said," Candace again took the reins. Everything you need to know, from the timeline to the technical, is in the brief. Feel free to grab one from the stack on the table. I will put the onus on you to read it and get up to speed because, again, to echo what Dr. Rollins said, time is not our friend."

There was a mix of excitement, stress, and a little fear on the faces around the room as Candace could see them connecting the dots in their heads. This was a big deal; big planning and responsibilities come with big deals.

"Mayor Southridge, I will need you and your office to schedule a news conference for 10 a.m. tomorrow. Just call it an important update in the fight against GLU. Enough of a tease to make it important but nothing more."

The mayor nodded. The time for power struggles and the "I don't take orders from you" B.S. had passed, and she was smart enough to realize that.

Candace then turned to Javon and Lt. Col. Bradford.

"Javon and Lt. Colonel, I need the two of you and your respective departments to work in unison to establish heavy security, not only for the news conference but for the following hours, days, and weeks. Make no mistake: This anti-virus is right now the most precious thing on the planet, and there will be parties who want to get their hands on it legally or by other means. Your job will be to prevent that while still being able to maintain the day-to-day secure operations of this hospital."

"Seems easy enough," Javon said as part of his usual efforts to lighten the mood. On the inside, he was freaking out. The monumental undertaking that lay before him may as well have been Mt. Everest.

"Dr. Kora Bandjin is our shark expert. Any and all matters pertaining to the catching, sedating, well-being of the sharks, and harvesting what we need from the sharks is her baby."

Candace looked at the mayor and her chief of police, "Please understand this isn't a power struggle, but for the sake of efficiency, Mayor Southridge, I need you and your police force to follow her lead and give her authority to make decisions pertaining to any and all activity down by the harbor."

"You don't expect me to…." were the only words the police chief could utter before Candace cut him off.

"This is not a request or suggestion, chief. In order for all this to work, I need you to be on board."

Javon flashed her a look that, if Candace didn't know any better, was a combination of being impressed and a little turned on by this version of Candace he hadn't seen since they met on the hotel's second floor in Juneau. It was "bad bitch o'clock" again and it looked good on her.

The rest of the meeting was filled with a few more questions, everyone thumbing through the report, and then it was over. 10 a.m. tomorrow morning, the world would change. GLU's demise was at hand.

50
A BIG TO-DO ABOUT GLU

Spencer was sitting in his office, his tablet connected, and waiting for the news conference to begin from Streaky Bay, Australia. The wheels of commerce were being greased with each passing second that approached the mayor's big moment, and Spencer knew he stood to make a shitload of money. Considering all the help he had given Javon and Candace to get to this point, he didn't feel the least bit guilty about angling for his position.

10 a.m. came quicker than expected. Outside the hospital, news vans, socially distanced reporters in masks, tripods, cameras, microphones, police blockades, and military and emergency vehicles dotted the city scene like some sort of twisted scavenger hunt game on the computer. The only thing missing was Waldo.

Mayor Southridge approached the podium; there was a squeal of feedback; the crowd didn't need to be told to quiet down. The sound of digital cameras taking rapid-fire stills of the moment echoed in the streets outside the hospital. It was the sound of history in the making. The mayor began:

"Good morning." She tried not to think about the fact that the news feed was global, not just for the people of her town or the country of Australia. "Yesterday will be a day remembered as the day Streaky Bay, Australia, became the epicenter of this global war on GLU. A few months ago, GLU didn't exist until it did, and in that short amount of time, it has had an irreversible effect on so many lives. Lives we can't bring back, lives that will never be the same.

It's those lives the team here at Streaky Bay Hospital was focused on to make sure that they did not die in vain. They did not. As of yesterday, we have a cure for GLU."

She paused not by choice, but by the deafening vocal wave that was a mixture of cheers, sobbing, questions, and more camera shutters. She waited for it to subside to continue.

"You will all be provided a copy of our report that will explain everything, but let me run down some of the highlights. The anti-virus was created from a byproduct found in one of the oldest living things on the planet; older than this virus, it was found in the Great White Shark. It is something we can harvest without killing a single shark and all steps will be taken to assure the safety and well-being of both the sharks and those doing the harvesting.

My team will work around the clock and as fast as possible to manufacture enough anti-virus for everyone here in Streak Bay. To expedite this effort, Doctor Staunton and Doctor Chatterjee will be working hand in hand with Spencer Grendhall, founder and CEO of biopharmaceutical firm Kadima. He has almost limitless resources to provide everything from logistics to financial backing.

In the meantime, centers will be created to donate blood. All types are needed, especially O negative. I ask that anyone able to donate blood do so because this will be an important piece to ensure every patient's recovery.

Finally, this anti-virus is now the most important resource on the planet and will be treated as such. We have a plan for mass production that will be followed. Anyone attempting to make their own plans and circumvent the rules will be dealt with harshly, swiftly, and without prejudice. We are now in a position to win the fight against GLU; we don't need any other outside forces working against us.

This is not just a Streaky Bay matter; it is a matter of global security and safety, and it will be treated as such. Thank you for your cooperation. There will be more updates through the media as they are made available." With that, the mayor dismounted from the podium and stage and walked off.

CHAPTER 51
FEAR SELLS

There was no denying that GLU was good for business. In the two weeks that followed the creation of the anti-virus, a sustainable plan to move forward was agreed upon. Great White Farms would go up on Cape Cod in Harwich, Massachusetts; Coos Bay, Oregon; San Diego, California; and, of course, Streaky Bay, Australia.

They would serve not only as a place to bring captured sharks and harvest the Ampullae of Lorenzini but Kora also suggested that they eventually act as hatcheries and research facilities because, as she put it, "What else don't we know about the great white shark? If it can fight GLU, who's to say a cure for cancer isn't hiding behind all those teeth."

Spencer Grendall and Kadima funded it all not entirely out of the kindness of his heart. In striking a deal with the United States and Australia, he built the "fish farms," as he liked to call them, at a fraction of the cost, and in return, he was awarded sole, proprietary rights to the production and distribution of the anti-virus. One condition: he must keep his word to Candace; it must be sold cheap. Furthermore, 40 percent of the profits were earmarked for families who lost loved ones, cleaning up and rebuilding some of the harder-hit areas where civil unrest and panic caused the worst damage.

Spencer wasn't an unreasonable man. Honestly, he knew how bad it would look if he were to cash in on the misery that GLU had created. $100 a dose, whether you had GLU or didn't want to catch it. Unlike Covid from years past, which was always changing, it was a one-and-done. No boosters, no updates, just one shot, and you were cured and protected.

Sure, that seems like a lot, but governments offered assistance to offset the cost to the public and to ensure Spencer got paid and paid he was. Even after the 40 percent he promised to give back, the man who already had more money than he knew what to do with had even more.

If Spencer's parents were still alive, they would be so proud of their son. The son of a Maine lobsterman who grew fast, Spencer was a self-made man who was not only rich financially but also had an abundance of compassion and empathy that reflected his desire to not just sit on his fortune but to do something good with it. In this case, he'd be helping to save the planet.

Soon, when there was a reserve of the anti-virus, the harvesting would stop, and the 'fish farms' would be 100% converted to research facilities. That was the end game; the journey to get there would not happen overnight, but as the name of Spencer's company, "Kadima," encouraged, FORWARD was finally the direction the world was headed.

CHAPTER 52
DATE NIGHT

The doorbell echoed throughout Natalie's apartment. She was just putting the finishing touches on her makeup and looking around to make sure her apartment was tidy. She lit a couple of candles and cracked a window as he walked toward the front door. The chill of the Australian winter blanketed Streaky Bay, but the wing speed of the butterflies in her belly was generating plenty of warmth. Her cheeks were flush, and her palms were a little sweaty. "Crikey Sheila, get it together, he's just a boy. Don't give him this sort of power," she whispered under her breath as she opened the door.

Dylan had made an amazing recovery in the weeks following the discovery of the anti-virus. He became very adept with his prosthetic leg. Life was almost back to normal for him—as normal as could be for a guy who many globally still considered a savior of sorts. He would have been knocking on Natalie's door sooner, but the initial demand for interviews made him feel more famous than Taylor Swift.

With the help of a PR person, he managed to be very gracious with his time, but he needed a break. No, he needed to see nurse Natalie. So, he put his interview schedule and speaking engagements on hold and focused on a promise he made to her when he was in his hospital bed.

Natalie smiled when she laid eyes on him. Slacks, nice shoes, clean white shirt. It all screamed, "I want to look good for you, Natalie, but

I wanted to be comfortable around you." He held a bottle of wine and a conservative bouquet in one hand, nothing too aggressive. On the other hand, a basket with all the fixings for a fantastic bowl of popcorn. Kernels, M&M's, a jar of caramel, salt, even bacon and cheese powder. It was a popcorn charcuterie. If that wasn't a thing, it needed to be.

Looking back through the door, Dylan was in trouble because his hands were full, which meant he had no way to pick up his jaw, which had dropped right after his eyes popped out of his head. He had only ever seen Natalie in her scrubs. While they did hug her hips and butt as most scrubs tend to, he never really got a chance to fully appreciate her curves.

Now, Natalie was standing before him in a plunging sun dress that she wore for two reasons: one, to think warm thoughts and try to usher spring to Australia a little quicker, and two, to create warm thoughts for Dylan. She was no Punxsutawney Phil when it came to predicting spring, but the secondary effect was clearly achieved.

"Y-y-y….ou..are magical," he stammered.

"Magical huh?" she said

"Yeah, because you just made every other woman on this planet vanish."

Did it sound a little like 'a line'? Sure, did it work? Well, the confident, vibrant, strong, and cheeky Natalie was left speechless for the first time in her life.

Whatever small part of her self-control she was clinging to was ripped from her hands when Dylan followed that up with, "Are you going to let me in, or is the 'no-no square' education you promised me going to take place outside".

Natalie smiled and said, "Look what I can do."

She knew it wasn't fair because his hands were full, but she leaned forward through the threshold of the door, kissed him ever so softly on the cheek, and whispered, "Don't forget about the danger zone." He walked in, the door closed, and class was in session.

CHAPTER 53

KAYAKS

It had been nine months since the discovery of the cure. Candace had returned home to Wichita around the first of the year. As you can imagine, she was the talk of the town, and there was still a high demand for interviews from local TV stations and local radio stations. Her favorite was KFDI, a local country station. She liked the morning guy, JJ Hayes, so just as Dylan had granted only one interview to the local news guy in Streaky Bay, Candace gave only one radio interview to her favorite country radio DJ.

The Ninnescah River is a little over 56 miles long, and all of it is in Kansas, a tributary of the Arkansas River. In Kansas, that's pronounced the 'Are-Kansas River' as in 'our-Kansas'. It was a weird territorial thing, a Kansas thing, and every time friends and family from out of town visited, she had to explain that.

It didn't matter though, because at that very moment she was home. Her mom and dad were safe; they had their dose of the anti-virus, and Kahl was back where he belonged, riding shotgun in the kayak with Candace.

Spring was storm season in Kansas, and even though "tornado alley" seemed to be shifting further east one season and back to the west the next, it had been pretty active this year.

A lot of storm warnings, lots of golf ball-sized hail, an abundance of much-needed rain to offset the drought of the last few years, and a few tornadoes, mainly in the middle of nowhere. However, one, an EF-3, did make a rare appearance just west of Wichita. It leveled several neighborhoods, but thanks to basements and plenty of storm coverage from Wichita's most trusted meteorologist, Ross Jannsen, there was no loss of life, just property damage, and cleanup to contend with. Candace always watched Ross because he was a dog lover like she was. From time to time, his corgi "May" would make an appearance on TV and steal the show.

"You know, after all that time on the water catching sharks, you've become quite good with boats," she said, looking over at Javon, who was in the Kayak beside her.

Javon was still Spencer's employee, but even Spencer recognized he needed to give his top guy a few months off.

Javon had been shot at, broken more than one law and military regulation, and put himself in danger so many times he lost count; he needed this. He needed Candace.

When the world was saved, his feelings for Candace became clear. He needed her to know that he didn't just care for her because she may have been the last face he ever saw. Now, he wanted her to know that her face was the first thing he saw when he woke up and the last face he would see when there were no more tomorrows. Lucky for him, she felt the same.

"Now that I'm in this thing, I'm getting the hang of it, but I'm just not sure how I'm supposed to get out," Javon said.

Candace laughed, "I'm not sure either, but you can be damn sure I'll be shooting video when you try."

"Don't you dare," Javon protested.

"No, really, what better way to learn for next time than to go back and watch the video to see what you did wrong. Football players watch tape all the time to learn about the other team and about their mistakes. I'm only trying to help."

"You saved the world doc; I think you've helped enough for a while."

THE END

Made in the USA
Monee, IL
02 November 2024

68289314R00111